The Gentleman & The Witch

BRANDY SHAW

To Grandma
You always read my stories, even when they made you blush.
I think you would have liked this one.

Chapter 1

LONDON, 1815

Sir James Marley bit back a groan as the line of carriages in front of them moved at a snail's pace. He would prefer to be anywhere other than stuck in a carriage, listening to his father drone.

"There will be many young women here tonight seeking a wealthy, titled husband. You have a title, lowly as it is, and our family has plenty of wealth. Tonight is about meeting people and making connections. We will wait a few weeks before selecting the chit to be your wife."

"And you believe these ladies will accept a proposal from me, lowly as my title is?"

His father, oblivious to James's mood, laughed heartily. "Desperation, my boy! Once these débutantes come to understand how few of them will actually win a wealthy, titled husband, they'll look to other options."

James drummed his fingers on his thigh and gazed out the window, willing the other vehicles to move. "How flattering to know I will be marrying a lady who has run out of options. Sounds like the makings of a spectacular match."

His father continued to ignore him, too caught up in his own brilliance. "I have made a list of women I wish for you to acquaint yourself with. None of the families have male heirs, and they are all lines where the title can pass through the mother to your son."

"That seems specific. I can't imagine your list is very long."

"There are three ladies whose families are in such circumstances."

"And we are gambling that none of these ladies will make a match before I propose, and will thus be open to my suit?"

"Of course not! It is possible Lady Eliza Hargrove could make a match. She is quite comely, and her dowry is not insubstantial. But Lady Cecilia Manning's family is penniless. With an impoverished line on the brink of extinction, you might be able to win her hand quickly. I am sure they would be more than willing to entertain your proposal."

James huffed a sigh. He was granted a brief respite from his father's diatribe when their carriage finally stopped in front of the stately home of Lord and Lady Pearson. They exited and made their way toward the entrance.

"Now remember, you may not have a distinguished title, but we have something more important." His father's tone was surely meant to be a whisper, but he could be heard by any of the people milling about.

"And what is that?"

"Money!"

James bit his tongue and questioned the sanity of going along with his father's scheme.

The old man had made a fortune importing goods from lands in the east and had spent the last two decades attempting to break into the upper class. He'd managed to enter the gentry with the acquisition of an estate in Suffolk, but that had only been one part of his plan. The next step was to gain a foothold within *le bon ton*.

Proper society detested trade, and most men in his situation would have cut their business ties. Edward could not fathom that, so he was attempting to make his son an idle gentleman. Unfortunately, James, to his father's unending disappointment, did not want that life.

Industrious from an early age, James would never have been satisfied with an idle existence. Following school, he'd purchased a commission in His Majesty's royal navy. He'd been a part of the battle at Trafalgar during his first year, but, apart from a few specialized missions on the continent, most of his career had consisted of running blockades, first against France and then in the recent conflict with America. After being injured, he'd suffered a terrible fever and had been sent home. Once recovered, he'd sold his commission, unwilling to return to running blockades after nearly a decade of taking part in the destruction brought on by war.

Shortly after his recovery, he had been knighted for saving the life of a senior officer at Trafalgar. He'd barely recalled the incident, but the family of the man he had saved was close to the king, and somehow they'd persuaded the monarch to bestow the honor on James. Though he could not confirm it, he suspected Edward had had something to do with the affair.

James had initially thought to work with his father after resigning his commission, but the old man had adamantly refused. So, instead, he had started an engineering firm with his friend Tom Reynolds. Tom was a brilliant inventor, and James called upon his own strategic skills to run the business side of the operation. The world of engineering was constantly evolving, and James was excited to be building something that would improve the lives of others.

Unfortunately, their fledgling business needed capital. James had approached his father to discuss a standard investment scheme, but Edward had proposed a different arrangement. He would invest, but only if James found a wife from a noble line. The elder Mr. Marley was determined to solidify their family's place among the aristocracy.

James enjoyed the idea of marriage, but he hadn't pictured marrying any particular woman. He liked the idea of living with a pleasing partner, so it had been no great sacrifice to go along with his father's plan. He'd begun to regret his easy acquiescence. It was possible his own shortcomings might mean that his marriage would not be as amiable and pleasing as he had pictured.

"Are you listening to me?" His father's rebuke pulled him from his musing.

James scowled. "You know this is in opposition to the usual order of things, don't you?" he whispered as they progressed toward the majordomo.

"How so?"

"Usually, the ladies want to impress the available men, not the other way around."

"My boy, if you want your boon, you must first give me mine. A match among the ton is a business deal. You are showing them the merchandise."

"I don't appreciate being thought of as merchandise," James grumbled, as his father turned to speak with an acquaintance.

"Marriage is a matter of more worth than to be dealt in by attorneyship."

The honeyed words sent a shiver down his spine. James turned and encountered a most stunning woman. Her big brown eyes were framed with thick lashes against soft beige skin, and several tendrils of auburn hair curled down the tempting slope of her shoulders. James resisted the urge to touch one of those curls and see if it was as soft as it looked. He swallowed thickly.

"It is not nice to eavesdrop." Her eyes flared and her cheeks flushed most becomingly. James had no idea who she was, but he hoped she was on his father's list.

"Forgive me, sir. I meant no offense."

James smiled. "I have taken no offense. Was that Shakespeare?"

"Yes," she replied, giving him a shy smile in return.

"*Henry VI?*"

"Yes!" Her mouth widened into a grin. "Have you read much of his work?"

"Nearly everything."

"Surely not everything," she said with a coquettish tilt of her head.

"Indeed." He rubbed the back of his neck. "I've had much free time in the last several years."

"Most gentleman can find more interesting things to do than read plays," she teased.

"It's more difficult when you're on a ship for several weeks at a time."

Her brow furrowed. "Are you a sailor?"

James smoothed the collar of his jacket. "I was an officer in His Majesty's Royal Navy."

"I see," she replied, an indecipherable expression on her face.

His father turned back and cleared his throat disapprovingly.

"Pardon the intrusion, my lady." James indulged in one more glance of her rosy cheeks before facing forward.

"I can't believe I have to say this, but *do not* break protocol," his father hissed. "None of the ladies will entertain your suit if there is the slightest chance you could ruin them."

James gritted his teeth and stared forward, his posture rigid. He would need to find a suitable wife soon, if for no other reason than to stop attending social events with his father.

❦

Anabel repressed a sigh as the man turned away. He was one of the most attractive men she'd seen in a long time—tall, broad-shouldered, and with soft light-brown hair a bit shorter than was the fashion. The dim lighting made it difficult to determine the color of his eyes, which strengthened her desire to interact with him again. Their brief conversation had piqued her interest. She'd had little opportunity in her life to get to know men who were not related to her, let alone a man she felt a connection with.

Noting her brother Isaac's absent gaze, she tried to subtly scratch at her hip through the layers of her clothing. She hated wearing all the frippery required on formal occasions. Anabel never envied her cousins more than when she was at a society event.

If society knew of her extended family, it could ruin her and her brother. The family traveled to town fairs all over the kingdom, selling their wares and performing shows, but that was not the most scandalous thing about them. They were also witches.

Her grandmother had decided long ago that the best way to protect the family was to hide in plain sight. No one expected proper behavior from a traveling band of entertainers and peddlers. Anabel had lived with that branch of her family for years. She'd befriended town folk, servants, and other nomads like the Roma and Irish Travelers all over the kingdom but had steered clear of the wealthier class.

She'd left high society behind, expecting to never return, and yet here she was, attending lavish parties and displaying herself to a social crowd that would judge her every movement. She had to prove herself as an acceptable young lady. If the people knew about her family, or that she had her own talent... She shuddered to think of the consequences.

She'd been back in London for only two weeks, and, so far, she'd been able to conceal her abilities, mostly by only attending daytime events. As the reclusive sister of a duke, she was a curiosity. She was also older than the other débutantes and was considered a spinster at the ripe age of one and twenty. She tried not to need the approval of others, but it hurt that they treated her like an oddity.

She and her brother were finally to the front of the line, set to be introduced after the handsome man she'd spoken with briefly. She stole another glance at his broad shoulders and noted how elegantly his coat framed his muscular torso. He wore trousers, a new fashion that not all men had adopted, and she appreciated how they encased his thighs. She wondered how his legs would appear in close-fitting breeches.

Anabel couldn't help but notice the sneers of disapproval from some of the people milling about in the room below, as Sir James Marley was introduced after his father, Mr. Edward Marley. They only tolerated the presence of a mere knight here, which meant he must be wealthy.

Anabel tugged on her brother's arm and pulled him from whatever reverie he'd been lost in. Isaac nodded to her and stiffened his posture, donning what Anabel liked to refer to as his "duke face." He was no longer her brother Isaac. He was the Duke of Montgomery, and he was ready to perform.

Isaac looked to the majordomo and led his sister up to the top of the stairs. Anabel fought back a wave of dizziness as she peered down at the crush. The ballroom was already packed, and there were at least fifty more people waiting to be introduced behind her.

"His Grace, the Duke of Montgomery, and Lady Anabel Montgomery." The majordomo's voice rang out across the ballroom, drowning out the din of conversation. Anabel took a deep breath and sent up a prayer to keep herself from tripping, then held onto her brother's arm and stepped down into the stately ballroom.

James could not stop himself from following Lady Anabel's descent. Her elegant figure was draped in a pale green gown in the latest fashion which displayed her figure to perfection. She was more well-endowed than some of the other débutantes. James had always appreciated a lovely pair of breasts. Beyond admiring her physical beauty, however, he wanted to continue their conversation. He was interested to hear more of her opinions on the Bard.

"Stop staring." His father subtly jabbed his elbow into James's ribs.

"Apologies," James said, reluctantly tearing his gaze from Lady Anabel. He racked his brain to recall protocol within the ton. If she had been married to the man she was introduced with, they would have been announced together. The fact that her first name was mentioned indicated she was unmarried. He failed to suppress a smile.

"You are much too low to court the daughter of a duke, and anyway, she is not on the list. Her brother has already inherited the title, and if he died without an heir, the title would go to some distant cousin. No sense in even trying to pursue that avenue. Come, let me introduce you to Lady Cecilia."

Lady Cecilia was tall with dark-brown hair pulled back in a simple, severe style. Her eyes were sharp as she scrutinized James. He couldn't blame her. His father had made no secret of his motivation when he had approached Cecilia's father, the Earl of Ravenswood. The two men spoke as if they were brokering a business deal. James could talk business with anyone, but he hated the idea of being the commodity in a deal.

Making the best of it, he turned to Lady Cecilia, quickly securing her hand for the next dance. As he escorted her onto the floor, he was grateful for the dance lessons his mother had forced upon him.

Lady Cecilia was a technically proficient dancer, but it was obvious she found no joy in the act. After several minutes of awkward silence, James tried to start a conversation.

"Is this your first season?" He immediately cringed. He should have complimented the lady. He was already bungling things up.

"Hardly." Cecilia scoffed, narrowing her eyes.

"Please forgive my blunder," James said, attempting to inject as much sincerity into his words as possible. "This is my first society event, and I'm afraid I'm making that very obvious."

Her face softened with a half-smile, and he felt a slight victory.

"I find your honesty refreshing, sir." Her smile bloomed fully, and James found the expression pleasing. "I'm in my third season. The gossip is that I'm too old to be married."

James smiled in return. "Apparently I'm not the only one with a penchant for honesty."

"Oh, I tried to simper and be the perfect débutante my first season. Even a little bit last year. But this season I will be nothing less than myself."

"I can only respect that."

"I'm glad to hear of it."

They parted for a moment while they paired off with others for the next sequence of the dance, before coming back together.

"I should tell you," Cecilia began when they reunited, "I have no desire to marry this year or any other. My father will undoubtedly try to convince me otherwise. He would very dearly appreciate a financial rescue for our estates, but I don't intend for him to obtain that on my back."

Another young lady dancing nearby overheard Cecilia and threw her a reproachful look, but it had no effect. Cecilia complained about her father for a full minute, saying she would not allow him to use her to rectify his mistakes.

When she finally paused, James studied her. "If I didn't know better, I'd say you were trying to scare me off."

"Are you certain you know better? Because that's exactly what I'm doing."

"Well, I'd say you failed, because all you've achieved is to pique my interest. I'd love to know more."

She frowned as she met his eyes. Their conversation paused as they moved through the couples to the end of the line. Bewildered, James noticed that the music had stopped, and the couples were dispersing.

"I'm afraid we'll have to continue this conversation another time." Cecilia said, taking his arm. "Our dance has come to an end." Before he could respond, Cecilia subtly pushed him to the side of the ballroom where their fathers stood.

Anabel caught sight of her friend Lady Cecilia leaving the dance floor and changed her path, hoping she could arrange an introduction. She'd watched her friend and Sir James with great interest and a bit of jealousy. She had a strong compulsion to become acquainted with the man, but she also did want to see her friend. She enjoyed Cece's company and was glad for a chance to reconnect.

"Lady Cecilia!" she called out as she maneuvered around people in her way. The place seemed to be littered with groups who had no regard for anyone trying to move through the crowd.

Fortunately, Cece heard her and turned in Anabel's direction. Squeezing behind another man she did not know, Anabel approached. She took the other woman's hands in hers and gave her a quick peck on the cheek.

"Hello, dear! I'm glad to see you. How is your evening?"

"Much improved, now I am with you." Anabel looked over her friend's shoulder at the tall man standing nearby. He was just as handsome as he'd appeared in the dim entryway. "I don't believe I've met your companion." She knew she was being terribly forward, but she was too curious to care.

Thankfully, Cecilia took up the charge. "Sir James, please allow me to introduce one of my dearest friends, Lady Anabel Montgomery. Lady Anabel, please meet Sir James Marley."

The man bowed at the introduction. Anabel reciprocated with a shallow curtsy. He escorted them to where Cecilia's father was deep in conversation with another older man and settled them onto a nearby settee.

"Might I fetch you ladies some refreshments?" James offered.

His voice sent a thrill through Anabel. She felt her cheeks heat.

"Some lemonade would be lovely, thank you," Cecilia said.

Sir James nodded and retreated. Cecilia opened her fan and fluttered it toward Anabel's face.

"He is quite handsome," Anabel said when she was able to catch her breath. Privately, she thought him more than handsome. His eyes were particularly striking. Their color changed with the light, from green to brown.

"I can agree somewhat. He is a pleasant-looking man, and his clothing is fine without being extravagant."

Cece's droll tone made Anabel want to gasp, but she stopped herself. "Are your fathers acquainted?" she asked, clearing her throat.

"They are now. Sir James is the latest victim my father would like to sell me to."

Anabel gaped at her friend. "Don't say that as if you are some great burden! Any man would be lucky to have you."

"Indeed," Cecilia replied with a wry smile, "but would I be lucky to have him?"

Anabel gave an awkward laugh. "He is not the worst candidate we've seen."

"No, although he may be more interested in you than me."

"Surely not," Anabel replied. She failed to quash the warmth spread through her chest. "He just finished dancing with you."

"Only because he hadn't had a chance to ask you first." Cecilia shifted her body slightly to face Anabel head-on. "You are a beautiful woman who is accomplished, well-dowered, and sister to a duke. You are certainly a more valuable prize than me."

Anabel scowled. "Well, I'm not here to find a husband."

Cecilia leaned in closer, lowering her voice. "Then why are you here? I've been trying to puzzle it out since we first reunited. I was sure that when you escaped from Mrs. Marlow's academy, I would never see you again."

Anabel sighed. Although she'd been back in London for a fortnight, she hadn't made time to pay her friend a proper visit. "Isaac is looking for a wife."

Cecilia gasped. "He is?"

Anabel nodded her head slightly. "He doesn't want that to be common knowledge because he is trying to avoid being swarmed by match-makers."

"I can't blame him for that." Cecilia adjusted her fan to hide her mouth as she spoke. "However, the real question is, where have you been for the last five years?"

"I was visiting my family in the country." Anabel looked away as she spoke the falsehood. She couldn't very well tell the truth.

Cecilia stared at Anabel for a long moment, her brow furrowed. "Are you sure helping your brother is the only reason you've returned?"

Anabel swallowed past the tightness in her throat. She'd felt so lonely since returning to London. Could she confide in her old friend?

"I..." she paused and looked away toward the ceiling before continuing. "I suppose I also felt out of place among my family. They are a different set."

"Are they the sort of relations that detest having to come to London for the season?"

It was as good of an explanation as any other. "Yes, they lead a different life than we do here."

"Most country families do." Cecilia turned to peer at the crowded ball-room, releasing a weary sigh. "So, you thought coming back here might feel more natural?"

"I suppose I did, although I'm not finding this any easier."

At that moment, Sir James returned, handing each lady a dainty cut crystal glass filled with lemonade. Anabel's hand brushed Sir James's when she took the glass, and she felt a tingle run along her arm.

Cecilia took her glass and calmly took a sip. "Surely you have other young ladies to charm this evening," she said to Sir James, her eyebrows raised.

"At the moment, I do not." He replied with a grin that made Anabel's heart race in her chest. "However, I would not be opposed to another dance if you feel so inclined, Lady Cecilia."

"I am not inclined," Cecilia replied, setting down her glass. She looked at Anabel with a twinkle in her eye. "But I am sure my dear friend would love a turn." Before Anabel could protest, Cece grabbed her wrist and lifted her dance card. "Oh look, this next dance is free." Cece hastily wrote Sir James's name and nudged her friend.

Unable to say anything without being rude, Anabel sent her friend a surreptitious scowl before reaching for Sir James's outstretched hand. They stood in silence for a moment before the orchestra began the next song. Turning, he led her to the dance floor.

Chapter 2

James fought to remember the steps as he danced with Lady Anabel. In addition to coping with his own nerves, he couldn't help but notice the frequent looks thrown their way. They were not friendly.

"They are wondering how rich you must be to dance with the sister of a duke," Anabel said, as if she had read his mind.

James smiled sheepishly. "I'm sure I am nowhere near as rich as the rumors say."

"Nevertheless, you have been noticed. I hope you don't mind having all of society watch you."

"I mind terribly. I am not a part of society, not really. I'm the son of a merchant who earned a knighthood through service to the Crown. Hardly anyone of import."

"Well, I am sure at least part of their interest lies with me. I am an unusual choice of partner for any man."

"And why is that?"

She gave him a wan smile, and James nearly missed a step. They separated as they paired off with others for the next movement. When they reunited, he held her hand a bit longer than the dance required. She smiled again, the expression more natural. They continued their dance in silence for a few moments, Lady Anabel moving through the steps with admirable grace. She made no move to speak, and James felt compelled to repeat himself.

"I am still awaiting a response, my lady."

She cocked her head. "Are you?"

"I am," he confirmed with a nod. "Why would you consider yourself an unfit partner?"

"I think nothing of the sort, but it is not my opinion you're asking about, is it?"

"I suppose not. Why would others consider you unusual?"

"I'm sure you'll hear plenty about it as soon as our dance concludes. I should save my breath, since you will likely not be given a choice in the matter."

"Society gossip is not something I'm interested in. I'd rather hear the story from you."

They parted for the next movement of the dance, standing far enough apart from one another that they couldn't continue their conversation without others overhearing. Lady Anabel observed him the entire time. When they reunited, she gave him a determined look.

"Sister of a duke I may be, but I am also a walking scandal. I disappeared from finishing school when I was sixteen and only resurfaced a few weeks ago. Everyone is aflutter with theories about what I was doing during the five years I was missing."

James furrowed his brow. "And what's the true story?"

Her gaze darted away, looking at the other dancers as she responded. "I was staying with family in the country."

"You are a terrible liar, my lady."

Her eyes flicked back to meet his, her gaze burning hot. They joined separate lines for the next part of the dance, and she glared at him with her chin raised. When they came back together after several minutes, she held his hand but would not meet his gaze.

"I have blundered," he observed, his chest uncomfortably tight.

She glanced back at him, then dropped her eyes to the floor. "I do not wish to continue this conversation."

James wished he could pull her aside and continue the conversation in private. "Please accept my apology, my lady."

She replied with a tight-lipped smile.

At the end of the dance, she dipped into a shallow but respectable curtsy, and James returned it with a much deeper bow. She sighed heavily before walking over and taking his arm.

"Lead me toward that tall, finely-dressed gentleman with dark hair."

He saw the man she'd entered with. Her brother, the duke. He seemed extremely displeased. James gulped audibly, and Anabel peered at him, her lips quirking.

"I take it you are acquainted?"

"Not formally, but I saw you enter with him. He does not look happy to see me escorting his sister."

She giggled, and a weight lifted from his chest. "He isn't so bad. Come. I will introduce you, and you will see. He'll likely enjoy your company more than mine. He's not exactly pleased with me either."

The mystery around this woman was tantalizing, but they reached her brother before James had an opportunity to respond.

The expression on her brother's face amused Anabel, helping to further dispel her anger. James hadn't been wrong. She was a terrible liar, and that was something she needed to improve.

Isaac's jaw was firm, and his posture was rigid. Her amusement faded to weariness. She had told him multiple times that she would only agree to help if he promised to not try to control her behavior, but it seemed he had not taken her seriously.

"Isaac," she said when they reached her brother, "please allow me to introduce Sir James Marley. Sir James, this is my brother, the Duke of Montgomery."

"Sir," Isaac said in his most intimidating tone.

"Your Grace," Sir James responded, bowing respectfully. "I thank your sister for bestowing the honor of a dance upon me."

"Indeed," Isaac said in return.

They stood in awkward silence for a moment before Sir James bowed again and excused himself before disappearing into the crush.

"I thought we had agreed that you were to behave respectably," Isaac muttered when James was out of earshot.

"I was respectable. What part of what I just did was not respectable?"

"You danced with a man you had not been introduced to."

"Nonsense! Cece introduced us."

"An introduction from another lady does not count if the lady in question is another débutante."

"Well, that is a stupid rule. I can't control the gossip, and anyhow, there are much more interesting topics for the gossips when it comes to me."

"Be that as it may, it will not help society's opinion of you, and by extension me, if you keep flouting their rules."

She gave him an incredulous look. "You're worried about society's opinion of you?"

"Of course. I have a reputation to maintain. I have an important place in the House of Lords and hundreds of people depending on me. I must be above reproach."

"Isaac, that's just it. You are a duke and rich as Croesus. Society has no choice but to respect you. You could have your choice of any débutante here. Their mamas would throw them at your feet. You don't really need me."

"I don't want débutantes thrown at me. That is why I need you. It's easier to observe potential brides if others assume that I am merely reintroducing my sister into society."

Anabel turned to watch the current procession of dancers. "I did not want to be a part of society. That is why I fled."

Isaac scoffed. "There's more to it than that. And anyway, Bel, you cannot spend the rest of your life traveling to town fairs, peddling herbal tonics and tinctures."

"I wasn't peddling tonics and tinctures. I peddled exotic cloth and ribbons. Suraya sells the herbal concoctions."

"Regardless, you were not meant for that life. You are the daughter of a duke. It is your responsibility to take your place in society."

"I'm only the daughter of a duke because our mother used less than honest means to marry one old enough to be her great-grandfather."

"Which I am grateful for. It saved you and I from a life as—"

"Do not say that word!" Anabel hissed. "Our family does not descend from the Roma, but if we did I would be just as proud. I have met a few, and they are some of the kindest individuals I've ever encountered in my travels."

"They are swindlers and tricksters, just as our family is."

Anabel's body flushed with anger, and then she sensed it. Someone was watching her. Of course, there were many eyes on her this evening, but ever since she'd left the safety of her family, she'd felt as though she was being followed. Her pulse pounded and sweat broke out all over her body. She knew she should not feel this fear and anger in a ballroom. The candlesticks on a nearby table begin to levitate just slightly. She turned her head to observe them directly, and the flames sputtered, though they continued to float.

Isaac looked in the direction she was staring. "Bel! Stop that this instant!"

She took a deep breath and willed her magic to gently place the candles back on the table.

"What was the purpose of that?!" Isaac asked, his face red and his nostrils flaring.

"I didn't do it on purpose" she replied curtly. "You know very well I struggle to control myself when I'm under stress. Perhaps you should think of that side effect before arguing with me further."

He relaxed his clenched jaw until his mouth hung open. "I did not intend to upset you, dear sister. I just need you to see the importance of your proper place. You were not born to live with our grandmother, traveling from town to town and never setting down roots. You were meant to live in a grand house and to be a part of society."

"I just told you. I don't want to be a part of society! I am here to help you find a suitable bride who will give you a herd of children to protect your succession. Once that is done, I will return to our family of peddlers and travelers."

"Enough," Isaac said with a scowl. "We will discuss this matter in further detail when we return home. For now, let me introduce you to some proper gentlemen to dance with in the hope of restoring your reputation."

Anabel considered continuing the quarrel, but there was no use arguing with Isaac when he set his mind to something. His ability to compel others to do his will exacerbated his domineering nature. His gift did not work on Anabel, but sometimes she wished it did. She would feel better about going along with this farce if it had been against her own free will. She pasted on a smile when Isaac introduced her to an acquaintance of his from Oxford and resigned herself to complying with her brother's wishes for the rest of the night. It could not be over soon enough.

After leaving Lady Anabel with her brother, James returned to his father's side. The man was deep in conversation with another associate of his, but he quickly ended the discussion when he caught sight of his son.

"You have been neglecting your responsibilities."

"Have I? I danced with Lady Cecilia."

"Yes, and then immediately secured a dance with the lady I told you not to pursue."

"She is Lady Cecilia's friend, and it would have been rude of me not to ask her to dance."

His father grunted but did not rebuke him further. "Well, come, we have others you must meet. Lady Eliza and her family are here."

"I was under the impression that Lady Eliza was likely to make a good match and wouldn't need our money badly enough to accept my overtures."

Mr. Marley glared at his son. "Watch your tongue, my boy. These walls have ears. There is no harm in introducing you."

They made their way to Lady Eliza, who was indeed very pretty and well-mannered, but James found no pleasure in dancing with her. Her speech was vain and dull. She was much too young for James to consider. She was only seventeen and had just debuted a few weeks prior. He felt odd courting a woman ten years his junior.

Next, he met the third lady in question, Miss St. John, the daughter of a baron. The poor girl seemed nervous and uncomfortable no matter what James tried to put her at ease. He felt sorry for the lady. Her discomfort was almost palpable, and he didn't see himself making a match with her either.

After meeting and dancing with all three ladies from his father's list, he was led around the room to meet the children of Edward's other acquaintances, resulting in another five dances. By the end of evening, James was exhausted and longed for nothing so much as a hot bath to dip his feet in. He struggled to keep his posture straight as he followed his father to their waiting carriage.

The old man appeared full of vigor as he took his seat across from his son. "Well done, my boy. Other than the one flub early in the evening, you behaved admirably."

"I'm so glad you approve of my behavior."

"Whom do you wish to court, now you have met all the ladies?"

"None of them. They are all much too young for me. Furthermore, I don't believe any were inclined to better our acquaintance."

"They won't have much choice if their fathers approve of the match."

"I am already wary of this plan. If you tell me I need to force a young lady to marry me, I will walk away."

"There's no forcing! Once their fathers tell them to marry you, they will fall in line. All young ladies wish to be married. It is their dream in life."

"Surely not all of them," James replied, thinking of Cecilia.

"All of them," his father retorted. "What else does a young lady have? It's not as if a woman could take up an occupation."

Edward conveniently forgot about his own mother, James's grandmother, who had been widowed young and had continued to run her husband's shop while raising three children. His grandmother ran the shop to this day, although she was ceding more responsibilities every day to her oldest son and his children. Sometimes James envied his cousins who ran the shop with her. They were not quite as successful as his father, but they had a comfortable home, quality belongings, and most importantly, did not have to attend high-society events.

Leaning his head back, he reflected on the evening. His father disapproved of the one lady he wanted to pursue further. His abstract ideas about marriage were solidifying, and the wife he now pictured had reddish-brown hair, striking brown eyes, and a mysterious nature.

A loud cough from his father interrupted his reverie, and he met the man's eyes in the darkened interior of the carriage.

"If you were thinking of the duke's sister, put her out of your mind. Nothing good will come of that."

"And what is so inappropriate about her?"

"Other than what we discussed earlier?"

James nodded, but said nothing.

"I have heard concerning stories about Lady Anabel."

James thought of her absence from society. He did not know the reason, but he suspected he was about to hear some wild theories.

"The girl disappeared five years ago. No one knows where she went, but the prevailing opinion is she had an inappropriate liaison and found herself burdened with a bachelor's son."

"And what evidence is there of that?"

His father scoffed. "There doesn't need to be evidence. Her disappearance is reason enough. What puzzles me is why they've brought her back with no ceremony. They must know there is gossip, and none of it good. It was very poorly done on Montgomery's part."

James chose not to respond as he leaned back in his seat and closed his eyes once more. His father harrumphed before doing the same. Annoying as the old man might be, he knew when his son was done listening

The moment they walked into the house after the ball, Isaac and Anabel were bombarded by their mother. The woman was supposed to have spent

the entire season on the continent, which was why Anabel accepted her brother's request. After spending much of her childhood being ignored by her mother, she had no desire to spend time in the woman's presence. Now Anabel stood, frozen in place as the woman approached, wishing she could become invisible and escape to her room.

Rowena Montgomery was a handsome woman in her mid-forties. Her fawn-colored skin complimented her thick, dark-brown hair, so dark it was almost black. She had big brown eyes framed in thick eyelashes—the same eyes Anabel, her brother, and most of the extended family shared. Everyone else's eyes seemed warm, but Rowena's were cold and calculating.

She stopped a foot away and stared, crossing her arms over her chest.

"So, you're back." Her tone was neutral despite her hostile stance.

"As are you. I thought you were going abroad?"

Rowena waved a hand above her head. "I changed my mind when I heard about your reappearance. I thought we'd never see you again."

"You needn't see me now," Anabel snapped. "It's not as if you did so when I lived here as a child."

There was a brief flash of something in her mother's eyes, but the lady quickly composed herself. "If that is how you are going to speak to me, you can get out. I will not tolerate being disrespected in my own home."

"No," Isaac said firmly, shocking both Anabel and their mother. "I have asked Anabel to return, and she will be staying in *my* home." He emphasized the word, reminding their mother he was the one who owned the property, along with everything else belonging to the dukedom.

Rowena's manner changed in an instant. "Of course, darling," she cooed, although she pinned Anabel with a sharp gaze once he turned away.

"We were not expecting you, Mother, but since you're here, we may as well speak." Isaac led the way to the drawing room without further ado, and Anabel and Rowena reluctantly followed. Only after they had settled and sent a servant to fetch refreshments did Isaac speak again.

"I have asked Anabel to come home. It was time for her to stop acting like a—". He paused at Anabel's sharp look. "It was time she stopped living like a nomad and took her rightful place among society."

Rowena contemplated them both suspiciously. "What did he offer you in exchange?"

Anabel flushed. "Nothing! I missed my brother and wanted to see him." She gathered from his careful statements that their mother did not know about his plans to wed. She would not like knowing she'd been left out of her son's plans, particularly as the responsibility of helping a son find a bride generally fell to the mother.

Rowena eyed them both. "There's something you're not telling me, but I'll let it go for now. Don't think I'll forget about it, however."

Anabel had no doubt. Rowena had a particular talent for ferreting out secrets.

After an awkward cup of tea, Anabel excused herself to head to her room. Her maid, Mary, helped her out of her gown and out of the lovely but painful hairstyle. She left Anabel's hair loose, as was her habit.

Needing help dressing was a little embarrassing after having so much freedom—and so little privacy—in the last half-decade. She'd shared a tent with her friend Suraya when they were on the road and shared a room with Suraya and her cousin Fiona at the family's winter-house. Anabel thought of them as she sat in front of the mirror and wound her hair into a loose braid over her shoulder. She missed her loud, boisterous family. When she first went to stay with them, it had been a shock to be surrounded by people, particularly after having spent so much time alone as a child. However, she came to love the open affection and caring they all showed one another.

Being back in her cold, quiet home was lonely. She crawled into bed, the luxurious arrangements foreign after so many years of humble accommodations. The family had slept on pallets, made comfortable thanks to her uncle Fergus's gift. His talent made even the scratchiest bed of straw feel like a down-stuffed mattress.

Anabel wished she had some of Fergus's magic now. The bed might be fine quality, but she was lonesome in the solitude of the cavernous room. As she drifted off into a fitful sleep, she thought back on her evening. The ball had been difficult, although she had enjoyed seeing Cecilia and meeting Sir James.

She recalled her argument with Isaac and of the sensation of being watched. Ever since leaving the safety of her extended family, she had felt a tingling on the back of her neck wherever she went. It was disconcerting. Sometimes her imagination even conjured a voice in her head.

She scoffed at her paranoia. "No one is following me," she said aloud to the room.

Are you sure about that?

Anabel closed her eye at the menacing whisper and concentrated on driving away the awful sound. That was just her subconscious, wasn't it? The voice she'd heard had never addressed her directly before.

So afraid. I can even feel it from where I am. Poor dear. So alone among all those people. Someone is going to find out your secret eventually. It's only a matter of time.

"No," Anabel said, sitting up and staring into the darkness. Her heartbeat thrummed in her ears, and she struggled to repress her trembling.

Suddenly, she felt euphoric, as if she were freed from all the burdens of society, all the burdens of life. It was delicious.

I can give you what you crave, the voice cajoled. *Just a simple ritual and you'll be one of us. You'll have the family and freedom you've always longed for.*

Her eyes flew open. She didn't trust this strange, disembodied entity. "In exchange for what?"

You don't have to give anything up. Just join me. I can show you the way.

The delicious feeling remained. She was tempted to revel in it, but it had to be a trick. "Leave me alone!" she cried, squeezing her eyes shut. The image of a sturdy door like the one on Montgomery House came into her mind. It was open, and she mentally slammed it shut. A moment later, she opened her eyes. The feeling of being watched was gone.

Was she going mad? Was she possessed by some sort of demon? She wished she knew how to do a protection ritual. She considered getting a book from the library, but she wasn't even sure what to look for. For now, she reminisced about warm summer nights with her cousins spent playing games around a fire. It was several hours before she fell asleep.

Chapter 3

Despite his late evening, James arrived early the next morning to the office he and Tom leased for their engineering firm. After Edward forbade him from working in the family business, James had tried to please his father and live the life of an idle bachelor, but he found the lifestyle tedious. He longed to do something industrious but struggled to determine what that was. Then he met Tom Reynolds.

Reynolds was not from a wealthy family. His father had been a mining captain in Cornwall, and, as a boy, Tom had been fascinated with the steam engine used to pump water from the mine. He had studied steam engines of all designs, and his first job had been working on the equipment in the mine where his father worked. He continued to study, learning about inventors making improvements on the steam engine design. It had been a natural progression for him to create inventions of his own.

His drive to invent had led him to a mechanical exhibition in London, where Reynolds decided there was no better place for him. He wrote to his family and informed them that he had no plans to return. An engineering firm had hired him, and he spent several years allowing another man to take credit for his inventions. James had met Tom by chance one evening at a pub. The two had become fast friends and decided to create their own firm.

James invested all his own savings in the business, and they did well at first. However, when Tom's former employer became aware of their existence, they were threatened and intimidated by the larger firm. They'd lost clients because of these tactics and now were struggling. James wanted their venture to succeed, so he'd reached out to his father for support.

Edward Marley had made his fortune in shipping, becoming known as a supplier who could obtain nearly any goods desired by his clients. While he had plenty of legitimate business lines, his true fortune came from smuggling, which had thrived during the war. His father could afford to grant them a loan to help his firm recover from their recent setback. Even if he never received a return on his investment, he wouldn't miss the money. But Edward only agreed to provide support if James went along with the marriage scheme first.

James was sitting at his desk, working through his correspondence, when his father walked in.

"What have you got there, my boy?" he asked as he settled into a chair in front of James's desk.

James bit back a retort. Unfortunately, it was not unusual for the man to drop by unannounced, as if he owned the engineering firm himself. "It's a letter from one of my chaps at Cambridge. He has some information I've been eagerly anticipating."

"Oh?" Edward spoke in a flat tone as he examined his nails.

"Yes. He writes about recent developments in steam locomotive engines and how they are being used to haul goods. Some great advancements have been made."

Edward looked at James, his eyes wide. "Locomotives? Those death traps? I've heard stories of them exploding. Why would you be interested in such a volatile project?"

"They aren't as dangerous as they once were. There are some fellows over in Leeds who have been using a stable locomotive to haul some of their goods. These engines are faster and more efficient than horse-drawn conveyances."

Edward peered at him with a furrowed brow. "How efficient can they be? I've heard about tracks buckling under the weight of the engine and freight. It doesn't seem like a solid investment."

"That capability is coming, father. Tom has heard of new designs that can better bear the load."

"Seems a waste to me. Let them create an engine that doesn't blow up first. One that can haul more than a team of horses."

"Tom has been working on just such a design. If we could get your investment, I'm sure he could come up with a workable prototype. You'd make your money back ten-fold if we were able to lease the design."

"None of that. You know my conditions for investing."

"But—" James began.

'Enough!" Edward said. "You are aware of how I feel about you continuing to engage in trade after everything I've done to elevate our family. Anyway, I have a more important task for you today. You must go visit the ladies you danced with last night."

"Visit?" James asked, bewildered at the change of subject.

"Yes, visit. They will be at home to acquaintances, as is customary after a ball. This is the perfect time for you to see the ladies again, gift them a bouquet of flowers, and press your suit."

"I will be bringing them flowers?"

"Aye, my boy. I have a bucket of them waiting in the carriage. One for each of the three ladies. Taylor has his orders and the directions to each of the ladies' homes. All you need to do is present them with the flowers and be somewhat charming. The rest should take care of itself."

"What does that mean?"

"Never mind. Now, straighten your cravat and put on a dab of cologne. You're otherwise presentable enough."

James resisted his father's fussing. The thought of visiting the homes of nobility was not appealing.

"Must I do this?" He asked his father warily. "I have so many things I could be doing here."

"Allow Reynolds to handle the business. That is his place."

"Reynolds is the inventor. I'm the one who manages the business side of things."

"Then leave the work and come back to it later!" Edward eyed his son sharply, a calculating expression on his face. "I can see you need more incentive than the temptation of a pretty wife and a title for your son. I will provide you with a small investment today to help cover your immediate expenses." James began to smile, but his father held out a hand to stay him. "But only after you complete your visits."

James dropped his smile. He wanted to refuse, but he couldn't turn down a chance to settle with some of his creditors. He left the office with a sigh, his father trailing behind and fussing like a mother hen.

When they reached the carriage, he turned and faced the man once more. "Will you be coming with me?"

"Indeed not," Edward gruffed. "I have my own responsibilities to tend to."

"How fortunate," James replied, keeping his tone as neutral as possible. He glanced pointedly at his father. "Perhaps you can excuse us, then. I would like to discuss our route with Taylor before we begin."

"Ah, yes. Very good. Just don't appear too eager. We want these women to know *they* need *you*, not the other way around."

"Indeed," James intoned as his father turned and walked away, hailing a hackney carriage without a backward glance. James turned to his father's driver, Mr. Taylor, to review the list with each lady's name and her direction. "Let's start with Lady Cecilia, shall we?"

"But her home is in the middle of the route, sir. We'll need to double back."

"Be that as it may, Lady Cecilia is the woman who most piques my interest."

Taylor's eyes lit up briefly, and James felt a small pang of guilt at deceiving the man who'd been serving his family for so many years. But, if he must visit all three of his potential wives today, he would start with the one whose company he could most tolerate.

After a fitful night of sleep, Anabel woke earlier than usual. She dressed without the help of her maid, although she debated whether she should unbutton the gown and allow the maid to assist after all. Now that she was no longer among her relations, she needed to be more careful. A casual use of powers was incredibly common within the family, but they hid their abilities from outsiders. Although the capture, torture, and murder of those accused of witchcraft was not common these days, there were still plenty of people suspicious of magic.

Anabel missed her family. Using her magic helped her feel connected to them. Her family members had a wide range of gifts, and each member had one or two particularly strong abilities. Anabel's predominant talent was moving objects with her mind.

Her power made it very easy to dress herself, but she should allow the maid to do so. The last thing she needed was servants spreading gossip about her. Anabel was unfastening the gown when her maid knocked, and she quickly turned to face the door just as it opened.

She tried to continue loosening the buttons but only managed two more. The dress was half-buttoned, and Anabel could tell Mary was confused as she assisted her with her toilette.

After Mary finished, Anabel headed downstairs, relieved to see only Isaac in the dining room. With any luck, their mother was still sleeping, and Anabel would be able to avoid the duchess for the rest of the day.

As she sat, a footman brought her a cup of hot water. She'd requested one the morning after her return, and the man now brought her the same cup every day. Anabel thanked him, pulled out a small pouch from a hidden pocket, and scooped two spoonfuls of the special tea she always kept with her.

"What is that?" Isaac asked after the footman had retreated.

"It's a special tea blend Suraya prepares."

"It's very fragrant. What's in it?"

"Several herbs and flowers designed to ease pain for women."

"Only for women? Is it not effective for men?"

"Men do not experience the type of pain this tea is meant to affect."

Isaac seemed puzzled for a moment before understanding dawned.

He pointed to the teacup in her hands. "Why do you carry the tea with you? Why not just have the kitchen store it?"

"Because my supply is limited, and I don't know when I will see Suraya again. She gave me the receipt for the blend, but I don't know if I can combine the ingredients in the proper order. Truthfully, Raya has the talent for these things."

"Perhaps we should invite Suraya for a visit."

Anabel could not stop herself from laughing. She loved Suraya dearly, but her friend was the antithesis of a typical Londoner. She wore loose garments, went barefoot as often as she could, and often wore her hair unbound and adorned with flowers.

"I don't think that would be wise," she said once her laughter died down. "Suraya is a bit of a free spirit. I don't believe she would take well to the stringent requirements of a London season."

Rowena entered the room wearing a scowl. "I can't believe Mother puts up with that heathen child. She's not even truly related to our family." The duchess scoffed and took her seat, fixing Anabel with a pointed glare. "Are you already planning your escape?"

"The thought had crossed my mind, yes."

"Oh really?" Rowena perked up.

"I don't think I'm cut out for society and its pressures."

"Of course you aren't," Rowena began.

"You can't leave!" Isaac cut in.

Anabel chose not to respond and finished her tea. She set the cup down on the table and used her spoon to scoop the leaves from the cup into a handkerchief. Rising, she faced her brother. "Isaac, I would prefer if you and I discussed this alone."

Anabel stood as Rowena protested. She ignored her mother as she headed toward the garden. Isaac fell into step behind her.

"Where are you going?"

"At this moment? I'm taking these leaves out to the garden."

He kept up with her as they walked the path that ran through the heavily manicured gardens. Anabel wove through the abnormally shaped shrubs until she came to a patch of newly tilled earth where the gardener had planted some seeds the day before. Kneeling, she opened the handkerchief and scattered the wet tea leaves over the earth. She muttered a few soft words of gratitude before standing again.

Isaac watched her carefully the entire time. "What did you just do?"

"Gave back to the earth as it gives to me." Anabel wiped her hands on the kerchief and folded it before tucking it into her reticule. "And now I am going to call on Lady Cecilia. I would appreciate it if you found a way to keep Mother away from me. I don't relish the thought of being in her presence again."

"She is our mother, Anabel," Isaac chastised.

She turned to face him. "That term means different things to you and me. I spent the first half of my life trying to get her to notice me, and I was always rebuffed. I will not allow myself to end up in the same circumstances now. If you want my help, keep her away from me."

Without another word, Anabel exited the garden and walked inside to grab her bonnet and spencer. She was eager to escape the suddenly suffocating atmosphere of her brother's house.

The carriage stopped a few paces down the road from Lady Cecilia's townhouse, just outside Hyde Park's Cumberland Gate. It was a highly coveted address and spoke to the former wealth of the Earl of Ravenswood. The road was already starting to back up with carriages entering the park, although it was not yet the fashionable hour.

James was idly observing the congestion when he noticed another visitor entering Ravenswood House. It was Lady Anabel. He grabbed two of the bouquets from the bucket on the carriage floor and emerged from the conveyance. A moment later, he was greeted by a dour-looking butler.

When he announced he was there to call on Lady Cecilia, the servant seemed momentarily shocked. Based on their prior conversation, James gathered that Lady Cecilia did not have many gentlemen callers. He waited with the bouquets as he was announced before being led into a comfortable—if somewhat outdated—parlor.

"Sir James," Lady Cecilia said, standing up.

"Lady Cecilia," he replied, handing her one of the bouquets. He handed the other to Lady Anabel, who still sat on the settee, and met her gaze. "Lady Anabel."

She took the flowers and covertly smelled them before settling them in her lap.

"Please, have a seat," Lady Cecilia said. "I've sent Stokes for tea."

James sat in a chair perpendicular to the two ladies and smiled.

"Do you regularly bring two bouquets with you when calling on young ladies, sir?" Lady Anabel's voice broke the awkward silence.

"As it so happens, I had an extra, and when I saw you entering, I thought it would be rude to only bring flowers for one of you."

"Indeed," Lady Cecilia replied. "Your visit is a surprise, sir."

James was puzzled. "I'm not sure why. I enjoyed our conversation and wanted to deepen our acquaintance."

She raised her eyebrows as she met his gaze. "Truly? That is not the typical response from a gentleman of my acquaintance."

James sat back, considering. He wasn't exactly enamored of Cecilia, but she was obviously intelligent and witty, and he wouldn't mind knowing her better. "I suppose I am not a typical gentleman, then."

"I suppose not," she replied, the corners of her mouth quirking before she looked away.

James was unsure what else to say, and Cecilia did not seem inclined to elaborate, so they sat in uncomfortable silence until a maid came in with a tea tray. Lady Cecilia busied herself with pouring tea, then sat back and shot her friend a nervous look.

Lady Anabel cleared her throat and met his gaze. "So, tell us about yourself, Sir James. I believe you said you were in the Royal Navy?"

"Yes. My family owns a shipping company, and I spent much of my youth on ships. After I left Cambridge, the navy seemed a natural fit."

"Did you participate in the war with France?" Lady Cecilia asked.

James paused. He'd been taught that war was not something a man should discuss in the presence of ladies. However, he appreciated how openly he could speak with these two women, so he decided to ignore the rule. "I did, although most of my time was spent running blockades. I also participated in the American war for a time."

"And you are no longer enlisted?" Anabel asked.

"No, I sold my commission when I returned from the war. I've gone into business with a friend now."

"You openly engage in trade?" Cecilia asked, her mouth agape.

"I'm not good at conforming to society's expectations of me," he replied. "My friend Mr. Reynolds is a brilliant inventor. He is working on a new design for a steam locomotive."

"Locomotives!" Anabel leaned forward, and James swallowed as he tried to avoid staring at the tempting slope of her breasts. "There was a locomotive display set up in Bloomsbury several years ago. I wanted to ride in a carriage it pulled, but my brother told me that it derailed frequently."

James nodded. "Yes, that was Trevithick's Steam Circus. Unfortunately, the track had some design flaws, but those are being improved upon. I look forward to the day England has passenger railways."

"Passenger railways?" Lady Cecilia replied. "Imagine the thought! I'm not sure if I would trust it. I have enough troubles with horses. I can't imagine traveling at the speed of those railway carriages."

"You are not fond of riding, then?" James asked.

"No. I do not interact well with large animals."

Lady Anabel reached over and rested a hand on her friend's arm. "You just need to know how to approach them. Horses are very sensitive."

"Does your family in the country have horses?" Lady Cecilia asked. "Because when we were in school together, you were just as wary of horses as I."

Lady Anabel cleared her throat again. "They do, as a matter of fact. They have several horses. I got to know them well."

"You must be a very accomplished rider," James observed.

Anabel's cheeks were rosy as she met his gaze. "I'm afraid I did not spend much time riding. I interacted with the animals often, but I could not get up the courage to ride. My cousin Fiona often tried to get me on a horse, but I refused."

"Fiona," James commented. "That's not a name you hear often. Scottish?"

"Um, yes. That part of my family is Scottish."

He was eager to know more, but didn't want to be rude to his hostess. "Well, it sounds like you have an interesting family."

Anabel gave him a slight smile in response. "Most assuredly."

James decided to bring Cecilia back into the conversation. "Now, Lady Anabel, you mentioned you read Shakespeare when we conversed last night." She blushed at his words. James felt a corresponding warmth in his chest but pushed it down and turned to her friend. "Have you read much of his work, Lady Cecilia?"

Anabel chuckled softly. "She was the one who first introduced me to his works."

Cecilia smiled, and they discussed the Bard before the conversation moved to various novels they'd read recently.

After they finished their tea, James took his leave, proceeding to the other homes his father wished him to visit. He also stopped and made a brief visit to a florist to replace the bouquet he'd given Anabel. The arrangement was not as handsome, but that went to Lady Eliza, who already had an abundance of bouquets on display. There was a long line to visit with her, so James decided not to stay. He left the flowers and his card and continued his calls. He doubted that Lady Eliza would mind his absence.

He spent a quarter of an hour with Miss St. John, though the lady was no more at ease than she'd been during the ball. He couldn't help but think of Lady Anabel the entire time they were speaking. His mind kept wandering to how her eyes had glowed when she spoke of her family and her love of literature. He wanted to learn as much about her as he could.

As the carriage rolled home, James noted they were once again driving past Ravenswood House. As if his thoughts had conjured her, Anabel emerged from the house. She straightened her gloves, opened her parasol, and briskly crossed the street toward the park, a maid trailing behind her. He had a pile of work waiting at the office, but James could not turn down this opportunity to see her again. He thumped the roof of his carriage to signal Taylor to stop, and he was out of the carriage and at the entrance in a flash, just in time to intercept her.

Chapter 4

"Lady Anabel. How lovely to see you again so soon."

Anabel's heart jumped at the sound of the voice she had not been able to get out of her head all morning. "Sir James. What a surprise!"

"Well, I will confess I saw you leave Ravenswood House. I would love a chance to continue our conversation, if you are not opposed."

She considered his proposal. Hyde Park was often crowded, especially at this time of day as people gathered in anticipation of the fashionable hour. The wisest choice would be to forgo taking a stroll, but she was not ready to go home yet. Despite the crowding, there were several small, wooded areas in the park that provided her a respite from the busyness of the city.

"It appears now is not a good time for company. If you will pardon my impertinence, I will take my leave." James said. He sighed and turned to leave, his shoulders slumped.

Anabel felt a tightness in her throat. "Sir James," she said. He turned back and met her gaze with shining eyes. She noted the fullness of his lips, and her mouth went dry with the sudden urge to feel those lips on her own. She cleared her throat in an attempt to clear her thoughts. "I would welcome some company, sir."

"Splendid," he said, giving her a toothy grin.

Anabel smiled in return but noted the crowd in the park. "I should warn you, our walking together may end up in the gossip sheets tomorrow."

James straightened his shoulders and turned toward the entrance. "I am willing to take the chance." He offered his arm to Anabel, and they proceeded along the path. Mary followed, carrying the lovely bouquet Anabel had received from James earlier.

They came upon a crowd, and Anabel gently steered her companion through the crush until they reached the copse of trees she sought. She saw Mary settle on a bench nearby and stepped off the path. The maid caught Anabel's eye and lifted the flowers, giving her a wink.

"This is lovely," Sir James observed.

Anabel released his arm and headed toward her favorite tree. She placed a hand on the young birch and felt the pulse beneath her fingertips. While she primarily levitated objects, Anabel could also feel energy. She mostly used the ability with plants, sharing energy with them. Closing her eyes, she felt the soft hum of the exchange. She took a deep breath and murmured a word of thanks before she opened her eyes. James watched her with keen interest.

"I feel at home here," she offered lamely, not sure how else to explain her behavior. It was as if she'd been mesmerized by the tree and forgotten she wasn't alone. Thankfully, the ritual was not an obvious use of her powers.

James smiled at her. "You previously mentioned your time with your family in the country. I take it city life does not suit you?"

"I wouldn't say that. I suppose I prefer quieter settings, which are hard to come by in London. Although, my family is anything but quiet."

"I see," he replied. He adjusted his posture so that his hands were behind his back and leaned in slightly closer. "Would you tell me about them?"

Anabel was cautious when it came to discussing her family, but she wanted to continue reminiscing. "They are my mother's relations. This is not common knowledge, but my mother was not good ton before she married my father."

"Are they one of those families who have fallen on hard times?"

"No, not like that." They were far enough removed from the crowd that their conversation would not be overheard. "I haven't been entirely honest about them." She began pacing the small area. "There are things about my family that would not be accepted by society, but I'm not ashamed of them. I love them as they are."

"I know we only just met," James said, "but I would be happy to listen." He reached out for her but quickly pulled his hand back.

Anabel stopped pacing and stared at him for a long moment. "I feel silly for thinking this, but perhaps you, as an outsider, would understand more than others. Can I trust you to keep what I'm about to tell you a secret?"

"Of course," he said. He observed their seclusion, then grabbed her hand, giving it a squeeze. "I will keep your confidence."

Anabel took a deep breath and squeezed his hand in response, reluctantly letting go. "My mother is not from a society family. Our relations are..." she tried to decide how to word her response. "They are merchants."

James smiled. "That's not so bad. I'm the son of a merchant."

"Not like your father. He's a tradesman. The goods he acquires are sold to other vendors, are they not?"

"They are."

"My family buys the wares they sell, at least in part, from those vendors."

"Do they have a shop?"

"In a sense. They travel to various towns throughout the country to sell their goods."

His face relaxed. "They are traveling merchants."

"Among other things. My cousin, Fiona, whom I mentioned earlier, is a trick horseback rider. She puts on shows at town fairs. She's built a name for herself within the show circuit."

"I see. So, your family travels with Fiona and sells their wares while supporting her performances?"

"Some do. Some of my cousins perform other shows or operate amusements like games of chance."

"What a unique family you have."

"I do. And I miss them terribly. I was not made for society life. The only reason I'm here is to help my brother find a wife. He takes his responsibility as the duke very seriously and has decided he must marry."

"There are many who neglect their duties. His diligence is to be admired." He paused, looking down before continuing. "May I ask... that is, if I'm not being impertinent..." He took a deep breath before continuing. "How did your mother come to marry a duke with such humble origins?"

Anabel bit her lip. She could not be completely honest. "She obtained an invitation to a ball and enchanted him so much he pursued her." The enchantment in question had been a spell to make the duke lust for Rowena above all other women, but Anabel couldn't share that. "They were married within two weeks of meeting."

"That's very quick."

"My father was in his sixties and had no heir. He was looking for his third wife and felt there was no time to waste."

James's eyes widened so much she thought they might pop out of their sockets. "In his sixties! How old was your mother?"

"Eighteen."

He swallowed. "That is quite the difference."

"Yes," she agreed. "Perhaps not a frequent occurrence, but not unheard of."

"Very true."

Anabel saw his hand resting by his side. Her skin still tingled where they had touched, even through the layer of her gloves. She looked up, and her breath caught at the intensity of his gaze.

A light breeze swirled by them, and James stepped closer. "Lady Anabel," he said, fingering a lock of hair the wind had blown into her face. He tucked the strand behind her ear and held her gaze.

A loud noise broke the spell, and Anabel leapt back. "I believe it is time for us to make our way home," she said, stepping away. She caught Mary's eye, and the maid closed her novel.

"May I offer you a ride?"

Anabel knew she should refuse. Her hand still tingled, and her neck reddened when she remembered the light touch. But she was not ready to leave his company. Taking a deep breath, she squared her shoulders. "Thank you. Mary and I would love an escort."

She made sure to sit next to Mary during the ride home.

The small loan from James's father allowed him to settle with some of his creditors and gave him enough funds to purchase new materials Tom desperately needed. He arrived the next day to accept the delivery and left the packages in Tom's workshop. He was writing letters when Tom entered his office a short while later.

"Have we obtained a new investor?"

"Good morning to you as well," James replied.

"Yes, yes, good morning." Tom never cared for etiquette. "Well," he continued, raising his eyebrows. "Do we have a new investor?"

"Why do you ask?"

"Because two days ago I was disassembling old inventions to repurpose materials, and now I have a surplus of parts."

James looked off in the distance. "We do not."

"Then where did you get the funding for new supplies?"

"Why are you concerned? Aren't you happy to have the items you need?"

"I'm concerned because I fear you may have made an unscrupulous deal to obtain them."

It was James's turn to raise his eyebrows. "I would never put you or our business at risk."

"You're evading," Tom stated. "I would like a plain answer, if you please."

James muttered a curse under his breath. "I have convinced my father to invest."

"In exchange for what?"

"Does there need to be an exchange? You don't trust my ability to get the old man on board?"

"No, I do not, because I have met your father. I know he wouldn't do anything without obtaining something for himself in return."

James opened his mouth to argue but promptly closed it. He could not disagree with Tom's statement. He hesitated for a moment longer before deciding to confide in his friend. "He is requiring that I marry."

Tom furrowed his brow. "Well, that's not so bad," he said as he took a seat in front of James's desk. "I've been pestering you for a while now to find a woman to share your life with." Despite his practicality and curt manners, Tom was a romantic at heart.

James rested his forehead on his hand. "If only it were that easy. In his continued quest to enter the nobility, father has mandated that I must marry a woman from a family where the title can pass through the female line."

Tom laughed dryly. "Is that even a possibility? I thought all nobs had to hand their titles down to a male relative."

"It is possible with some of the older titles, but there are less than a hundred in all the kingdom. And even fewer where a daughter is actually in a position to pass the title on."

"How many are there at present?"

"Three, and I have been directed to court each one."

Tom sucked in a breath through his teeth. "That seems an impossible situation."

"Well, if I can find a suitable bride, my father will solve all of our financial worries."

"At the expense of your happiness!"

James waved his friend off. "Marriage is not the key to my happiness. I will be happy when our business is financially solvent. And my father will be happy because his grandchild could be an earl." He turned his head and swallowed hard.

Tom observed him for a moment before his face lit up. "You've met someone you fancy, haven't you? And she must not be on the approved list, or you wouldn't appear so conflicted."

James looked at his friend sharply. "Why would you ever think that?"

"Call it intuition," he replied with a wink. "You've always said my intuition is what makes me such a good inventor. Perhaps it benefits me in other ways as well."

He was just about to reply when the shop bell rang. He and Tom both rose, walking to the front. Lady Anabel stood there, illuminated from behind. The golden light spilled around her from a high window and brought out the red tones in her hair. James's fingers itched once more to touch the soft strands framing her face.

Tom's boisterous chuckle broke James from the spell of his astonishment. His partner patted James's shoulder. "I'll let you handle this one." He turned and headed back toward his workshop.

"Lady Anabel," he said, wincing internally when he heard the breathiness in his voice.

"Sir James," she responded.

"Please, I insist you call me James."

She gave him a small smile. "Only if you will agree to call me Anabel in return."

"It would be my pleasure." He stepped closer, once again noting the pesky lock of hair that never seemed to stay in her coiffure. He tucked it behind her ear. "How can I help you today?"

She blushed and dipped her chin, but did not step back. "Actually," she replied, reaching into her reticule and handing him a folded piece of paper, "I'm here to help you."

He carefully straightened the page, laying it out on the counter to read in the light from the windows. It was a scandal sheet, like those his father collected.

An interesting development occurred in Hyde Park yesterday, when the mysterious lady A.M. was seen promenading alongside Sir J.M., a newly conferred Knight Bachelor. The two were seen unchaperoned and in close conversation in a secluded area of the park, before leaving the park in the M. family carriage. One wonders what illicit trysts may have occurred away from the watchful eyes of the ton. Will we be hearing wedding bells for the lady and her knight? Or will Sir J. turn out to be a rake of the first order?

James grunted and squeezed the paper in his fist. "What utter rubbish. Your maid was with us the entire time. We were not alone in the park or the carriage."

She swallowed, temporarily distracting James with her slender throat. "This is why young ladies are cautioned to avoid even the appearance of impropriety. I should not have accompanied you in the park. My maid was not an adequate chaperone."

"This," he said, holding up the paper. "Is nothing but flimflam. They have no proof I compromised you."

"Nevertheless, the rumor is out there." Her eyes brimmed with unshed tears. She blinked rapidly several times before looking over to the counter that James and Tom used as a repository for books and unimportant papers. Anabel cleared her throat before continuing. "I came to warn you. I've managed to keep this from my brother for now, but the rumors will reach him. He will most certainly pay you a visit."

"Will he insist that I marry you?" James tensed at the thought of another forced marriage. Although marriage to Anabel might not be so bad.

Her gaze darted back to him. Her mouth was open, but she gave no response. Color rushed to her cheeks, and James idly wondered if she would blush as deeply if he kissed her. He shook his head to remove the illicit thoughts. He did not need a forced marriage, no matter how attractive the lady was. He turned his head to face her but noticed a slight movement out of the corner of his eye. To his astonishment, one of the books appeared to be floating a few inches above the counter's surface.

He gaped, glancing at Anabel to see if she also saw the levitating book.

"What is it?" she asked, a tremor in her voice.

"It's..." James pointed to the counter, unsure how to describe what he saw. The book, however, was once again lying flat on the surface

Tom emerged from his workshop, moved to the counter, and picked up the very same book. "Sorry to interrupt," he said. "Just needed to retrieve this."

James gave him a distracted nod before looking back at Anabel, but she was gone. He ran out of the shop, determined to stop her. He checked in both directions but could not see her. Tom stepped outside as well. "She fled," James observed, his mind racing.

Tom laid a hand on his friend's shoulder. "You'll see her again." He looked up at the sky before continuing. "I suppose she is the one you fancy?"

James was too bewildered to prevaricate. "Yes."

"Wise choice, my friend." He gave his friend's shoulder one more squeeze before dropping his hand. "Shall we take a break and go get luncheon?"

James allowed Tom to steer him back inside. He nearly told his friend that he needed to leave and find Anabel when his stomach growled loudly.

Tom handed him his coat. "Let's eat first, then we can discuss what you should do next." James nodded and followed his friend.

❦

Anabel was flustered as she entered her home. She'd run away from James as fast as she could when he'd looked back at the counter, furious with herself for nearly revealing her power. Part of her had wished to find a place where she belonged in London, but she was hopeless when it came to life apart from the family. As out of place as she felt among her relations, perhaps it would be best for her to return to them.

She started walking toward the stairs, but then heard a loud voice coming from the open door of the sitting room. "I insist, Your Grace."

"That's not necessary, Mr. Marley."

Marley? Curious, she slipped toward the sitting room, staying out of view of the occupants.

"I disagree. And anyway, it's already done. I'll not have my family name slandered."

"Did Fergus's nasty daughter teach you to sneak around and spy on people?"

Anabel jumped and turned to see her mother standing with her hands on her hips, looking at her with raised eyebrows.

"I was just…" Anabel trailed off, not wanting to admit she'd been eavesdropping.

Rowena looked over her daughter's shoulder into the room, which had become very quiet. She shot Anabel one more withering glare before walking through the doorway. Anabel followed in her mother's wake.

"Mother, Anabel," Isaac said as both men rose. "Allow me to introduce Mr. Edward Marley."

"Your Grace," Mr. Marley said as he sunk into a respectable bow. "And Lady Anabel. You honor me with your presence."

"I do, indeed," Rowena replied, her posture stiff. "What is your purpose in being here today?"

"I've come to tell His Grace I have already taken care of the libel printed about my son and your daughter in today's gossip sheet."

"Oh, there's no need for that," Rowena replied.

"Exactly as I said," Isaac replied with a nod.

"Yes." Rowena sat in a chair and carefully arrayed her skirts. The men and Anabel also sat. No one said a word until Rowena finished arranging herself and regarded them once more. "There is no need because my daughter is already a walking scandal. What's one more on the list?"

"Mother," Isaac said through clenched teeth. "Perhaps this is not something we should discuss in front of company."

"Oh please, Isaac," she said with a wave. "It's not as if Anabel has a good name to save."

"But my son does!" Mr. Marley interjected. Rowena's eyes flashed, but she allowed the man to go on. "My coachman can attest the two were never alone, in the park or the carriage. The girl's maid can no doubt corroborate the story. The paper will be printing a retraction tomorrow stating the story was written in a misleading manner and there is no scandal.”

“How did you get them to do that?” Anabel asked. Three pairs of eyes looked at her, as if they had all forgotten she was in the room.

Marley cleared his throat. “I bought the paper.”

“You bought the paper?” Rowena stared at the man with wide eyes.

“Aye,” Edward replied. “As I was saying to His Grace, I will not have my family’s name dragged through the mud. My son is a respectable gentleman and would never take advantage of a lady. He was kind enough to offer Lady Anabel a ride home after she had been visiting with a woman my son called on, Lady Cecilia Manning. There was nothing untoward about the meeting.”

Isaac rose and approached the other man. Marley stood to meet him. “I appreciate you informing me of this solution, Mr. Marley.”

“Of course, Your Grace,” Marley responded.

“We need to discuss this as a family. You will leave now,” Isaac said, staring into the man’s eyes.

Mr. Marley turned and walked away without further comment, his movements stiff and unnatural. A footman met him, and Isaac softly closed the door behind them.

Anabel squirmed as her brother took his seat once more. “I suppose now is a bad time to tell you about the gossip sheet?” she asked, giving him a small smile.

Isaac was not amused. “Were you ever planning to tell me?”

“I was,” she assured him. “I just wanted to warn James first.”

“James? Do you mean Sir James?”

She shrunk back. “Yes?”

“And where exactly did you meet with Sir James?”

“At his office.”

"His office?" Isaac stood again and stalked over to her chair, his long legs allowing him to reach her in two strides. "You went to the east side of town? Did you at least bring a servant with you?"

She mimicked his posture. Her brother was nearly a foot taller, but she would not let him intimidate her. "No, I didn't bring a servant. I'm faster on my own."

"So, you didn't take the ducal carriage?"

"No. I took a hack."

"What?!" For the first time since she had found Anabel snooping, Rowena showed a modicum of emotion. She strode over to them. "You rode in a dirty hack?"

"Yes," Anabel replied, biting back a smile.

"And you sat on my furniture?" Rowena cried. "You must go upstairs and change out of that filthy gown. Have Mary send for a bath as well. You need to get that stench off you."

"What stench?"

"You reek of common folk." Rowena pinched her nose and looked away.

Anabel wanted to be offended, but a bath did sound lovely.

"A moment, Mother," Isaac interjected. He moved in closer to Anabel, looming over her. "You are not to leave this house alone anymore. Do you understand me?"

"But, Isaac!" She started to protest, but he cut her off.

"No, Anabel! Your reputation may be in tatters, but you are still a part of this family. We have a name to protect. You may not value it, but I do."

"It's not that I don't," she began.

"Your brother is right," Rowena picked an invisible speck of lint from her gown. "You cannot be trusted to do anything with sense. You are asking someone to take advantage of you. We should send you away to one of the country estates where you can't—"

A vase sitting on a pedestal in one corner flew across the room, crashing into the opposite wall.

"Anabel!" she cried, turning to her daughter. "That was a Ming vase gifted to the second duke by King James."

"Enough!" Anabel yelled. "I am not responsible for another's lies about me, and I don't deserve your scorn. I am going to my room, not because you want me out of sight, but because I need some quiet. I will not countenance such treatment again."

She marched to the door, wrenching it open. She encountered Hawkins and instructed him to send up water for a bath, as well as her maid. She would take a bath, but only because she was angry and needed to calm down. She wasn't sure what to do about this treatment from her mother and brother. She didn't feel comfortable among her extended family, nor did she feel comfortable under the thumb of her mother and brother. Sir James's words came back to her. Would Isaac force him to marry her? Marriage would get her away from her mother, but James didn't seem very pleased about the idea. She was not ready to examine why that made her sad.

Chapter 5

The next morning, James made his way to his office, still fixated on his meeting with Anabel. It had been a strange encounter, to be sure, but he was most disappointed by the sudden loss of her company. He and Anabel had a connection. She was beautiful, intelligent, kind, and the most intriguing woman he'd ever met. He felt a pleasant warmth at the fact that she'd trusted him with one of her secrets during their walk in the park. He was no longer angry at the thought of being forced to marry her, instead he had a strong desire to be the person she entrusted all her secrets to.

James had not grown up with a good impression of marriage. His parents weren't acrimonious, but they were not a love match. His mother was the daughter of a gentleman who owned a small estate in Suffolk. Edward made no secret of the fact that he'd bought his wife by paying her father's gambling debts. When her father died, James's mother inherited the estate, which went to Edward, who turned his attention toward acquiring a neighboring estate as well as several properties in the nearby town. James rarely saw the family estate growing up. His parents did not spend much time outside of London. His mother seemed content to live a life of luxury, participating in social engagements all over town. Both his father and mother had their own pursuits, and James was often left on his own during his childhood. He had never known affection or acceptance the way Anabel seemed to with her family.

James wondered if his father could be convinced to settle for a connection to a duke. His grandchild might not be directly in line for a title, but there was a possibility the duke would not have an heir, which could make James's son eligible to inherit. It was a long shot, since Anabel had disclosed her brother's search for a wife, but perhaps it was worth a try.

He was playing out scenarios in his mind when Edward walked in.

"Woolgathering, are you?" the old man said in lieu of a greeting.

James shook his head to release the thoughts. "Good morning, Father. What brings you in today?"

His father sat across from James and glared. "I fixed your little problem with the gossip sheet."

"Pardon?"

"The paper is printing a retraction. The scandal should also die down rather quickly, as a juicy tidbit about the Countess of Bellamy is running today."

"And how did you manage that?"

"I purchased the paper, of course. It's high time I bought one anyway. It's a worthy investment."

"I see." James pushed back from his desk, unsure how he felt about that information.

"Some gratitude would not be out of order, son. I saved you from making an inappropriate marriage."

James took a breath and decided to be honest. "What if I didn't find the marriage in question inappropriate?"

Edward's face screwed up. "I'd say you'd better know what you're doing. If you want my support, it will only come from marrying a lady of my choosing."

Leaning back, James met his father's gaze head on. "Perhaps I don't need your support. There are other ways to get investors for our business."

"Not if I tell them not to invest with you. I may not be a nob, but I have sway among the businessmen of London," Edward said, leaning back in his chair. "If you want your little venture to survive, then select one of the women from my list. The Marleys will become part of the aristocracy, dammit!"

"I'm a knight, father. Technically, I am part of the aristocracy."

Edward scoffed. "A knight is the lowest of all titles. I know they look down on us for my inferior birth. Never mind that I could buy and sell them all in a day. The whole rotten lot of them have nothing but their pride."

"If you dislike them so, why are you so eager to join their ranks?"

"They will not have me! No one denies me what I want. I will laugh in all their faces when they see someone from my line inheriting one of their precious titles."

James leaned forward, placing his elbows on the desk. "Society is not so much about titles as connections. Surely it would be better to ally ourselves with a dukedom, even indirectly, than an impoverished earldom."

Edward stood and leaned over the desk so that he was looming over his son. "You want to marry Montgomery's sister? I won't allow it. You could not have picked a worse match."

"Why? She's a duke's sister. If you want to force the nobility to accept you, having the support of a duke would be beneficial."

"Not a puppy of a duke like Montgomery! The man is only just six and twenty. He has no influence and no idea what he is doing. And that family is riddled with scandal."

"What do you mean?"

"Montgomery's mother seduced the late duke and stole him from another woman of good quality. No one knew her or where she'd come from. She mysteriously appeared and enticed the late duke away from his betrothal. He jilted a good lady and married the scab within two weeks. There are rumors she used nefarious means to entrap him."

"Nefarious? What on Earth does that mean?"

"Some sort of a love spell or enchantment. No one knows for sure, but that's how witches operate. They sow seeds of mistrust until no one is sure of anything."

James couldn't believe his ears. His father had never been the superstitious sort. "So, you are saying the lady used witchcraft? That's preposterous! And regardless of how she got the position, she is a duchess now. What sense is there in discussing things that cannot be changed?"

"Duchess she may be, but she is still a woman with no past. No one knows where she came from. And there are worse rumors about the lady than the circumstances of her marriage."

"What rumors?" he asked, trying to keep his voice steady. He braced himself to hear Anabel's secret. Was the fact that her family were traveling fair folk common knowledge among the ton?

"There are those who say the duchess killed the old duke with her foul witchcraft."

James sat back, silent as he processed the words. "Surely, she didn't kill the man! The old goat was in his sixties when he married." He couldn't help but laugh at the absurdity.

"He was in perfect health! He married the chit, and less than a decade later he's dead. That is suspicious, is it not?"

"It's not. He was past the age of seventy by the time he died."

His father grunted and waved his hands at his son. "You're impossible to talk to when you're like this. You will defend the family, no matter what I say, because you are besotted by the girl. Put that out of your head right now! She is not for you. If the mother uses witchcraft, you can be sure the daughter does as well. And anyway, the girl is a walking scandal. I heard so from her mother's own mouth."

"When would you have heard that? I wasn't aware you were acquainted with the duchess."

"I was introduced to her yesterday when I paid Montgomery a visit to tell him I'd fixed the problem."

James leaned forward once more. "You visited the duke?"

"I did. And you should be grateful that I saved you once again. If you want to continue to receive my assistance, get that little witch out of your mind and pick a bride from my list!" He turned and left the room before James could say anything more.

James's chest tightened as he replayed the conversation. Anabel had shared how her mother had met the duke, but what had the lady done to catch the duke's eye? How had the old man been so besotted that he would have jilted a respectable match? A young man may behave that way, but a man past the age of sixty on his third marriage was not likely to be swept away. Had there been unnatural forces at play? That was ridiculous, wasn't it? Magic wasn't real.

Still, he couldn't silence his doubt. If Anabel's mother could enchant a man, would her daughter do the same? After all, James had only met Anabel a few days ago, and he was already considering marrying her. He couldn't stop thinking about her, and he wanted to break with propriety every time they were together. Could his obsession be the product of some spell?

Anabel awoke the next day with heated cheeks at the memory of her childish display in the drawing room. She wished she could go back and stop herself from smashing the vase. Her brother was surely waiting to lecture her on respecting the history of the dukedom, but he needn't bother. She was already saying everything to herself. The disappointment in his voice would crush her, so she resolved to stay out of his sight for as long as possible.

Her room was boring, however. She perused her small collection of books, thinking to pass the time by reading. She'd read all the books in her possession, but one of her favorite authors had recently published a new story. Could she sneak away to the bookshop without being noticed?

Resolved, she grabbed her spencer and bonnet and stepped out of her room, closing the door with a quiet snick. She tiptoed down the stairs and paused in the entryway to tie on her bonnet.

"Where are you going?"

Anabel jumped at Isaac's voice. Breathing slowly to calm her racing heart, she turned to face her brother. He wore a frown on his usually stoic face.

"I am going out," she replied, holding her chin high.

Isaac eyed her suspiciously. "Out where? And why don't you have your maid with you?"

She scoffed. "Really, Isaac! I don't always need a chaperone. I know how to care for myself."

"We discussed this," he replied. "Considering the recent scandal that nearly forced you to marry a stranger, you shouldn't ever leave the house without a proper escort." He lowered his voice and leaned in, suddenly changing from the disapproving duke to her concerned brother. "You need to show propriety in your every action. I will never find a bride from a good family if everyone thinks my sister is a hoyden."

Anabel sighed and stared at her brother for a long moment. "I don't claim the title of hoyden, but I agree that I'm unusual. I won't ever be considered proper by society."

She expected her brother to continue arguing with her, but his face fell, and he looked at her the way he had when they were children and he wanted her to do something for him. She could never refuse that expression. "I need you to try, please, for my sake. Hundreds of people depend on our family for their livelihood. I have a duty to them, and that includes marrying and producing an heir to ensure they will continue to be cared for."

When he put it that way, Anabel couldn't say no. "Fine, let me call for Mary."

"I'm here, my lady," Mary said suddenly. She must have been waiting just out of sight. "Hawkins found me in the kitchen a few moments ago and informed me you wished to go out."

"Thank you for your concern for your mistress, Mary," Isaac said, and the young maid blushed. "Your diligence is greatly appreciated."

Isaac insisted they take the carriage and a footman. Anabel sighed as they waited for the carriage and longed for the simpler days when she was traveling.

After a long while, they finally arrived at the bookshop. Anabel tapped her fingers rapidly as the footman arranged the stool and helped her exit. She entered the bookshop with Mary dogging her heels—the maid having promised the duke that she would stay close to her mistress.

Isaac's duty to marry and the part she had to play in it ran through her mind while she perused the shelves. If she could find a suitable match, she could leave her brother's house, and he could focus on his own marriage. Marriage had never been a goal of hers before, but she could see the value, particularly with a well-suited man. A tall man perhaps, with light brown hair, captivating eyes, and tantalizing lips. Someone with whom she could speak openly and share her interests.

She'd never met anyone that made her feel the way she felt around James. They had only known each other a few days, but she'd spent more time than she liked to admit imagining a life with him. She itched to know more about the things she'd seen in his workshop. Would he teach her? Or even let her have a hand in his business? She'd always been good at organizing things, and she'd learned much from helping her Uncle Fergus manage the administrative tasks that accompanied their family's trade. Perhaps she could help James's business prosper.

She shook her head to clear the wayward thoughts. She was not going to marry a London man and stay in town. She was not suited for city life. Even if she were, she was still experiencing issues with her powers. She remembered the sound of the vase crashing against the wall, and her throat choked up. She could never tell James about her unreliable magical talent.

Don't forget that you also hear voices.

The words echoed in her mind. She hadn't heard the voice since the other night, deliberately choosing not to dwell on it. Was that thought her own, or was the voice speaking to her again? She pretended to read titles to calm the shaking in her limbs, occasionally touching the spine of a book. Her thoughts drifted back to James. He had been so understanding when she told him about her family. Perhaps he would accept her powers? He was a kind man. If she took the time to get to know him, would he understand?

She scoffed. How could he understand her when she didn't even understand herself? She imagined him staring at her with horror, and her eyes watered. She spun way from the shelf and cradled her head in her hands.

The silence of the shop was interrupted by a loud clatter. Anabel lifted her head and saw five books scattered at her feet. Horrified, she noticed empty spaces on the shelves and saw that every book came from a different shelf, and each was one she'd physically touched. It was as if a string was connected from her fingers to each book, and when she'd turned away, the string had pulled taut.

She lifted her head warily, praying no one had seen the incident. Luck was not on her side, because she met the shocked eyes of Mary, who glanced at the books and then back at Anabel.

Mary lifted her hands to cover her mouth, but Anabel heard her whisper as if she'd shouted it throughout the shop.

"My lady," Mary said. "What just happened?"

Before she could even begin to consider how to respond, the voice was back.

She will tell others your secret. They will come for you. You must run. Come find me, and I will shelter you.

Anabel's knees wobbled. She knew those were not her thoughts.

"No!' She yelled, slamming the door in her mind. The minute she did, a terrible headache started to bloom. She doubled over and bit her lip to avoid crying out.

"My lady?" Mary asked again.

Anabel looked up at her maid, and everything turned black. The last thing she heard was Mary crying out as she fell to the floor.

After a restless night, James awoke with a head full of doubts. His father's gossip weighed heavily on him. The words repeated on a loop all morning as he sat in his office, moving through his daily routine. By mid-morning, he'd given up on accomplishing anything. He needed to investigate further, and decided the best place to do so was his father's private library.

Joining the British aristocracy had been a long-term goal for Edward Marley, and he'd begun collecting information on them early in his life. His personal library was filled with copies of Debrett's. He had also amassed an impressive collection of newspapers and gossip sheets. James was sure there was a museum somewhere that would welcome the old man's collection, but today he would use it to put his mind at ease.

His mother and father were not at home, and he thanked his good fortune that he was able to proceed unimpeded. He greeted his parents' butler, declined the offer of refreshments, and headed to the library.

He started with Debrett's, researching the Duke of Montgomery. He learned the date Anabel's mother had married the old duke. With that date in mind, he turned to the newspapers. His father meticulously organized his collection, so it was no trouble at all to find the issues from that period. He found three separate newspapers with a write-up about the wedding. All were unhelpful. They mentioned the particulars of the event, the number of attendees, and the distinction of the Montgomery line, but none had much to say about the bride. The gossip sheets were also unhelpful, although they used slightly more colorful language to hint at the bride's origins. One sheet referenced an edition from the previous month, and James returned to the files.

He found two sheets released on the date referenced. Both described a mysterious, dark-haired young woman who had appeared at one of the more influential balls that season. The lady, referred to as Miss H., was described as uncommonly beautiful, with rich dark hair, dark eyes, and an abundance of grace. They also mentioned that "His Grace, Lord M., could not take his eyes off Miss H., despite his recent betrothal to Lady A.W." James was not sure who Lady A.W. was, but it was clear who the other parties had been.

He was crestfallen. All the information confirmed what his father had told him. Anabel's mother had most certainly lured the duke away from his betrothed. He had no idea how Miss H. had convinced the duke to marry her in such a short amount of time. The gossip sheet described the lady as having 'bewitched' the duke, backing up the rumor his father shared. James still struggled to believe it. Sorcery and witchcraft weren't real. They were superstitions from a time when people did not understand how science worked. James scoffed as he put the materials away.

He settled into a chair in the library to consider what he had learned. There must have been some other reason the duke had jilted Lady A.W.

But, as he pondered, his mind kept returning to witchcraft. Had Anabel enchanted him? He had a hard time believing she would deliberately do so. Perhaps she had some unconscious ability that drew him to her? After all, a few days ago he had not cared at all whom he married, and now he was devising ways to convince his father to support the match. Was that not proof enough?

He laughed at this train of thought. There was no spell craft at work here. He'd just been caught up in the first genuine attraction he'd felt in a long time. That was it. It had been some time since James had been with a woman. He'd had an arrangement with an understanding widow, but she had moved to the country some six months before. James had not had the time nor the inclination to find another companion.

He resolved to put Anabel out of his mind. He needed to be more objective in the process of finding a wife. This was a business transaction, after all. No need to get feelings involved. In time, he and his spouse might come to love, or at least esteem, one another, but he did not expect passion in the beginning. James never let himself get caught up in excitement. The only way to get ahead was to be pragmatic. That was how he'd achieved his success, and it was how he would find a wife. His father would get the noble connections he'd craved, and James would save his business and support Tom's work on locomotives.

His purpose renewed, James stood and straightened his coat and cravat. He had much work to do to make up for his idleness that morning. He ignored the knot in his stomach and heaviness in his limbs at the thought of Anabel's sweet smile. He was determined to remain objective.

Chapter 6

Anabel twisted her fingers as Mary arranged her hair. Her fainting spell yesterday had caused quite an uproar in the bookshop. For the remainder of the day, Anabel had refused to answer any of Mary's questions. She should have just denied outright that she'd had anything to do with those books falling off the shelf. Most people witnessing magical incidents were happy to convince themselves that what they'd seen was not reality. If Anabel had said, "I don't know," when Mary had asked what happened, there would be no awkwardness now.

The voice had not returned. She'd awoken from her fainting spell with a headache that had not abated. The pain originated from the same area as the voice. Had she done that? Or had the voice hurt her as it was pushed away?

She was more disturbed by the voice than she was comfortable admitting. No one in her family heard disembodied voices. Her cousin Fiona heard animals speak, but they were always nearby. Anabel worried she was touched in the head.

Her headache and racing thoughts prevented Anabel from showing her nerves overtly, but Mary kept shaking and dropping things. More hairpins had scattered on the floor than were on Anabel's head. The process of having her hair arranged, usually soothing, had been almost unbearable tonight.

Mary secured one last pin and stepped back. She wouldn't meet Anabel's eyes in the mirror. "May I help you with anything else, my lady?"

"No," Anabel sighed. Mary started to exit when Anabel whirled around. "Wait," she called. Mary froze, but did not turn.

"Yes, my lady?"

Anabel cautiously approached her maid. "Mary, I want to…" She wasn't sure how to put her emotions into words. Swallowing, she began again. "Mary, let's talk about what you saw yesterday."

"I'm not sure what you mean, my lady. I saw nothing."

"You and I both know that's not true. There was an incident at the book shop, and I handled it poorly."

Mary took in several deep breaths before meeting Anabel's gaze. "I'm happy to say whatever you ask me to say, my lady." Anabel would have believed her, if it weren't for the tremor in her voice.

"Mary, I feel like we were building a friendship, and my actions yesterday damaged that relationship. What you saw—"

"Was a practical joke. Or a strange wind blowing through the building. Or mayhap your fingers were sticky, and the books stuck to them."

Anabel wrung her hands. "I don't want you to be afraid of me."

Mary stared at Anabel for a long moment. "I ain't afraid of you. I don't know what I saw, and I'm afraid of that, but it don't make me afraid of you."

"Then why are you so shaky?"

Mary looked at her hands as if just realizing how much they were trembling. "Perhaps I am a bit scared."

Anabel grabbed her maid's hand in a light grip and was heartened when the girl did not pull away. "Mary, I have…" she hesitated. "I have unusual abilities. I was born with them, but I don't like to discuss them for fear of what might happen to me if people knew."

Mary gripped Anabel's hand tighter. "I didn't think about that, my lady. I ain't said nothing to no one. I'll keep your secrets."

"Will you?"

"I didn't know what I saw, but I said nothing to none of the other servants."

"Thank you, Mary. I appreciate your secrecy. England is only just beyond the time of witch hunts."

They were silent for a few moments, then Mary let out a short giggle. "Can I see it?"

Anabel smiled at the girl's light tone. "A display of what I can do?"

"Can you control it?"

Anabel was glad to hear Mary's natural accent. She wanted to protect this fragile intimacy. Her eyes landed on a book sitting on the bedside table. Anabel widened her grin and opened her hand. The book glided from the table to Anabel's outstretched palm. The maid's eyes were as big as saucers as she took the book now being handed to her.

"Gracious me!" Mary paged through the volume for a moment before snapping the book shut. "That's how you buttoned your dress by yourself!"

Anabel laughed. She felt so much lighter now that she had been honest with someone.

"Do you do anything else?"

"Like what?"

"Spells and the like. My gram talked about a woman in her village who could do spells, for a price. Everyone was careful when they asked her for a favor. Sometimes what they got didn't turn out good."

"I personally don't do spells, although I know some people that do."

"Are they like the woman in my gram's village?"

She hesitated, because she wanted to protect her family's privacy. It was one thing for her maid to know about her abilities, but quite another to know there was an entire family with magical powers. "They are a bit like that, yes."

Mary looked at the book again before meeting Anabel's eyes. "So, you just move things with your mind?"

"Yes. I can also help plants grow, although that's not as strong of an ability."

"How did you learn it?"

"It isn't something I learned. It started happening around the time I turned fifteen. I had a hard time controlling it at first, but it got easier with time." Anabel gently grabbed Mary's hand and met the other woman's eyes. "Please don't share this with anyone. I am not a danger to others, but people fear what they don't understand."

"I'll keep your secrets," Mary repeated, meeting Anabel's gaze earnestly.

A knock caused them both to jump. Mary went to open the door. Isaac stood there and, although he could not have known what they were discussing, gave Anabel an accusing glance.

"Did you need something?" she asked.

Isaac scowled toward the clock on the mantel. "I told you to be ready a quarter of an hour ago. We are going to be late to the Greystones' dinner party."

Anabel felt her tension return, but Isaac prided himself on his punctuality. "Of course. Let me grab my reticule and shawl, and I'll be ready to go."

"Here you are, my lady," Mary said, handing the reticule to Anabel the placing the shawl around her shoulders.

Anabel felt sad to hear Mary's proper accent and style of address return. "Thank you, Mary," she replied, giving the maid a sincere smile.

Isaac coughed loudly from the door, and Anabel frowned at him. "Shall we?" she asked as she took his arm.

He gave her no reply but led her downstairs to the waiting carriage.

An emergency at the office delayed James, and he was almost unforgivably late for the Greystones' dinner party. He entered just as their hostess had begun pairing up couples to move into the dining room. The Greystones were not nobility, but they were a wealthy, highly-connected family with ties to several aristocratic lines. Obtaining an invitation to this dinner was a coup d'etat his father had boasted about for weeks. Though the old man wasn't here, James couldn't help but feel like his father was watching him as he apologized for his tardiness.

Mrs. Greystone only smiled and teasingly chided him. She led him over to a small group of people standing near the fireplace. Lady Anabel and her brother stood with Lady Cecilia. It would be a challenge to be in the presence of both Anabel and Cecilia. After resolving to be more pragmatic about marriage, he'd chosen Cecilia from his father's list. Now he needed to woo the lady while not letting his attention linger too long on Anabel.

Mrs. Greystone made perfunctory introductions, glad to hear they were all acquainted, and informed James he was to escort Lady Anabel into the dining room. It felt like the Fates were testing his resolve.

"Now, Your Grace," Mrs. Greystone began, as she threaded her hand under the young duke's arm, "I simply must introduce you to the young lady I have paired you with. I believe you will get along famously."

Anabel seemed amused as she watched her brother be escorted away.

"That poor man," Cecilia said in a droll tone. Anabel giggled.

No sooner had James greeted both ladies than the dinner bell rang, and another man made his way to Cecilia's side. He appeared roughly the same age as James, with ruddy skin, grey-streaked brown hair, and kind eyes behind a pair of spectacles. Cecilia's face brightened upon his approach. She was more animated than James had ever seen.

"Sir James," she began, "please allow me to introduce Mr. Matthew Bradley. Mr. Bradley, this is Sir James Marley."

"I am pleased to meet you," Bradley said, giving James's hand a vigorous shake. "I read about your knighting ceremony. Your deeds at Trafalgar were commendable."

"Thank you," James replied awkwardly. He never knew how to respond when someone congratulated him on his war record. As a member of the Royal Navy, he'd been spared the worst of the conflict with France, but the battle at Trafalgar had been hellish. Even a decade later he still heard cannon fire in his sleep. Whenever someone brought up the war, James's changed the subject as quickly as possible. Fortunately, it was their turn to enter the dining room, so he offered his arm to Lady Anabel and made his way inside.

Since he'd entered with Anabel, he would be seated next to her. He was glad to see Cecilia on his other side. However, they were seated at a table set up in a darkened corner of the room. A few others were seated there as well, but no one of note.

"Welcome to the black books," Cecilia said under her breath, as she settled her napkin in her lap.

"Pardon?"

"The black books," Anabel replied. "Those who are out of favor."

"I hadn't realized I'd been in society long enough to fall out of favor."

Bradley laughed. "Sir James, you have much to learn. Society has an opinion of you long before you set foot among their ranks."

"How encouraging," James replied in a monotone. Anabel laughed, and he failed to repress the thrill of joy he felt. He stole a quick glance at her while their wine glasses were filled. He could not deny the pull he felt toward her. There must be some unconscious force driving his behavior.

Next to him, Cecilia, laughed openly at something Bradley said. His initial impression had been that she was witty but dry, so it was a pleasant surprise to see her carefree and energetic. When she let her guard down, she was quite charming.

The soup course was served, and after a few sips, he leaned over to Cecilia. "May I ask about your connection to Mr. Bradley?" He hoped he didn't sound jealous.

Cecilia's smile widened as she looked back at the man in question. "I've known Mr. Bradley most of my life. His family lives near my father's estate in Hampshire."

Bradley leaned forward with a genial smile. "The lady is too kind to me. My father is a tenant farmer on her father's land."

Cecilia's face blanched. "But Mr. Bradley is being too humble," she said as soon as he'd finished. "He is a chemist and a member of the Royal Institution where he has worked with Sir Humphry Davy."

"You flatter me, my lady. I had the privilege of assisting Sir Humphry at one of his last lectures at the Institution. Most of my work today is assisting Mr. Brande."

James opened his mouth to ask about Bradley's work, but Lady Cecilia spoke first, asking the man's opinion on a scientific lecture they'd both recently attended. Their easy affection was obvious, and James didn't have the heart to woo the lady while she enjoyed the company of her friend. He turned to his other dinner companion.

"It is nice to see you again, my lady," he said, after catching Lady Anabel's eye.

She smiled warmly at him. "And you, sir. I did not know you were invited."

"My father was to attend, but he was injured today and begged me to go in his stead."

"Oh no! I hope he's not too badly hurt." She placed a hand on his forearm, and the touch seared through to his skin. He simultaneously wanted to keep her hand there forever and to run to keep from falling back under her spell.

He shook his head to clear his mind. They had been discussing his father's injury. "I believe he will recover soon. Just a sprained ankle."

"Make sure he is elevating it. And if he needs relief and does not want to take laudanum, willow-bark tea can help reduce pain. I've also seen a tincture made from the turmeric root from India help with pain relief."

"Interesting. My father has a shipment of turmeric root in his warehouse."

She smiled at him. "It might be easier to purchase from an apothecary. It is a bit time consuming to make yourself."

"Is this something you've made?"

"Only under the instruction of my friend. She has a knack for medicinal remedies. She would also tell you to bathe the injury in cool vinegar at least two times a day, and after the third day, soak the ankle in a salt bath."

"Fascinating," James said. "Your friend should open her own apothecary shop."

Her face lit up with a grin. "That is her wish."

"Well, let me know if she needs investors. I am sure she could do much good."

Anabel laughed. "Try her remedies first and let me know how they work. It's been some time since I've dealt with a sprained ankle."

James laughed before he realized she was not jesting. "Seen many of them, have you?"

"There are many children among my extended family. Injuries are inevitable."

"Are you injured, my lady?" The companion on Anabel's other side, Lord Rossmore asked.

Anabel laughed and changed the topic quickly, discussing inane things with Rossmore. If James recalled correctly, Rossmore was a rake with an annoying habit of getting foxed at every event he attended. The man's attention toward Anabel incensed James. No doubt he had his sights set on the beautiful lady. It would not be the first time he had tried to ruin a débutante.

Silently fuming, James continued his meal when all he really wanted to do was plant a facer on Rossmore.

After dinner, Mrs. Greystone led the ladies to the parlor, where tea was being served. The fashion was to serve tea after the gentlemen joined them, but Mrs. Greystone believed that ladies should not have to wait for their refreshments.

Anabel was sad to lose her dinner companion. She'd had a delightful time talking with James, and the interaction had only strengthened her attraction to him. She settled next to Cecilia on the settee as the other ladies found their seats.

She had not uttered one word before Mrs. Greystone approached. "Lady Anabel," she said. "You would do me such an honor if I could introduce you to my friend, Lady Whitlock, and her daughter Lady Caroline." She looked expectantly at Anabel, who threw a pleading glance at her friend. Mrs. Greystone saw the exchange and raised an eyebrow. "If Lady Cecilia can spare you."

"Of course," Cecilia replied. "I see my friend Miss Walker over there. I haven't spoken to her in an age. I will go say hello."

"Splendid!" Mrs. Greystone proclaimed, her cheery demeanor returned. "I do so love it when my parties bring people together."

Turning from Cecilia, Mrs. Greystone steered Anabel toward a severe woman with sharp cheekbones, blond hair pulled up in a tight hairstyle, and a well-made, if slightly out of fashion, gown. Lady Whitlock, Anabel supposed, and the younger woman sitting with her must be Lady Caroline. Caroline appeared more sophisticated than the other débutantes. If Anabel recalled the gossip she'd overheard, Caroline had been out for two seasons, which would make her nineteen or twenty, not much younger than Anabel herself.

Presumably Mrs. Greystone intended for them to be friends, but Anabel suspected she would not be friendly with Lady Caroline. The young woman was in the full bloom of health, with milky white skin artfully dusted with just a hint of rosiness on her cheeks. Her golden hair was arranged stylishly, and she wore an ivory-colored gown in the most current fashion. Her appearance contrasted sharply with her stiff posture and pursed lips.

Short introductions were made before Mrs. Greystone took a seat and urged Anabel to do the same. Once she was sitting opposite Lady Caroline, Anabel realized she was the woman who'd been paired with Isaac for dinner.

"Did you enjoy the meal?" Anabel asked tentatively.

"Oh yes," Lady Caroline responded. Her voice was breathy and light, almost certainly an affectation.

They sat in awkward silence for a few moments before Mrs. Greystone interjected. "Lady Whitlock, you were just telling me the other day how much you admire Montgomery House."

"Indeed," the lady replied. "Such a handsome residence in the most fashionable part of town. Situated just far enough from the road to ensure privacy, but not so far back as to be an inconvenience."

Anabel wasn't sure how to respond to praise for a house built by her family two generations ago, but desiring to avoid the appearance of rudeness, she muttered a thank you. The silence resumed. Why had Mrs. Greystone asked her to join this group?

"Do you play an instrument, Lady Anabel?" Lady Whitlock finally asked, looking at her with a raised brow.

"I do. I play the pianoforte."

"My Caroline plays the pianoforte and the harp exceedingly well." Lady Whitlock said, beaming at her daughter.

"I concur wholeheartedly," Mrs. Greystone replied. "And her voice is like that of an angel."

The amount of praise being heaped on Caroline was making Anabel uncomfortable. The young woman's smug expression was even worse, as if she expected total adoration. Anabel caught on to their scheme. These women were trying to exhibit how suitable Lady Caroline would be for the role of Duchess of Montgomery.

Anabel knew Lady Caroline and her brother would never suit. Isaac had a big heart. He would never be drawn to someone as self-centered as Lady Caroline.

Anabel picked up the teacup Mrs. Greystone poured and took a small sip, trying to calm the shaking of her hands. The other ladies continued heaping praise on Caroline. She breathed deeply, trying to calm the swirling in her stomach. Caroline pointedly ignored Anabel and picked up her own cup and took a sip, and settled it back in the saucer, holding both in her lap.

Don't you want to take these shameless women down a peg or two?

Anabel flinched at the sound and pretended to sneeze to cover the involuntary movement. Her heart was racing, and a feeling of arrogance and disdain rose in her chest. This was the first time the voice's menace had been directed toward another. Her cheeks heated as she admitted to herself that she agreed.

Anabel kept her eye on the teacup in Lady Caroline's lap, barely hearing anything else. She was not sure if she was afraid of the voice speaking, or if she wanted it to belittle the other ladies again. She longed for the gentlemen to join them, both as a distraction, and so the Whitlocks could bother Isaac directly. No sooner had she had the thought than the door to the room opened, and the men walked in. Anabel jerked her head up, away from Caroline's teacup, searching for Isaac and Sir James.

A shriek tore through the room. Caroline bolted up, dropping her teacup to the floor. A stain was spreading quickly on the skirts of her ivory gown.

"Oh dear," Mrs. Greystone said. "It appears you've spilled your tea, Lady Caroline."

The proper thing to do would be to excuse herself to the retiring room to try and salvage her dress. Caroline, however, had no concern for propriety.

"I did not spill my tea! I never spill my tea. Something lifted the saucer from my hands." She pointed an accusing finger at Anabel. "She made it happen! I don't know how, but she did it."

Lady Whitlock did not reprimand her daughter. She scrutinized Anabel instead. Anabel's throat tightened as she realized all conversation in the room had come to a halt and everyone was staring at her. A cold sweat broke out on her forehead.

Run, the voice said.

Isaac hurried Anabel from the drawing room as quickly as he could while respecting propriety.

"What a silly chit," he muttered as they rode home in the carriage. "As if you reached over and dumped the teacup in her lap. She couldn't admit she was being clumsy. Instead, she cast doubt on you and started unnecessary rumors." He shook his head before gazing out the window.

Anabel swallowed, needing fortification before confessing to her brother. "She was being silly, but I think I may have been the cause of the issue."

"What?" He turned from the window to look at her in the dim light. "You used your powers again?"

"Not consciously!" Anabel protested. "Mrs. Greystone insisted I sit with her, Lady Whitlock, and Caroline, and then they spent the entire time praising Caroline." She paused—not ready to tell her brother about the voice—and cleared her throat. "It was such a dull conversation that I focused on her teacup to keep from falling asleep. When the men came in, I lost my concentration and must have caused the spill."

All signs of mirth dropped from Isaac's face. He was quiet for the remainder of the ride. Only when they were out of the carriage and in the foyer of the house did he continue. "Did she see you concentrating on the cup?" he asked in a low whisper.

"I don't think so," she whispered in reply.

"So, it's just conjecture? Her story has no merit?"

"I don't know if anyone else was watching, but would they even be sure of what they saw?"

"The only witnesses were Lady Whitlock and Caroline?"

"I'm almost certain Lady Whitlock didn't see anything."

"Lady Whitlock?" Their mother asked, entering the foyer. "She's such a nosy busybody. I heard she was encouraging her daughter to set her cap toward you, Isaac."

"Toward me?" Isaac looked at Rowena with wide eyes.

"Of course. Lady Whitlock is not an imbecile, so she sees your charm and good looks. But what she wants is the title of Duchess of Montgomery. She couldn't get it for herself, so she's trying to get it for her daughter."

Anabel peered curiously at her mother. "What do you mean, she couldn't get it for herself? Was she your rival?"

Rowena laughed heartily. "She was certainly not qualified to rival me. She was engaged to Montgomery, but he took one look at me and knew we were destined for each other."

"More like he was caught by your lust spell and would have done anything to have you," Anabel corrected.

Her mother shrugged her shoulders. "Either way, I grabbed him from her clutches, and she's been bitter ever since."

Bile rose in Anabel's throat as the meaning of the woman's hostility became clear. If it weren't for Rowena's machinations, Lady Whitlock would have been the Duchess of Montgomery. Had she had feelings for the old duke when she was younger? Anabel found that hard to believe, but it wasn't impossible.

"I'm going to bed."

"Perhaps you should stay there for a few days," Rowena said. Anabel scowled at her mother before giving her brother a pleading look.

Isaac cleared his throat. "She may be right, Bel. You should stay out of the eye of society for a few days."

"Isaac!" Anabel cried, moving to her brother's side.

"Don't argue, dear," Rowena said. "Your brother is right. And anyway, the duke's word is law in this house. Go to your room and stay there until we tell you it's safe to emerge."

Anabel glared at her mother. "You mean 'go hide yourself so we can forget you exist,' right? That's what you did my entire childhood. I'm ashamed I thought you would be any different now."

Rowena sneered. "You have nothing without your brother's charity, so do as he says and go play least in sight."

Anabel gave her brother one last pleading look, but he refused to meet her eye. With a huff she turned and ran up the stairs.

Chapter 7

James hesitated as the carriage stopped. He was about to change his life forever, closing off paths he wasn't ready to let go of. His hands were tied, though. If he didn't act soon, he and Tom could very well lose their business.

He'd decided on this course that morning, after he realized he would never be able to save the business on his own. He had come to understand this when he opened the bill for Tom's materials. The cost was double what they'd been charged in the past. As soon as he'd recovered from his shock, James had nearly run to the supplier's warehouse.

Their discussion had been less than fruitful. Mr. Smith, the supplier, maintained that his costs had increased and therefore he needed to increase the cost to his customers. After some badgering, Smith begrudgingly admitted he'd been approached by a representative from Walton & Bolt, the engineering firm where Tom had gotten his start. They were larger and more prosperous than Marley & Reynolds, but Mr. Bolt held a grudge against Tom for striking out on his own. Bolt was the most likely reason James's firm had lost several lucrative contracts, leading to their current dire straits. Now the man had resorted to bullying James's suppliers.

James convinced Smith to agree to a slight discount, but it was still far above their previous rate. He needed to do something about Walton & Bolt's intimidation tactics, but that had to wait for another day. For now, he needed to increase their capital, and the easiest way was to fulfill his father's wishes.

A sudden banging on the roof of the hack pulled him from his thoughts.

The hackney man slid the small driver window open. "You gonna keep sittin' on your arse, or are you gettin' out? The fare don't include lollygaggin', even for a swell."

James exited the carriage at once, handing the man a good tip for his troubles. It was quite a trek from his offices to Mayfair.

Standing alone on the streets, he could feel eyes watching him. Society thrived on gossip, and his mere presence in the area would end up being a topic of conversation. He did his best to ignore the sensation as he approached Ravenswood House and knocked on the door.

The butler admitted him and bade James to wait in the entry while he was announced. He took a breath to bolster his resolve. His major regret was that he would no longer be able to pursue Anabel. She remained a mystery to him, especially after the Greystones' dinner party. The incident with Lady Caroline Whitlock's tea had cast a pall over the rest of the evening. Blaming Anabel for the incident had been ridiculous. How could anyone cause another to spill their tea? Even with his doubts about her mother, James couldn't believe Anabel would do such a thing.

It didn't help matters, however, that Montgomery absconded with his sister shortly after Lady Caroline's departure. Gossip had spread through the room, some repeating the rumor that the duchess was a witch. It was all so ridiculous. He'd spent the rest of the evening speaking with Lady Cecilia and Mr. Bradley, trying to ignore the rumors swirling around them.

The servant reappeared and escorted him to the drawing room where Lady Cecilia sat. He thought they were alone until he heard a soft snore and turned to see an elderly lady dozing in a chair near the fire.

"Sir James," Cecilia said, "I don't believe you've met my great aunt, Angela Manning. She is my chaperone this season."

"I see," he replied. The woman stirred in her sleep but appeared nowhere near waking up. He turned back to Lady Cecilia. "Perhaps I should return when your aunt is more alert."

"No, please, do sit," she said, gesturing to the settee.

He obliged her since the door was open, and technically, they were not alone. He needed to make everything as scandal free as possible.

Cecilia poured him a cup of tea. They sat in awkward silence for a moment.

"Sir James," she began at the same time that he said, "I've come here today." They both paused, but then Cecilia grinned. She was lovely when she didn't appear overburdened.

"Is Mr. Bradley anyone important to you?" he asked abruptly. He immediately regretted the impertinent words, but he needed to understand their connection before proceeding.

She blushed and lowered her gaze. "He is no one. Just an old acquaintance."

"So, there is no understanding between you?"

She looked at him, her eyes wide. "What? No, nothing of the sort."

"Good, because I would like to formally declare my intentions toward you."

Cecilia's blinked at him open-mouthed. "Me? You have intentions toward me?"

"Indeed, I do. I would like to officially court you."

"Why?"

He couldn't very well tell her he was being pressured by his father and circumstances beyond his control. "I enjoy spending time with you. You are lovely and witty, and I believe we could have a good partnership."

"Forgive my impertinence, but I thought you would want to court Lady Anabel."

"Lady Anabel is pleasant, but I do not think she and I would suit." His tongue felt thick, and his stomach churned, but he needed to save his business.

"I see." She stared into her teacup. "You understand I have no dowry?"

"I do. Just as I have no noble birth. It is an exchange of sorts, is it not?"

She gave him a wan smile. "I suppose it is." She gazed out the window. "I'm not sure how I feel about this."

"I do not expect an answer now. I understand you will need time to think."

She gave a small nod, and they sat in silence while they drank their tea. James needed to do more to convince Cecilia to accept his suit. He needed more time with her, which meant public outings. He took another sip of his tea and immediately coughed as he contemplated making society aware of their courtship. Would Anabel be upset when she heard the news?

Cecilia gave him a worried look as he continued to clear his throat. His coughing even awoke her great aunt for a moment, and the woman simply stared dazedly before falling back into her slumber.

Straightening his spine, James allowed one more cough to clear his throat. There was nothing for it. He had to declare his intentions toward Lady Cecilia publicly to satisfy his father. "Why don't we plan an outing? Our fathers are friendly. I'm sure mine would invite your family to attend the theater with us. He has a box for the season."

She looked down at her lap, wringing her hands. Just when James decided he would need to leave and try again another day, she nodded. "I think that would be acceptable."

Despite his misgivings, James felt buoyed by her agreement. He planned the outing for another quarter of an hour, before taking his leave.

Hurt feelings and a nagging desire to appease her brother kept Anabel hidden in her room, but after three days, she was becoming restless. She was used to roaming freely, not keeping to her chambers like a hypochondriac.

She waited for her brother to return from the House of Lords. Despite her restlessness, she was not ready to venture out on her own. The voice had not spoken to her since the dinner party, and she wasn't sure if it was another entity, or if her mind was playing tricks on her. She's researched madness in some of the medical books in the family library but had found nothing of use. What she did find convinced her she should never tell anyone about this affliction.

Three days without the voice had softened some of her anxiety, and she longed for an escape. Perhaps if she went somewhere with her brother, he could lend some of his mental fortitude. And keep her from blundering again.

Mary kept watch for the duke, and she alerted Anabel upon his return. Anabel flew downstairs to his study. "Welcome home, Brother," she said as she entered the room, her breathing heavy.

Isaac eyed her suspiciously. "Thank you, I suppose."

Anabel settled onto a chaise lounge near the fireplace. She never bothered with ceremony when it came to her brother, so she curled her legs behind her and tucked her feet under the hem of her skirts. Once she was satisfied with her arrangement, Isaac was seated behind his desk, reading his correspondence.

"Do you have anything planned for tonight?"

Her question startled Isaac. He blinked at her for a moment before he seemed to understand her question.

"As a matter of fact," he finally said, "I am taking Mother to the theater."

"Oh, that's perfect!" Anabel replied, clapping her hands.

He raised an eyebrow. "You're happy Mother asked me to escort her to the theater? What do you have planned?"

"Nothing!" she replied, rolling her eyes. "I am tired of being sequestered at home. I need to get out. I would like to join you at the theater."

Isaac's mouth fell open. "You want to join us?"

"Of course. What's so wrong with that?"

"The fact that you are currently the subject of rumors about possessing unearthly powers."

Anabel stared at her brother. "Surely not! That was three nights ago. I can't imagine there are people walking around Mayfair discussing my so-called unnatural abilities when there are so many more interesting topics to discuss."

"You underestimate Lady Whitlock, dear sister. Some of my acquaintances have advised me that she is the last person you want to upset. She has an uncanny ability to ruin a person socially should she choose to do so."

Anabel scoffed. "That is ridiculous. She saw nothing of substance. The only way to overcome this is for me to return to society. Hiding will only fan the flames."

Isaac considered her. "You seem rather confident today. It's quite a change."

"I can't spend another evening eating from a tray in my room and reading. I need to get out of this house, Isaac."

Her brother threw up his hands. "Fine. You may join us."

Anabel squealed in delight and made her way to her brother's side. She threw her arms around his neck, enveloping him in a hug. Isaac simply patted her arm, not returning the embrace.

"Thank you," she said. "I'll go begin my preparations for tonight."

She made it to her room and threw herself onto her bed, squealing with glee.

Careful child. You might learn something that will make you regret asking to be a part of this outing...

The raspy, all-to-familiar tone made her hair stand on end. Ignoring the risk of a headache, she again pictured slamming the door in her mind and buried her head in the pillow. Perhaps a nap was in order.

Edward had been elated when James had asked about taking Lord Ravenswood and his family to the theater. He'd even given his son money to help cover their increased expenses, no questions asked. The bestowing of funds based on his father's whims left James feeling like a beggar, but really, what choice did he have?

As they made their way into the box, Edward insisted James and Cecilia sit together in the front row, with only her great aunt as a companion. James could feel the eyes of the patrons in other boxes, scrutinizing his every move.

Cecilia looked lovely today. Her hair was in a softer style than she usually wore. Had he not met Anabel, James could easily have fancied Cecilia. He wasn't distracted by thoughts of kissing her, as with Anabel, but he enjoyed her company. He didn't admire the slope of her neck, or the delicate curve of her ear, or the piercing quality of her eyes, but they had a camaraderie that he believed would be a good foundation for marriage. Much better than simply a physical attraction. He rubbed his chest at the thought, ignoring the throbbing pain.

As the show progressed, he desperately tried to stay awake. Cecilia appeared to be enjoying the show, and James willed himself to remain engaged. Only a few moments later, however, he nodded off. A loud exclamation from the stage caused him to flinch, and he awoke with a start.

"What is the matter with you?" Edward hissed as he leaned forward and grabbed James's shoulder.

James suppressed a yawn. "Apologies, Father. I am overtired."

"Well, get over it," Edward commanded.

"Of course," he whispered in reply. "I just need to step away for a moment." He nodded to Cecilia when she looked up at him. She lowered her chin and returned her attention to the stage.

Stepping into the quiet of the hall was a relief. He decided to walk along the corridor to wake himself up and shake off some of his tension. He was nearly at the far end when the curtain to another box opened. He moved to the side to allow the newcomer more space, then stopped. The newcomer was Anabel.

"Sir James!" she stepped away from her box and gave him a quick curtsy. "I was just about to visit the retiring room."

James bowed in response, fumbling for words as he met her eyes once more. "Lady Anabel," he finally said.

"If I may just…" she gestured toward him. He was blocking her way.

The polite thing to do would be to step aside and allow her to pass. James was not inclined to be polite. He noted the sleek neck he itched to touch, the delicate ears he longed to whisper into, and the lush mouth he yearned to taste.

He saw they were alone, and there was a shadowy alcove a few steps away. A wild notion overtook him. He grabbed her hand, practically dragging her toward the alcove. Anabel seemed surprised, but did not protest. Once they reached their destination, he nestled her to one side, pleased to discover they were nearly out of view.

"Sir James," she said as he moved closer. He could feel her panting against his chest. He wrapped his arms around her and pulled her into a tight embrace. He could barely see her, but he felt her breath on his neck. He relied on his instincts as he bent his head down, sliding his nose alongside hers.

"Tell me no," he said, his voice gruff. He would die if she rejected him, but he wouldn't go any further without her consent.

"I..." Her hands, which had been trapped between them, slid over his coat and grabbed the lapels. Just as he thought she might push him away, she released her grip and encircled his neck. And then her lips were on his.

She kissed tentatively, with small, tight-lipped pecks on his mouth. James captured her bottom lip with his mouth and sucked lightly. Then he pulled back and used his teeth to nibble where he'd just kissed. The slight pressure made her gasp, and he wasted no time deepening the kiss. He sipped at her mouth, licking ever so slightly. There was so much he wanted to do with this woman, but he had to take it slow to avoid scaring her off.

He pushed her against the wall, and she canted her hips forward, rocking into him. He trailed soft kisses along her cheek and down to the slender neck he'd been dreaming of. She whimpered as he lightly sucked the soft skin just below her ear.

James wanted to disrobe her right there and grant her all the pleasure he could. Ravishing this woman steps away from society was extremely tempting, and he struggled to maintain his composure.

She gasped again as he nipped her earlobe. He returned his mouth to hers, kissing her with the ferocity that he restrained elsewhere in his body.

"James..." she moaned in his ear. He rubbed her thigh through the layers of her gown, wishing he could gather her skirts up and feel the creamy skin of her legs.

"James," she said again, this time sharper, a tremor in her voice.

Her tone broke the trance. He looked at her as best he could in the sparse light. It took a moment for his brain to catch up. When he realized what he'd been doing, he dropped his hands, pulling away from her as if he'd been burned.

"I apologize," he said, trying to step back more. Her hands drifted with the movement until they were back on his chest.

"Don't," she replied, playing with the edges of his cravat. "I'm just wary of being discovered."

Her touch was exquisite, and James couldn't stop himself from groaning.

"What does this mean for us?" Even without the light, James knew she was looking up at him with innocent eyes.

His heart pounded, and James struggled to respond. He felt the weight of her regard even in the dark, and he could not lie to her. "I...I don't know. I'm courting Lady Cecilia."

"What?" Anabel dropped her hands and stepped back as much as she could in the small space.

James's mind began to clear, and he reached for her. "I'll need to speak with her before I can offer for you."

"You're courting Cecilia, and you kissed me?!" she hissed.

James opened his mouth to reply, but he had no excuse. "I didn't plan for this," he said. "Something came over me."

"Oh, like a spell?" she scoffed.

The comment was so close to his thoughts that it was his turn to step back. *Had* she enchanted him?

The light from the hallway filtered into their alcove, and he could see her sneer of disdain. "Even if I could do a love spell, do you honestly think I would use it on you?"

"I don't know what to think! Everyone at the Greystones' dinner party said your mother was a witch."

She put her hands on his chest and shoved him hard. James stepped back out into the hall, Anabel fast behind him. Once she was free, she moved in the direction of the ladies' retiring room.

"Anabel, wait, please." He tried to grab her hand.

"Don't call me that. I will only ever be Lady Anabel to you. Goodbye, Sir James."

She disappeared before he could say anything else. Bewildered, James tried to understand the ramifications of what he'd just done.

Chapter 8

After her disastrous kiss with Sir James, Anabel hid in the retiring room. She sent one of the maids to inform her brother she was unwell and would need the coach. She had assumed Isaac would want to stay with their mother, but he met her in the hall outside of the retiring room.

He scrutinized her appearance but said nothing. He was quiet until they were safely ensconced in their carriage. Tears burned behind Anabel's eyes, and part of her wished her brother had allowed her to leave alone so she could cry in peace.

"Did someone say something to you?"

Anabel looked up at her brother with a furrowed brow. "Did someone say something to me?"

"About the rumors Lady Whitlock is spreading."

Her chest tightened. She'd forgotten about the rumors. "No. Sir James..." She was unsure of what to say.

"Marley?" Isaac asked, raising his voice. "I would not have expected it from him."

"No, he did not…that is to say…" She took a deep breath to calm her mind. "No one said anything."

"I see," he replied. The rest of the carriage ride was silent.

Once they pulled up to Montgomery House, Isaac remained in the carriage after Anabel exited.

"I'm returning to the theater to accompany Mother home. Get some rest. We will speak in the morning."

Nodding, she turned toward the house and proceeded to her room as quickly as she could. A chambermaid was stoking the fire. The girl caught sight of Anabel, and rather than simply bobbing a curtsy, she froze in place, her eyes wide. Anabel's mind raced. Did the girl know something? Had Mary shared her knowledge with the other staff?

The maid recovered enough to ask if Anabel required anything, and she asked the girl to inform Mary she wasn't needed. As soon as she was alone, Anabel sat on her bed, a splitting pain blooming on the right side of her head. She dropped her head in her hands and massaged her temples, her mind continuously replaying the girl's reaction.

They are all suspicious of you. It's time to make your escape.

Anabel shivered, feeling the voice's presence more strongly than ever before. She doubled over, her eyes welling with tears from both the pain and from the tension of the evening. The door opened and her head shot up. Mary stood there, holding a pitcher of water.

"Sorry to bother you, my lady," Mary said, averting her gaze. "I've just come to check on you and bring you some rose water. Let me just set this down and I'll leave you be." She moved toward the washstand.

"No!" Anabel cried, throwing out her hand. Mary froze, literally stopping mid-stride. The pitcher fell from her hands and shattered into several pieces, soaking the carpet with the fragrant liquid.

"My lady?" Mary asked, her voice shaking.

Anabel yanked her hand back, releasing her maid. She should apologize, she knew that, but she couldn't find the words. "Did you tell the other servants about me?"

Mary's eyes widened. "No, ma'am. Of course not!"

"The chambermaid seemed afraid of me. Why would she be if she did not know about my abilities?"

"That's Betsy, ma'am. She's Cook's niece, just arrived from the country. Not used to spending time around nobility. She'll get more comfortable over time."

Anabel was certain there was more to the girl's fear than an unfamiliarity with the upper classes. "Don't lie to me!"

The pottery shards flew in multiple directions, and one flew straight up to Mary's face. The maid gasped and put a hand to her cheek. When she pulled it away, there was blood on her fingers. Anabel gasped at the two-inch cut on Mary's cheek.

"Mary!" she cried, her rage dissipating at the sight of the injury. "I'm so sorry." She grabbed one of her handkerchiefs and handed it to the other woman.

Mary dabbed at her cheek, her eyes brimming with unshed tears. "Will you be needing help with your gown, Lady Anabel?" She asked, all familiarity gone from her voice.

"No. Mary, please..." Anabel reached out, but the maid darted away before she could say anything more.

See, you are a danger to those you care about. Come find me and I will give you sanctuary.

Anabel shook as she pictured the deep gash and the blood on Mary's fingers. Could the voice be right? Was she a danger to her loved ones? She needed answers. She must leave her brother's home.

She hurried to her wardrobe and quickly changed into a plain gown before packing an old valise with the things she'd owned before returning to

London. The only new possessions she took were two books she'd recently purchased. As soon as she'd gathered her belongings, she crept down the back stairs, escaping out the kitchen door.

As she walked along the darkened streets of Mayfair, she realized her headache lessened the further she got from Montgomery House. She felt a presence guiding her, silently propelling her toward the voice, but Anabel had another plan. She needed to get back to Gran and her extended family. They had ways to protect themselves against her abilities.

They were normally in Yorkshire around this time of year. If she could make it up there, she could find her family. The only way to reach them was to ride the mail coach along the Great North Road.

During the long walk to the posting inn, she reflected on her brief time in London. She felt guilty about leaving without a word, and she wished she could have apologized to Mary. Even if she had gossiped, Anabel was heartsick at the pain she'd caused her maid. She hadn't even left a note for her brother, and she knew Isaac would be sad. To say nothing of Cecilia. She had enjoyed reconnecting with her old friend. How would she feel when she learned Anabel had escaped yet again, most likely never to return?

Thinking of Cecilia brought Sir James to mind. She was furious with him for kissing her while he'd been courting her friend, but she could not stop thinking of their interlude in the alcove. Anabel knew more about lovemaking than the average Mayfair girl, thanks to her cousin's stories. Fiona enjoyed the sex act and made no apologies for it. She shared her knowledge with Anabel and Suraya, so Anabel knew how passionate some men could be. Even so, she'd never thought a proper gentleman would show such physical affection to a girl he intended to marry.

That was the problem though, wasn't it? He hadn't intended to marry her, at least not at the time they'd kissed. It had been a purely physical reaction, and he'd been openly courting Cecilia when he'd cornered An-abel. She wanted to be angry with him, to lash out. But she also wanted to experience those sensations again. She'd hardly had time to process her physical reactions, but now she recalled how her nipples had tightened and her core had clenched when he grabbed her thigh.

Part of her wished she hadn't run from him so quickly. His words came back to her as she walked.

"I'll need to speak with her before I can offer for you."

Did that mean he wanted to offer for Anabel? Was she running away from a man with whom she could be happy? Her feet felt leaden, and her stomach churned as she continued along her path toward the inn.

The following day, James took a rare morning off to meet a friend at White's. Elliot, Lord Asher, was a Viscount who recently came into his title, and one of the few nobs who'd been kind to James at Eton. They'd remained friends throughout their time at Eton and Cambridge and had recently reconnected after James resigned his commission.

Having been raised as a second son, Asher had been woefully unprepared to lead the family following the unfortunate death of his brother. Prior to his ascension, he had been James's opposite in many ways, spending most of his days in idle pursuits. He even took pride in his well-earned reputation as a rakehell.

Asher had taken the title but refused to take up residence in the ancestral homes of the viscountcy. His sister-in-law had revealed that she was with child shortly after her husband's passing. Asher was not married and had no intention of uprooting the widowed and pregnant viscountess. He continued to lodge in a bachelor's residence and was in no hurry to find a bride of his own.

"With any luck, Laurel will birth a son, and the lad can take this blasted title off my hands," he told James. "Although mother has been pressuring me to take a wife of my own so that I can 'secure the line.'" His voice rose as he imitated his mother. "I told her I see no need to muddy the waters if Richard has a son. Better to keep my own issue out of the picture."

"But what if you find yourself enamored with a woman?" James asked. Although he was curious about his friend's views, he also wanted to introduce his own dilemma.

"Lord, why would I ever do that?" Asher laughed.

"I seem to recall you being enamored of many fine ladies during our time at school."

"Infatuated, perhaps, but not enamored. I think I can safely say I have never felt love for a woman. I don't see that changing anytime soon."

"How fortunate you are," James muttered as he took a sip of his brandy.

Asher leaned back into his seat, assessing his friend. "And why do you raise this topic? I believe it may be more than just concern for my hypothetical nephew."

James took another fortifying sip before he began, sharing his business struggles and the condition his father required before he would invest. He withheld the situation with Lady Anabel for the moment.

"I see," Asher said once James had finished. He sat back and studied his friend. "And Tom believes that he can come up with a more stable design for a locomotive?"

James nodded. "He has studied the older designs and corresponded with other inventors. Tom believes he has found a way to solve the pressure issue that caused most of the dangerous accidents."

"But the railroads still need work. They need more infrastructure, and the engines aren't strong enough. It could be years, decades even, before you see any return on this investment."

"Tom wants to lease the design to manufacturers. They will pay handsome royalties for those rights, and we can use that money to fund smaller inventions and improvements to existing machines. My father has more money than he could spend in three lifetimes. He could fund us for several years and not feel the loss."

"But is it worth putting your own freedom on the line? The man is demanding a marriage, James. And not even to a woman you know or like. This is the rest of your life we are discussing. I know Reynolds dreams of making a name for himself as an inventor, but you don't need to sacrifice your freedom to achieve it."

"I have dreams too, dammit!" James slammed his fist on the table to emphasize his point. The action brought the head waiter to their table. James felt his face heat as he apologized. He knew his membership at White's was tenuous, at best. He'd only been able to join because Asher had sponsored him.

When they were alone again, James blew out a frustrated sigh. "I know my father desires me to be an idle gentleman, but that's not who I am. I believe in this business and in Tom, and I want to be a part of moving our country forward."

"I understand," Asher replied solemnly. "I may not understand how you can be so industrious, but I know you have no other way of being." He drained his glass before continuing. "What will you do about the marriage situation, then?" he asked, pointing the empty glass at his friend.

Anabel's rosy face appeared in his mind. "I have found I have a preference for a lady."

"One of those on your father's list?"

"Unfortunately, no. She is connected to a dukedom, but her children could never inherit a title. Father has blatantly told me to forget her and seek partnership elsewhere, but I cannot move on so easily." He recalled the sensation of holding her in his arms and warmth coursed through his body. "The lady has a hold of me, and I am not sure I want her to let me go."

"Is she well-dowered? Perhaps you don't need to use your father's funds to save your business."

James shook his head. "I know many men marry a wealthy woman and use her funds for their own gain, but I wouldn't feel right doing that. The dowry is meant to ensure the future for the bride and children. I can't use that money for something as risky as a railroad scheme."

"Then you are at a crossroads, my friend. If you want your father's support, you will need to marry a bride of his choosing."

"And if I want Lady Anabel Montgomery more, then my business will fail."

"Lady Anabel?" Asher asked, his mouth agape. "Isn't she the chit who ran off at sixteen, birthed a bastard, and tried to sneak back into society as if she never left?"

"Is that what the gossip mongers are saying?" came a new voice from behind James. He recognized that voice, although he hadn't had a chance to speak directly with the man since the ball where they had first been introduced.

Lord Montgomery strolled up to the table, shadowed by a footman who set down a chair for him. A glass of brandy was placed before the duke before he'd even had a chance to settle in his seat.

James felt all the blood drain from his face as he met the obsidian eyes of the Duke of Montgomery.

"Your Grace, please accept my apology. My friend spoke out of turn. I will not allow such slander of your sister and was about to tell him so before your approach." James glared at his friend to bolster his claim.

"Indeed, Your Grace," Asher concurred, slouching down in his chair. "I apologize for repeating such salacious gossip."

Montgomery took a slow sip of his drink before responding, his gaze pinned on Asher. "I will forgive the transgression this time," he said, turning to his other companion. "But only because I need a favor from you, Sir James."

"From me?"

"Indeed. I need your help with a situation involving my sister."

James's jaw dropped and he had to consciously lift it before meeting the duke's eyes. "You are asking for my help for Lady Anabel?"

Montgomery sighed and adjusted himself in his chair. He motioned to Lord Asher. "Would it be better if we took this conversation to a private room?"

James considered the offer. Despite his most recent gaff, Asher was a trustworthy fellow. However, gaining the duke's trust was important. "If you feel this information is confidential, then by all means, let's retreat to a private parlor."

Montgomery stood, and James mumbled a quick apology to his friend before following the duke through the dining room.

The mail coach rattled along, and Anabel burrowed closer to the wall on her left side. She'd made it to the inn early that morning, exhausted and weary. Her feet were so sore that she'd had trouble standing in the yard as she waited for the coach. When it arrived, the coachman had told her there was no room. She had paid nearly triple the usual fare for him to make an exception, and she had been packed inside with four other passengers.

Her travel companions consisted of two women, an elderly man, and a younger man who was obviously drunk. His cheap alcohol permeated the carriage interior, making it hard to breathe. Anabel tried to surreptitiously cover her nose and mouth with a handkerchief to dull the smell, but every time she did so, she received nasty glares from the other women. The old man was kind enough, but he slept for most of the journey, snoring loudly.

The drunk alternated between a wheezing slumber of his own and casting lascivious glances at Anabel.

The trip could not be over soon enough, but even with the speed of the mail coach, it would be another two days before they reached her stop in York. Once she left the coach, she would need to proceed on foot through the county to find the town fair her family was attending. Her blistered feet throbbed at the thought. Hopefully her time in the coach would allow her feet to heal.

Exhaustion pulled at her, and Anabel clutched her valise closer to her body, leaning her head against the side of the coach. The moment she closed her eyes, she was assaulted by negative emotions.

What are you doing in a mail coach, stubborn girl? Come and find me. You needn't go through all this trouble.

Anabel winced at the throbbing in her head. Every time she closed her eyes, the voice spoke to her. She closed the mental door once more, but that intensified her headache and added to her exhaustion.

A rustling next to her forced her to open her eyes. Blinking, she looked over, her tired mind expecting to see the women who'd sat beside her when the journey began. Her new seat mate, however, was the drunken lecher.

"What's a white ewe such as yourself doing on the mail coach?"

His breath was rancid, and Anabel had to swallow a few times to push back the bile that rose in her throat. She turned her head away, hoping he would pass out again if she paid him no mind.

"Don't ignore me, hoity-toity wench," he said, leaning in closer. "I'm trying to talk to you."

"Please, sir," she whispered. "I'd prefer to ride in peace."

"Sir?!" he said with a hiccup. "I ain't no damned sir." He leaned back slightly and scrutinized her. "Where'd you learn to talk like that?"

"Oh, leave off!" one of the women said. "It's obvious she ain't like us." She waved her hand to demonstrate the point. "She's probably some dumb chit thinking she could slum it with the poor folk before she goes off to get married." She turned slightly toward Anabel. "Not what you expected, is it love? You ready to head home yet?"

Anabel had to consciously stop herself from gasping at the woman's words. Was she truly that obvious? She met the woman's gaze head on. "I'm not running away from a marriage. I'm going to York to join my relations. I know this is not an adventure."

"I'll give you an adventure," the drunk said, leaning in once more.

Anabel closed her eyes and swallowed again as his scent wafted over her. When she opened them, the lady was staring pointedly down at her lap. It was just as well, considering the woman had been the one sitting next to her until a moment ago. The woman had obviously swapped seats with the drunken man, so she was unlikely to offer any further assistance.

The drunken man's hand landed on Anabel's thigh, gripping firmly. She feared she might have bruises, even with the layers of clothing between his hand and her skin.

"Please. Remove. Your hand." She choked out the words between shallow breaths, her heart racing.

"Come now." He breathed his hot breath on her neck. "I ain't gonna hurt you. Unless you ask me to," he added with a chuckle.

"Remove. Your. Hand." She repeated, shaky but firm.

The man just looked at her, his eyes hazy with drink. Anabel could focus on nothing but the man's hand. Angry thoughts rose up within her, and she closed her eyes again. In her mind's eye, she pictured him being pulled from her side and ejected from the carriage, his body tumbling as he rolled away from the vehicle. The unusually violent thought made her shiver.

"What the hell?!"

Anabel's eyes flew open just in time to see his hand fly off her leg, reaching for the opposite door. The movement looked unnatural, as if his hand was being pulled by an unseen force.

"Stop that!" the older woman yelled. "You're gonna hurt somebody!"

"It ain't me!" he yelled. His arm was yanked hard enough that he lost his seat and fell to the floor. His position looked oddly like the beginning of the vision she'd just seen.

"No!" she cried, and the man's hand fell like a leaden weight to the floor of the carriage. The commotion was over as quickly as it started.

"Bloody fool!" the old woman said, giving him a kick. "Get back in your seat or I'm telling the coachman, and he can remove you."

The drunk scrambled back in his seat, but he scooted as far away from Anabel as possible, given the limited space. There was at least a full inch between her body and his.

She gave a silent thanks that the other passengers attributed the erratic behavior to the man's inebriation. Anabel knew, however, that she'd been the true cause. The man appeared to suspect her as well. If he spoke of his suspicions, she could be removed from the coach. This was the strongest display of her powers yet.

She closed her eyes, thinking of her lady's maid, her friend. Tears welled up, but she fought them back. She needed to stay strong. There would be time for tears later.

You're going to keep hurting people, but I can help you. Get off the coach at the next stop and I will come to you.

The soothing words were undercut by a raspy, clipped tone. Anabel didn't believe that whoever was behind that voice would help her, but closing the door in her mind was getting more and more difficult. It was going to be a long day.

Chapter 9

James sat across from the duke as the man settled in his chair. He ordered two more glasses of brandy, and faced James silently. Only after the servant understood they were not to be disturbed did he speak

Montgomery was a few years younger than James, but he carried himself with the demeanor of a man twice his age.

"I suppose I should begin by apologizing to you," the duke said.

"Why would you need to apologize to me, Your Grace?"

Montgomery scoffed. "None of this 'Your Grace' business." He took a sip of his drink and met James's gaze. "I have been unfairly prejudiced against you. I made a snap judgment and have given you the cut when I've encountered you in other social settings."

James swallowed, unsure of how to respond. "Thank you," he finally said, after a period of uncomfortable silence.

Montgomery sighed and rubbed his hand down his face. "I need to engage your services as a military man."

James blinked. "I'm glad to help, but how can my tenure in the Navy assist you?"

"I've read the reports. You were one of the best strategists we had."

A thickness rose in James's throat. He was conflicted about his service. He possessed strong strategic abilities that had helped him during his career, but his stomach churned whenever he thought too long about the battles he'd participated in. "Are you planning to blockade something, Duke?" he asked, taking a sip of his drink.

Montgomery leaned forward. "I know you led the team that rescued Lacor from Verdun. Some say his leadership helped turn the tide on the peninsula, and the outcome would have been different had he not been retrieved."

James took a moment to consider. His involvement in the extraction of the Portuguese general was highly confidential information, but he supposed he shouldn't be surprised that a duke had been privy to it. "How does that relate to what you need?"

The duke lowered his voice. "I share this with you in full confidence and trust that you will not share this with another."

James nodded.

"My sister disappeared last night." He swallowed thickly, fidgeting with his glass.

James stiffened his spine at the thought of Anabel being harmed. "Has someone taken her?"

Rubbing the back of his neck, the duke shook his head. "I don't believe so. I think she left voluntarily."

James relaxed slightly. "Then I'm still not sure what I can do."

The duke cleared his throat. "I believe I know where she is going, but I cannot leave London at this moment. There are duties in Parliament I must attend to. And my mother..." he took another sip of his drink. "Let's just say it's better if I do not leave her to her own devices." He looked at James once more. "I would like you to go after Anabel in my stead."

"I'm flattered you thought of me," James replied. "But I'm not the best person for this job. There are investigators and Bow Street Runners who could accomplish the task much more efficiently."

The duke shook his head. "I cannot engage a Runner. Word would get out, and Anabel's reputation would be even more tarnished than it is."

"I understand your reluctance, but it's not as if I am closely acquainted with your sister."

"She has spent more time in your company than any other, apart from Lady Cecilia. My sister must trust you. She keeps her circle limited."

James considered this. "Where do you think she has gone?"

"She is most likely following the Great North Road. We have family who are normally in York this time of year."

"Is this the family that travels to town fairs throughout the year?"

The duke straightened as he took in James's words. "She told you about that?"

He nodded. "She shared some information with me."

"She trusts you more than I realized."

James reached for his glass of brandy, but it was empty. "Do you know why Lady Anabel decided to leave town?"

"She has a nervous disposition, and there was an...an accident with her maid last night that I believe my sister blames herself for."

"Is the maid all right?"

The duke waved his hand in the air. "Oh, yes. She's quite forgotten the entire incident."

Something about the way he said those words put James on his guard, but before he could ponder for long, his attention was pulled to the duke's eyes.

"You will do this favor for me," the other man said, not as a request but as a command.

James felt a slight tug in his chest, as if he wanted to do the duke's bidding, but he shook it off. This nob wouldn't be ordering him around.

"If I do, what will I get in return?"

Montgomery looked shocked at James's response, but rather than answering, he sharpened his steely gaze and met James's eyes. "You will do this task for me."

This time the tug was easier to ignore. James balled his hands into fists. "I will do nothing of the sort. I respect your sister, but I cannot simply abandon my responsibilities to chase her throughout the kingdom."

The duke looked at James for a long moment before schooling his features. "Apologies, Sir James. I am normally in a position to ensure others will do as I ask." For the first time during their conversation, the duke looked flustered. He took a sip of his drink before meeting James's gaze once more. His expression had softened considerably. "Forgive the intrusion, but I overheard your conversation about needing capital for your business."

James did not respond except to gesture for Montgomery to continue.

"I am fortunate to have ample funds and can pay you for your efforts. Name your price, and we can negotiate."

The sudden change in tack left James feeling dizzy. He wasn't sure he could achieve what the duke wanted, but he could not deny the opportunity. The same number he'd requested from his father flashed in his mind, enough for Tom to get the prototype running. Once they were leasing out the design, surely Walton and Bolt would stop their intimidation tactics.

"Five thousand pounds," he said, expecting Montgomery to balk.

"Agreed. I will provide some funds now for your journey and pay the remainder upon my sister's safe return." He extracted some bank notes from his inner coat pocket. "I assume this will suffice?" He handed five one-hundred-pound notes to James. The duke straightened his jacket and nodded. "I'll leave you to prepare for your journey. If you require anything more for expenses, please contact my steward. Anabel will likely be on the mail coach, which stops in Alconbury for the night. If you hurry, you should be able to catch them."

James had many questions to ask, but simply nodded.

Montgomery turned at the threshold to look at James. "I hope it goes without saying I wish for this task to be achieved as quietly as possible. The point is to avoid scandal."

"Of course," James replied.

Montgomery exited without another word.

James considered this turn of events. He was unsure why the duke had thought to engage him for this task, but he could not turn down the prospect of five thousand pounds, a sum large enough to insure his business for the next year.

He hated to neglect his responsibilities, but this was too important. His mind made up, he summoned a servant. After writing notes to Tom and his father, he made his way home to begin packing. He would need to ride fast to catch up with the mail coach before it got too dark. Although the duke seemed convinced Anabel was safe, James couldn't be sure. He needed to find her as soon as possible.

He considered stopping to call on Cecilia, but he did not have the time. He would need to make a point to see her when he was back in town. Even if he managed to retrieve Anabel without alerting society, he wasn't sure he could continue to pursue Cecilia. He didn't have to meet his father's demands now that he had another source of capital. Cecilia was lovely, but the thought of pursuing Anabel made warmth spread through his chest. Would he do his duty toward Cecilia, or follow his heart to Anabel?

"Wait! Stop!" Anabel called as the mail coach sped away from the inn. It had only been a few minutes since the driver stopped to change horses. Anabel had felt certain she had time for a trip to the privy, but apparently she'd taken too long. She tried to run, but there was no way she could catch up to the coach on foot.

"Bollocks." She'd timed how long the horse changes had taken at the last three stops and had believed she'd have roughly ten minutes to relieve herself before she had to be back in her seat. The stable hands at this particular inn must be very efficient, because it couldn't have been more than seven minutes.

What was she to do now? The coach was supposed to stop in Alconbury. She could try to walk there and catch the next morning's coach, but she would need to purchase another ticket. Her money would rapidly dwindle if she had to pay for a new fare or another bribe. And of course, walking so far alone would include the risk of highwaymen who might try to rob her or steal her virtue.

With a sigh, she headed into the inn and settled at a table. A serving girl came by, and Anabel ordered tea. Her blistered feet throbbed at the thought of walking to the next town. She could wait, but the next northbound coach would not arrive until tomorrow. She did not relish the idea of being stuck so far from her family when the owner of that voice came for her.

"Bollocks," she muttered again. She was woefully unprepared for this journey. She'd never traveled on her own, always having her brother, servants, or her family to accompany her. When she'd first fled finishing school to seek out her family, she'd only had to walk a mile to the nearby village hosting the fair. Having corresponded with Suraya for years, she knew her family would be there and had snuck away to visit them, only intending to stay for the afternoon. She'd never meant to run away from school, but she slept there that night and then went with them when they packed up the next day. Her abilities had just started to reveal themselves, and it felt so freeing to test them among her family members without worry of discovery.

And when Isaac had asked Anabel to return to London earlier in the year, he'd sent a carriage to convey her home. She'd traveled leisurely, not adhering to a strict schedule.

So today was her first time using transportation that was open to the public. Thus far, it did not have much to recommend it.

The heavy *thunk* of a mug shook her from her memories. She expected to see her tea, but saw a tankard of ale instead, held by a meaty hand. The hand was attached to a thick arm, which was in turn attached to an equally thick man.

"Now ain't you a pretty sort?" He was a large fellow. Anabel shook as she took him in. He was much larger than the lecherous drunk on the coach.

She willed her voice to stay steady. "Sir, I'm going to ask that you leave my table."

The man ignored her, sitting down on the bench opposite. "What's a pretty gel like you doin' here?"

"I'm just having a cup of tea before I continue my travels." She had no intention of letting this man know she was presently without a conveyance. She would deal with that problem later. Right now, her concern was getting him away from her person.

"Aw, come now love. I don't mean you any harm. I'm just curious as to why a nob is sittin' in a place like this with no chaperone."

Anabel felt her face go hot at his words. Anger was dangerous in this situation and might cause her problems, but she couldn't tolerate this man's impertinence. "I don't require a chaperone. I am perfectly able to care for myself."

"Is you? Cause I think you need a protector. I can be that for you."

"I appreciate your offer, but I must decline." She started to move to another table when his hand grabbed her wrist. His grip was punishing, and Anabel felt her power flare reflexively. "Please let go of me, sir." She tried to release herself from his grip, but he held tight.

"No need to be formal. Name's Wallace, and I can show a pretty little thing like you a good time if you'll let me."

"Again," Anabel responded, "I must decline." She refused to meet his gaze, and noticed a knife sheathed at his waist.

Wallace stood and stepped around the table, pulling her closer to him. His grip squeezed her wrist, and Anabel felt sure she would have bruises under her gloves. She struggled. He pulled her toward the side of his body that wore the knife, but her hands were far from the weapon.

She heard a gasp and saw the serving girl standing at the threshold.

"Help!" Anabel cried. The girl ran.

"Quiet, gel!" Wallace yelled, and he turned her, so her back was against his front. One hand still gripped her wrist, and the other clamped over her mouth.

Anabel fought back a wave of nausea as she tried to elbow him in the stomach. He released her mouth and caught her other arm, pulling her tighter against his person.

"Stop fighting love," he whispered in her ear. "I'll take care of you if you'll be nice."

Anabel grunted in frustration. She could not see the knife. Her powers always worked better when she could see the object she wanted to move. Her Uncle Fergus had pressed her to work on developing her talent without the ability to see. She wished she'd practiced more, but she closed her eyes and called on that training now.

She tried to see with her other senses. To smell the object and feel the vibrations coming from it. It was faint, but she could smell the metal on the knife. She inhaled the leather of the sheath and the knife handle. She focused on Wallace's strong scent on the grip and felt the vibrations as the knife slid out of the sheath.

A small thrill of triumph ran through her when the knife was free. She concentrated her will on the weapon, aiming the point at her attacker's leg. With all her might, she commanded the knife to embed itself in Wallace's thigh.

"Bloody hell!" The knife sank deep into his flesh. He released Anabel and fell back.

She should run, but she couldn't resist turning to see the result of her actions. The knife was squarely in the middle of his thigh. There was no logical explanation for how it had gotten there.

Wallace glared at her. "You're a bleeding witch, you is!"

At that moment, the serving girl returned with one of the stable hands. They both looked upon the scene with horror.

"This gel's a witch!" Wallace yelled, pointing to his thigh.

She should have stood her ground and laughed off his accusation, but now that she was free, panic overwhelmed her. She closed her eyes, and the throbbing in her head began, heralding the return of the voice.

Run, child, or these country folk will burn you at the stake. It's not too late to come find me.

With a yell, Anabel once more slammed the door in her mind. Gripping her forehead, she turned and ran out of the inn as fast as her legs could carry her.

James dragged himself to the next inn on his list. A travel guide had listed which posting inns were along the mail coach's route, and he'd been to them all. At each stop he'd asked if anyone had seen a young lady fitting Anabel's description, careful not to reveal her name or his. He'd dressed in his most worn clothing—which he only donned when helping Tom test a new engine design—but the townsfolk saw through his disguise. He could not hide his fine boots or the quality of his horse. They were reluctant to speak with him, but responded well enough when their palms were greased with coin.

He'd been to five inns, and night was about to fall. He didn't relish the idea of continuing his ride in the dark, but he might not have a choice if he wanted to catch the coach before it departed Alconbury the next morning.

Entering the inn, his attention was drawn to a sizable crowd in the back. In the center was a large man with his foot atop a bench, his thigh wrapped in a blood-soaked bandage, loudly recounting a tale. The slurring of his words hinted at the spirits he had likely imbibed to dull the pain of such an injury.

A serving girl was standing in the shadows, and he motioned to her.

"Can I get you something, sir?"

"A tankard of ale, please." He pressed a coin into her hand. The coin would be more than enough to pay for the drink, and he hoped she understood why he wanted her to keep the difference.

She nodded as if she understood. "I'll be right back."

James settled at a table near the loud patron, still telling his tale. He was only half-listening when the man described his attacker.

"She was a pretty little thing, with dark eyes and copper hair. Definitely a gentry mort. That's how these witches survive, you know. They hide among these noble families, so's they don't get discovered. But I knew her for what she was. I says to her 'witch, repent of your ways, and I'll take you to the Vicar to be baptized.' But she refused and said 'I'll never be baptized! I do the devil's work.' And then she called on Satan and he sent a demon to stab me in me leg. She laughed and ran off with the demon."

"She called a demon?" One of the other patrons replied in disbelief.

"Well, how else could she have stabbed me?"

"She could've grabbed your knife from your belt, that's how."

"No, this witch was clever. She didn't even get close enough to touch it. She was using dark magics, she was."

The serving girl scoffed as she set a tankard of ale in front of James.

"You don't believe him?" James asked. The attacker sounded like Anabel. Had he caught up to her? His heart started to pound.

"He's pulling the long bow. That ain't how it happened. I saw it. He grabbed that poor girl and tried to kidnap her. He's just sore she managed to throw him off and give him a licking."

"What did she look like?"

The girl looked at him skeptically. "Are you a magistrate? I swear, sir, she was only defending herself."

"I'm not going to get her in trouble. I'm trying to find her."

"Who is she to you?"

James pressed his lips tight. He finally had a lead, and he needed this girl on his side. He sensed if he said the wrong thing, she would deliberately throw him off course.

"I'm her brother. Do you know where she is?"

The girl hesitated, and James was afraid he'd hit a dead end. "Please," he asked, injecting his voice with as much need as he could muster.

"I don't want her hurt."

"I'm not here to hurt her. I just want to bring her home."

The girl hesitated a moment longer and then nodded. "She ran out of here after she fought Wallace off. I followed her because she left her bag. The poor thing was shaken up, so I led her to me mum's house. She's staying there for the night."

James breathed a sigh of relief. "Thank you. Will you tell me how to get there?"

She hesitated again. James extracted two coins.

"No, sir, you needn't pay me."

"I'm not," he replied. "This first coin is for my room here, which I'm reserving for the night. The second is for my sister's stay with your mother. If you don't need the funds, give them to the church, but I want to thank you for your kindness."

She gave him directions to her mother's home. James thanked her and promised to return after he checked in on Anabel. As he was leaving, he heard Wallace once more.

"I'm telling you, there's no way she could've touched the knife without some kind of demonic influence. It were out of her reach."

"How'd you know she couldn't reach it?" another patron asked.

"Because I held her hands."

Red flashed across James's vision, and it was all he could do not to turn around and give Wallace the pummeling he deserved. He wasn't sure how Anabel had overpowered the man, but he hoped the stab wound led to the man's death. If Wallace was still telling tales when James returned, he might finish the job Anabel had started.

Chapter 10

Anabel awoke in a tidy sitting room.

She'd run away from the inn with no real purpose. The serving girl, Nelle, had caught up with her and insisted on taking Anabel to her mother's house. Nelle's mother had taken one look at Anabel and brought her inside, made her a cup of tea, and sat her by the fire. It was so cozy that Anabel dozed off in the chair.

The sky outside the window was dark, and the fire had died down a little. She was in the same chair, covered with a lovely warm quilt. Nelle's mother sat on a settee, a basket of mending next to her.

Anabel sat up gingerly, anticipating the headache she'd felt after hearing the voice. Miraculously, the pain was gone. She pictured the door in her mind, adding locks and other impediments to bar it from outside intruders. It felt silly, but perhaps it would prevent the voice from returning.

"Oh good, you're awake. How're you feeling, dear?"

"Much better, thank you. I appreciate your hospitality."

"I wouldn't have dreamed of leaving you outside. That Wallace is a menace."

Anabel chuckled and sat up in the chair. "Very true, Mrs.— I don't believe I got your name. How rude of me. My gran would have my hide."

The lady laughed good naturedly. "I'm Mrs. Smythe, but you can call me Eleanor. My Nelle is named for me."

"Thank you, Mrs. Smythe, and you can call me Anabel."

"Eleanor," the lady corrected with a smile. "You introduced yourself before, but I believe you were too overtaken. It's nice to meet you once more."

"And you, Eleanor," Anabel replied, returning the gesture. She smoothed the blanket over her lap, taking in the room once more. "You have a lovely home."

"I'm sure it's nothing compared to the grand houses you're used to."

Anabel stiffened. "Why do you assume that?" She tried to keep her expression neutral.

"You may be wearing a plain gown, but it's made from fancy fabric with little wear. Poor folk can't afford something like that. And your boots are too clean for a dusty town like this. It's obvious you're quality. So, what're you doing riding the mail coach on the North Road?"

"My boots weren't always this clean," Anabel replied. An insufficient answer, she knew, but she disliked how so many people saw through her disguise.

"I'll keep your secrets, love. I don't wish to harm you. I just worry about someone as young as you traveling alone."

Anabel took a deep breath. She wanted to share some of her troubles with this woman. She couldn't explain it, but she felt safe here. "I was born into nobility, but I don't belong among them. My mother came from humble roots, and I have spent time with that side of our family. I recently left them to help my brother in London, but I can't stay there. I want to return to my relations, and they are usually in York this time of year. I want to catch up with them."

"Are they travelers?" Eleanor asked.

Anabel knew she was referring to the Roma who traveled throughout the kingdom, usually settling down for a short period before moving on. She'd met some of them when she was with her family. "We are not part of a tribe, if that is what you mean. We travel to town fairs throughout the country, offering entertainments and selling our wares."

"So, they live a life similar to my people."

"You're Romani?" Anabel could see it. She had dark hair with a few streaks of grey, and, although the lighting was dim, her complexion appeared golden. The lady's eyes were a stunning hazel shade and illuminated her face.

She smiled at Anabel's question. "I suppose you could say that, though I left that life long ago. I fell in love with the son of the town baker. His father said we couldn't marry, but when we learned I was with child, we did anyway. Nelle was the pride of our lives. That man loved his little girl."

"Do you ever regret leaving your life behind?"

"Not at all. I found another one here that I love just as much. A few years back, I thought about going back to my people, but Nelle was planning to wed. I wanted to stay to help her."

Anabel smiled at the picture of domestic felicity. "Have they married yet?"

A sad look came over Eleanor's face. "No, the poor dear. Her man enlisted to try to earn a little money before they wed and never came home."

"Oh, I'm so sorry to hear that."

"Sweet Nelle was only sixteen. She had to mourn the loss of her betrothed and the loss of her father."

The woman's suffering pierced Anabel's heart. "What immense sorrow. I am sorry for your pain. I wish I could do something to lessen it."

Eleanor covered Anabel's hand with her own. "It was hard, but we have each other. Lemon balm tea once a day helps ease the sting, but mostly it eases with time. No talisman can keep your heart from breaking. Only time heals it."

Anabel smiled. "My friend makes a lemon balm tea that she sells for that very purpose. She's a great healer."

"She knows the old ways. So much power in herbs. I share some blends with the village. It took a while, but they eventually accepted me, once they knew I meant them no harm."

"So even now, you wouldn't return?"

"No. Nelle and I have a home here. I miss the road sometimes, but I like my life here. It was not easy in the beginning, but I'm glad I kept at it. If I'd left, I would always have wondered what could have been. I don't have the opposite regret. I may not have had a lifetime with Henry, but I wouldn't trade the years I had for anything. Opening up to someone can be scary, but living in fear is worse."

The parallels to Anabel's own life were obvious, and she would be wise to heed the advice Eleanor was giving. She thought about James and the potential connection she was leaving behind. Was she being foolish running away from him? She hardly knew the man, but she felt such a strong pull toward him.

A knock on the door pulled her from her thoughts, and a chill rushed down her spine. Had Wallace come to finish the job he'd started?

Eleanor gave Anabel's hand a gentle squeeze. "Don't worry. I don't feel any malice coming from the other side of the door. Whoever is there doesn't mean us any harm."

She opened the door to reveal James standing on the threshold. Anabel met his eyes, and her chill melted as heat spread through her chest. Was Fate sending her a sign?

A cup of tea was set in front of James. His tension had fled once he had seen Anabel was safe and sound. She, in contrast, seemed to tense up more with each second as they sat in each other's company. The owner of the house, a kind woman who looked too young to be Nelle's mother, placed a plate of biscuits in the middle of the table and took a seat next to Anabel.

Once they all had their drinks, James felt a compulsory need to fill the silence. "Thank you, Mrs. Smythe, for caring for my sister."

Mrs. Smythe put down her teacup and eyed him. "That's not your relationship to her, but I'll not be the one to expose you."

The woman's scrutiny made him slightly uncomfortable. Her eyes were a strange color, and he imagined they would look golden in the sunlight. She was a beautiful woman, although Anabel was more beautiful.

"Why are you here, S—" Anabel broke off and cleared her throat, taking a sip of her tea. "Why are you here, James?"

The sound of his name on her lips without the honorific did something to him. "When I learned of your departure, I had to come after you. I can't let you leave, Anabel. Not when there is still so much left unsaid between us."

"I'll get back to my mending," Mrs. Smythe said, standing. "I'll be in the sitting room if you need me. The walls are thin in this cottage," she said, staring pointedly at James as she walked away.

She meant he'd better behave himself, but her tone was fonder than he'd expected. It was clear she wanted to protect Anabel, but she recognized he did too.

"Your brother sent me," James said in a low voice when Mrs. Smythe was out of earshot.

"But he didn't come himself," Anabel said, slumping back in her chair.

"No," he replied carefully. "He couldn't get away."

"He never can," she sighed and took another sip of tea. "I'm sorry," she said after a period of silence. "I'm not being fair. I appreciate what you've done, but I'm not ready to return to London."

"Is this about the rumors Lady Whitlock is spreading? I am sure they'll die down. Witch stories are fairy tales, and her insistence on telling them only makes her look ridiculous."

"It's not just about that." She set down her teacup, the look on her face so burdened James longed to hold her.

"What else is there? I'm sure I can help. Or your brother, perhaps. His title holds a considerable amount of power. Whatever we need to do, we can do it, but please come back to London." James met her eyes and tried to convey his sincerity.

There had been plenty of time to think during his ride today, and he wanted Anabel in his future. More than that, he wanted her to *be* his future, and he hers, despite what his father might say. The conversations with Asher and the duke had reminded him that he had options outside of Edward's narrow mandates. Why would he tie himself to another woman when Anabel was within reach?

Anabel sighed again. She pinned James with her stare. After a long moment she muttered "I wish I had his power."

"Pardon?"

She waved her hand. "Never mind. How did you find me?"

He told her about how he had come to the inn, and how Nelle had directed him here.

"Was there anyone else at the inn while you were there?"

"There was a man telling tall tales. It looked like he'd been badly injured in a fight. His attacker sounded like you. I didn't believe his lies, but the description gave me hope that I'd found you."

"What was he saying?"

"The man was foxed and told anyone who'd listen that you were a witch, and that you'd summoned a demon to stab him. I was ready to thrash him myself after he said he was holding your arms. Did he leave bruises?"

"Yes, but that's not important."

"The hell it isn't!"

Anabel rolled her eyes at his show of bravado. "I didn't summon a demon."

"Of course you didn't," James replied with a laugh. "It was fanciful nonsense."

She stood and turned her back to him, seeming to study the wallpaper. "You don't find it odd that you've heard two people accuse me of witchcraft?"

"Why would I? I know witchcraft isn't real."

Anabel hung her head. "How do I..." The air was charged with tension. She turned to face him. "I can't come back with you."

James stood suddenly, irritated by her stubbornness. "You would abandon your family and your future to go into hiding because of a few silly rumors?"

"They are *not* silly rumors!" she yelled.

A teacup flew past his head, sloshing warm liquid all over the floor, then crashed into the wall. The charming cream and pink wallpaper now sported a large brown stain. The cup's shattered pieces were piled up on the floor.

"What happened? Is everyone all right?" Mrs. Smythe asked as she walked into the room. Maybe she had thrown the teacup? But she was coming from the room on the other side of the wall that the cup had shattered against.

Anabel burst into tears. "I'm sorry. I didn't mean to break one of your beautiful teacups. I'll replace it, of course."

"Hush, darling," Mrs. Smythe said, enfolding Anabel in a hug. "It's just a teacup. I can buy another. The real question is, 'what has you so upset?'"

It took James a moment to understand what they were saying. "How could you have broken the teacup without touching it?"

Both Anabel and Mrs. Smythe looked at him. His cheeks heated under their combined stare. He thought back on the drunkard's tale.

"Anabel," he began. "How did you get free of that man's hold?"

Mrs. Smythe looked at the younger woman. "It's all right, dear. I sense he's safe."

Anabel sniffled before stepping out of the woman's embrace. She held up her hand. He heard a light *clink*, but before he could turn to see the table, the cup was floating next to his head. It carefully sailed through the room toward Anabel's outstretched hand. She caught the item and held it out to him.

James looked it over. Was this some elaborate ruse? Like the magic shows at Vauxhall? There was no string tied to the cup. No logical explanation for what he'd just seen.

"What just happened?"

Anabel took a deep breath and wiped a tear from her cheek. "That is how I got away from the drunkard. I'm a witch, James."

Anabel stood frozen as she waited for James to process her words. She was more nervous than she'd been in a long time. Before coming back to London, she had not shown her magic to anyone outside of her family. She'd been away from them for less than a month and had revealed her abilities to three people she barely knew.

Gran had told Anabel to trust her intuition when it came to judging a person's character, believing it was tied to her ability to sense and share energy. She had suggested that Anabel could learn to read a person through their energy, but Anabel had been reluctant to try. Sharing energy with plants was one thing, but sharing with people felt too intimate. Even among her family, Anabel had a hard time letting her guard down.

Standing in front of James now, she wished she'd developed the power more. She had no idea how he would react, but she was afraid he might be angry and push her away.

James set the teacup down and carefully turned back to Anabel. His face was unreadable. "You're a witch?" he finally said.

"Well, I don't call myself that, but it's what my kind have been labeled by other people. I would say magically gifted. I have a special ability."

"The ability to move things without touching them?"

"Yes," she replied, unsure of what else to say. Her eyes, only just starting to dry after the broken teacup, welled up once more from the possibility he might walk away from her. She turned away before he could see them.

She was taking a handkerchief from Eleanor when James's hands touched her shoulder. He gently squeezed, urging her to turn around, and she didn't have the strength to refuse. Once she was facing him, she kept her eyes down.

"I'll return to the sitting room, but call if you need me, dear," Eleanor said as she gave Anabel a quick hug. Anabel watched the other woman's feet as they left the room. Alone with James, she started to tremble.

James caressed her face before sliding his thumb under her chin and tilting her head up. Anabel closed her eyes, trying to keep her tears from falling.

"Anabel," he said, his voice rough. "Look at me."

"I'm afraid."

"Afraid of what?"

"Of what I'll see when I look at you. I want to trust you, James. I feel like I can, but I worry it may have been unwise to share my ability with you."

James pulled her close. She couldn't resist the urge to lay her head on his shoulder and inhale his unique fragrance. She caught notes of bergamot mingled with pine and the slight musk of sweat from his long ride. Anabel finally allowed herself to relax, her arms drifting up to wrap around his waist.

For a long moment, they simply held one another, but eventually James returned his thumb to her chin and lifted her head to meet his gaze once again. She blinked twice to clear the fog of tears. When she could finally focus, she saw, not coldness, but warmth in his eyes. He carefully dabbed the tears from her cheeks.

"You were not wrong. You can trust me," he whispered. Leaning forward, he pressed his forehead to hers, breathing her in. Anabel lifted her mouth to meet his, their lips less than an inch apart. Before she could settle what to say next, his lips met hers in a gentle caress.

She sank into the kiss, and the gentleness was quickly overtaken by heated passion. James pulled her closer to his body, one hand low on her back and the other threading through her hair. He pulled at the strands to reposition her head, and Anabel gasped at the pleasure of the sensation. The moment her lips parted, his tongue was there, licking into her mouth. She met his tongue with her own before he pulled away, nibbling on her lower lip.

His hand tugged her head back further, and then his mouth was on her neck. He kissed, licked, and nibbled all along her tender flesh, and Annabel lost herself to sensation. She heard a whine, belatedly realizing the noise had come from her own mouth. The sound broke the spell, and James buried his face in her neck as they panted for breath.

And a spell it had been. Anabel had lived among magic for the last five years, but nothing had ever felt as enchanting as kissing James.

"Forgive me," he finally said. "That was very ungentlemanly of me."

"I don't want you to be a gentleman," she replied. "If that was an ungentlemanly kiss, then I don't want you to ever kiss me in a gentlemanly manner."

He laughed and lifted his head to look into her eyes. "But you do wish for me to kiss you again?"

"Yes," she replied, lifting on her toes and placing a peck on his lips.

James returned the gesture. They stood, comfortably embracing, for a bit longer.

"So..." Anabel said after several seconds of companionable silence.

"So?" he replied cheekily.

"You are not angry? Or afraid of my ability?"

James pulled back just enough to meet her gaze. "Of course not, Anabel. I am the farthest thing." He rubbed his hands along her back. "I need to speak with your brother as soon as we get back to London."

The name of the city brought back her panic. Anabel stepped out of his embrace. "I can't go back to London, James."

"Why not?"

"I just showed you why not. I can't attend balls and dinner parties and the theater when I risk exposing my secret to society. There are already so many rumors. I would inevitably reveal myself. I need to reunite with my family. I left them too soon. I need to go back and work on concealing my ability."

James stepped closer and pulled her into his arms once again. "If that is what you need, then I will accompany you. My father's carriage should be at the inn by now. We can continue north to find your family."

"You would do that?"

"Yes. But understand, once this adventure is over, I intend to make you my wife."

Anabel raised her eyebrows. "I thought you were courting Lady Cecilia?"

"Not any longer."

"So, you are proposing to me?"

He smiled at her. "Not yet, love. I will, but not tonight." He released her and stepped back. "Now, I must return to the inn. I understand you will be staying here?"

"Yes, Nelle has offered her bed."

"Then I will be back in the morning so we can begin our journey. Please make my apologies to Mrs. Smythe. I'm not fit to be in her company at present."

Anabel was confused. "Why?"

James looked down and coughed. "She will understand."

Anabel followed his gaze, and her cheeks flamed when she saw the outline of his erect member against the front of his breeches.

James gave her a tight smile and chastely kissed her on the cheek. "I'll see you in the morning."

With that he was gone, and Anabel stood in the kitchen, reeling from the effects of James's magic.

Her eyes drifted to the stained wallpaper and broken china. She thought of Mary and shuddered. She hoped her maid was all right.

You're going to hurt him too. He will leave you when he learns what you really are.

Anabel slammed the door in her mind. She needed to figure out how to get rid of the voice before she could move forward with James.

Chapter 11

When Anabel woke the next morning, she had to take a moment to orient herself. Yesterday's events had exhausted her, and she'd slept deeply. She remembered the interlude with James, and her lips tingled as she thought of their kiss. Recalling his promise to return early, she forced herself to get out of bed.

She dressed quickly, reflecting on what Eleanor had said about her traveling dress. Even with the plain design, Anabel could see it was in much too good condition to belong to the lower classes. She thought about rolling around in the dirt but dismissed the thought. She packed up her bag and headed down the stairs to the kitchen, where she found Eleanor and her daughter breaking their fast.

"Good morning," Nelle said as Anabel took a seat opposite her.

"Morning," Anabel replied. "I'm surprised to see you awake. I heard you come home last night. It must have been late."

"Aye, 'twas. The mistress of the inn got called away, so I had to stay longer than usual. But it was for the best. If I hadn't been there, I wouldn't have run into you, my lady."

"Please, call me Anabel."

Nelle smiled. "All right, Anabel. I'm glad I was there to meet your handsome gentleman and send him your way." She winked and held up her teacup in a toast.

Anabel felt her face heat. "I had no notion that he was following me."

"Do you still plan to go to York to find your people?" Eleanor asked as she took her place at the table. She lifted the pot of tea and started to bring it to Anabel's cup.

"Actually, if it's not too much of a bother, could I have some hot water? I should be drinking my medicinal tea every day, and I missed it yesterday. I'm happy to get the water myself if you will point me in the right direction."

"No need, dear," Eleanor said. She stood up, walked over to the hearth, and wrapped a thick cloth around the handle of the kettle. She poured steaming water into Anabel's cup with a practiced hand.

"Thank you," Anabel said. She added a small measure of the tea to the water.

"What's that?" Nelle asked as she watched Anabel carefully fold the paper back up and return it to her reticule.

"It's a tea blend my friend Suraya made me. It has some herbs and flowers for feminine pains. I must take it daily for it be most effective."

"Suraya..." Nelle repeated, looking toward her mother. "I think I know that name."

"It's not one you normally hear," Eleanor replied. "I think we met your friend a few weeks ago, Anabel."

"You did?"

"Aye," Eleanor continued. "We went to the next town over to attend the big fair. The tea seller was about the same age as my Nelle here, with dark hair worn loose 'round her shoulders and bright green eyes."

"That's Suraya," Anabel said with a smile.

"She was lovely. There ain't many people who look like her. I thought she was Roma when I first saw her."

"She's from a small town near Mount Lebanon in the Levant. She came to England all alone when she was very young, and my grand-mother adopted her. I guess, technically, that would make her my aunt, even though she and I are the same age" Anabel said with a laugh. "I miss her terribly."

"I can see why. She lifts the spirits of all she encounters."

Anabel smiled at the description of her closest friend. "That she does. I'm glad you met her." Her tea had cooled enough that she took a sip of the brew before continuing. "I do intend to continue my journey north, although I'm reconsidering whether I intend to stay with my family long-term."

"Oh?" Eleanor asked.

She smiled to herself. "I suppose you both have realized Sir James is not my brother."

"*Sir* James?" Nelle asked.

"Um, yes. He was knighted after his service in the war with France." Anabel's neck went hot. She hadn't meant to reveal his title.

Eleanor smiled warmly. "It's fitting. He seems the noble sort."

The desire to share James's intentions burned in Anabel's chest. "He wants to make me his wife."

"Well, I should hope so," Eleanor replied, her tone playful. "It's not proper for an unmarried couple to travel alone."

"Oh, no, indeed," Nelle continued, her tone matching her mother's. "Quite scandalous, that is."

Anabel couldn't help but chuckle.

Eleanor's smirk dropped, and she grabbed Anabel's hand. "Do you want to marry him? He seemed supportive, but I want to know if you're comfortable with this arrangement."

"I'm not sure," Anabel replied honestly. "I do like him, more than I have liked any other man. Though, most of the men I have spent time with were related to me in some way."

"Trust your intuition," Eleanor said. "If you look inside, you'll find what you truly desire."

Anabel was normally filled with anxiety about her decisions, but a sense of calm came over her, seemingly from an outside source. She brought her other hand to the top of Eleanor's and squeezed gently.

"Thank you. I am so grateful to have met you both."

"I find we meet the people we need at the right time," Eleanor said, releasing Anabel's hand. "As they say, the Lord works in mysterious ways."

"That they do," Anabel replied with a nod.

"I have something for you," Eleanor said. She reached into her pocket, withdrew a stone, and handed it to Anabel.

Anabel turned it in her hands. It was smooth and slightly smaller than her palm, made of grey rock with bands of white. There was a hole in the middle of the stone, slightly bigger than a quill tip.

"My gran has stones like this. She calls them mare stanes. We hang them around the horses' necks at night."

"I know it as a hag stone," Eleanor replied. "I found that on a walk last week, and something told me to bring it home. I know now you're the one the stone was seeking."

"I don't understand. It was seeking me?"

"Hag stones find the person they're meant to be with. It's for protection, to keep away evil spirits."

She lies! Throw it away!

Anabel enclosed the stone in her palm, gripping it hard. The door in her mind, which she'd kept a watch on, now appeared with planks of wood across it, nailed shut. The feeling of being watched, which had been with her since the evening the voice first appeared, dissipated. Anabel marveled at the quiet in her mind, something she'd never appreciated before it was stolen.

She looked up at Eleanor with tears in her eyes. 'Thank you."

Eleanor wrapped her arms around Anabel's shoulders. "I don't know what you're fighting, but you aren't alone. Love always conquers hate in the end."

Smiling through her tears, Anabel nodded before pulling a handkerchief from her pocket and dabbing at her eyes.

Nelle grabbed another teacup and saucer from a nearby cupboard.

"I believe your young man has come to fetch you," Eleanor said, straightening.

Anabel was confused until a knock sounded at the front door.

"I'll get it," Nelle said, setting the cup on the table and moving to the door.

Anabel's heart swelled as she squeezed the stone. She met James's eyes with a relieved smile.

Exhaustion had helped James sleep well, but his passionate encounter with Anabel had influenced his dreams and he'd awoken with a erection. He had groaned at the sight, knowing he couldn't take matters in hand, as it were, because he wanted to get back on the road.

Before leaving London, James had offered Taylor a large bonus to follow him in the Marley carriage, stopping at each posting inn to check for a message. Edward would not have supported James taking it, but fortunately he had not been at the house when James arrived. He confirmed last night that the carriage had arrived, and Taylor had a warm place to bed down for the night.

Now he needed to clean up, check on Taylor, and retrieve Anabel. If he were riding alone, he could make the trip in two days, but with the carriage, it would take at least three days before they arrived at their destination. He was grateful the full-sized carriage had been available. His family's smaller conveyances would have had a difficult time completing the journey.

He gathered his things before returning to the dining room of the inn. A few people had slept in the common room, waiting for the next mail coach, so he kept his voice low as he requested his breakfast and for a basket to be made up. After confirming all was in order, he retraced the path to Mrs. Smythe's house.

He smoothed his lapels and straightened his cravat before knocking, wanting to be as presentable as possible for Anabel. She would be his wife someday soon. Part of him wanted to find the nearest bishop, apply for a special license, and marry as soon as could be arranged. But he knew Anabel would want her family in attendance.

He raised his hand to the door when it was opened by a breathless Nelle. "Good morning, sir," she said, bobbing a small curtsy. "Come to fetch Miss Anabel?"

"Good morning, Nelle. Yes, I have. May I come in?"

She opened the door wider, and he walked the short distance to the kitchen where Anabel sat at the table. She gave him a brilliant smile, and it took him a moment to notice Mrs. Smythe had set a cup in the same spot he'd sat before and was pouring him some tea.

"Do you have time to sit with us before you begin your journey, sir?"

He could not decline the kind offer from someone who'd been so generous to Anabel. "I do, thank you." He took his seat and watched Anabel spread jam on her bread.

"Good morning," she said. A pretty bloom rose to her cheeks, and the back of James's neck tingled.

"Good morning," he replied.

Mrs. Smythe and Nelle sat as well. The table was crowded, but cozy.

"I would like to apologize for my sudden departure yesterday evening, Mrs. Smythe."

The lady waved off his concerns. "I'm not offended. It was late, and I know you were worried about your..." she gave him a wry smile. "Your sister, you said?"

James cleared his throat. "Yes, my sister. Thank you for allowing her to sleep here."

"It was no trouble."

"Nevertheless, you have my gratitude." He turned to Anabel. "I hate to tear you from such pleasant company, but I would like to be on the road soon. We have a long way to travel to Yorkshire."

"Of course," Anabel said. She smiled at him, but her posture was stiff as she picked up her teacup and took a sip.

The memory of a brown stain dripping down the wall came to mind, and he couldn't stop himself from looking at the same spot now. To his astonishment, the wall looked pristine.

He hadn't forgotten about Anabel's confession, but the conversation had been eclipsed by the kiss they'd shared. He looked at the wall once more, and then back at the ladies, considering what to say next, when Nelle interjected.

"Did you meet your driver, sir? He arrived last night, and I gave him your note meself," she said.

"Thank you," James replied slowly. He decided it was better not to mention the stain. Though he was still processing what had happened, he understood Anabel was sensitive to the subject of her ability. "I spoke with him this morning. The horses are well rested. We can make it to York in three days if we move at a moderate pace."

"That will be fine," Anabel replied, and her smile returned. "It might be slower than the mail coach, but I'll be happy to not be packed in with other passengers."

"Will you ride in the carriage with Miss Anabel, Sir James?" Mrs. Smythe asked.

James regarded her with slight alarm. How did she know his title? He had not shared it with anyone in the town.

Anabel laughed, and the joyful sound soothed him. "I might have shared the true nature of our relationship with my new friends, as well as your distinctive honor."

James furrowed his brow when he thought of the potential for consequences. "Well, I would appreciate discretion. I don't want word to get back to London and ruin Lady Anabel's reputation."

"Lady Anabel?" Nelle repeated. "Are you a nob?"

Anabel laughed again. "By birth, although when I am among friends, I do not like the honorific. Please just call me Anabel."

"Well, Anabel," Mrs. Smythe replied, "please don't be a stranger. We'll expect a letter from you when you arrive at your destination. And if you come back to Graveley, please come visit."

"I would be happy to," Anabel said, and James could see her genuine affection for the two women. Whatever else happened on their journey, he was thankful Anabel had found some respite in this town.

The easy quiet was interrupted by a knock at the door. Mrs. Smythe opened it to find a grimy boy waiting there.

"Miss El," he said. "Wallace bid me come ask you to see him. He took a wound yesterday, and now he's got a fever. He said he's been cursed by a dark witch, and he needs your white magic to heal him."

"The stubborn fool isn't cursed," Mrs. Smythe replied. "Let me grab my bag and I'll go to him. Where is he holed up?"

"He's in Mr. Howell's barn. Mrs. Howell found him this morning and screamed something frightful when she saw him."

"Wait there a moment, Jimmy. I'll be right back."

Mrs. Smythe closed the door and turned to the table. "You may want to leave now. Wallace isn't well-liked by most in this town, but he does have friends. They might come looking for you if he dies."

"Oh no," Anabel said. "I wanted the man to leave me alone, but I never meant to cause his death."

The older woman waved a hand in the air. "This ain't your fault. He's receiving his recompense." She crossed the room and placed her hands on Anabel's shoulders. "Be well, dear girl. We will meet again someday."

Anabel hugged Mrs. Smythe and Nelle with tears in her eyes. They bid a farewell to the women and left the cottage from the back door, hurrying to the inn.

James's carriage was much more comfortable than the mail coach. For one thing, there was room for Anabel to stretch out. The vehicle was well sprung, and the road they traveled was well maintained, so there were fewer bumps to toss her about. They weren't traveling as fast as the mail coach had, but keeping the team healthy meant moving more slowly. Anabel was not worried about the time. Her family usually stayed in York for several weeks, as there were two fairs in the area held back-to-back. She should be able to catch them before they began their journey south.

The hag stone seemed to be keeping the voice away. Anabel turned it in her palm as she considered what to do. She couldn't rely on the stone forever, could she? She needed to share this burden with Gran. The old woman would not call her mad for hearing the voice and would also know how to get rid of the intrusion for the long-term.

Rest and a plan worked wonders for her mental state, and her mind wandered to more pleasurable topics. She looked out the window at James as he rode alongside the carriage. He'd said he was riding outside the conveyance for the sake of propriety, but she wasn't sure why it mattered. If they were going to marry soon, what did it matter if her reputation took a little damage beforehand?

She couldn't help thinking about their kiss. The books from Fiona had provided her with some carnal knowledge, but she now understood that they were not written from a romantic point of view. They were focused more on the man's pleasure, even if the story was written from a female perspective.

Anabel wished she had Fiona to speak with now. She was unprepared for what lay ahead with James. They still had several days on the road, and Anabel couldn't help but think about being alone with him. Would he insist that she keep her virtue intact until they were officially married? To her surprise, her sincere hope was that he would not.

A light drizzle began. James cursed the weather, and she saw an opportunity to change things to her advantage.

"Will you join me in here, sir?"

He met her gaze through the window. "It's not a heavy downpour, and the sky looks clear ahead. I can manage a little rain."

Anabel inwardly cursed. She didn't want the weather to hinder their journey, but she'd hoped to get him to join her. "I was hoping you'd ride some of the way in the carriage so we could talk," she replied, deciding honesty was the best policy.

"I'm not sure that's wise," he said, his voice uncertain.

She decided to be completely open with him. "If we're to be married soon, I'd like to spend some time with you. Once we're among my family, there will be little peace. This is our best chance to converse in private."

"That is a valid point. Give me a moment."

He rode ahead to speak with the driver. Moments later the carriage stopped. They'd pulled off the road onto a narrow patch of grass. Some kind soul had set up a small, fenced area, obviously meant for horses to graze. There was also a rustic wooden table with two benches.

James helped her down, and Anabel's fingers tingled. He retrieved the basket the inn had prepared for them and led her over to the table. Glancing at the sky, she saw the rain had stopped. The sun was peeking out from behind the clouds. The driver took care of the horses while James laid down a blanket on the bench for her and unpacked the basket.

"We may as well rest a moment before getting back on the road."

"This is lovely," Anabel replied.

"It is rather quaint," he agreed as he sat down across from her. "Now tell me, what would you like to know?"

Anabel found herself at a loss for words. She closed her eyes for a moment to distract herself from the contours of his face and the mouth which had kissed her so passionately the night before. Unbidden, her hand felt for the stone in her pocket and she rubbed her thumb along its smooth surface.

He will leave when he learns what you really are.

Her body went cold. The door in her head was still barred shut. The words she'd heard were not new. The voice had said them after her kiss with James in Eleanor's kitchen, and she'd just heard an echo of them. Even though the voice could not reach her, she felt the effects of its poison.

"What is it?" James asked. He reached across the table and took her hand in his.

Anabel considered her response. How could she share with him that she heard a disembodied voice in her head? Would he think she was mad? She gathered her wits and decided a change of subject was in order. "Have you always lived in London?"

James contemplated for a moment. "I have. My father owns an estate in the country, but we rarely spend time there."

"Do you like visiting the country?"

"It's been so long that I couldn't say."

She opened her mouth to ask another question, but he placed a gentle finger on her lips. The sudden touch caused her breath to shudder in her throat. His gaze sharpened, and he slowly withdrew his finger and settled back against his seat.

"I believe I should be able to ask you some questions as well."

Anabel laughed nervously. "I'm not sure what else there is to share, but I will try."

"What is your favorite color?"

Her lips curled up. It was a simple, almost silly question. But she found herself wanting to be honest with him.

"Pink."

"Interesting choice," he mused. "Why is that?"

"It's the color of the sky as the sun is setting on a summer day. The clouds turn pink where the fading light hits them. I have many fond memories of watching the sunset with my cousins."

"What a lovely thought. You'll need to show me this bejeweled sky some time."

"Happily."

He gestured to her. "I believe it is your turn."

A part of her longed to ask him about the kiss, and about the carnal pleasures he could show her. But this wasn't the time to press him. They were sitting out in the open with the driver only a few steps away.

Instead of bringing up something that might embarrass them both, she moved on to another mundane question. They spent the rest of the meal in pleasant conversation. Anabel forgot the voice as they chatted. Once they were finished with their meal, they rested for a while before re-entering the carriage. James still refused to sit with her, but he offered to ride alongside the carriage so they could continue their conversation. Progress was slow, and the rocking of the vehicle and her full stomach made Anabel drowsy. As her eyelids drifted closed, she recalled the sharp tones of the voice.

He will leave.

She couldn't help but wonder if there was any truth to the words. Would James truly wish to be with her the more he got to know her? She drifted into a fitful sleep.

Chapter 12

When they arrived at the inn that evening, James was exhausted. It had been quite frustrating to ride at such a slow pace, but he'd enjoyed his easy conversation with Anabel. He'd almost given in and rode with her, but he didn't trust himself. Visions of their encounter at the theater—as well as their kiss from the night before—repeated in his head, and he knew he made the right choice to keep his distance. He had no desire for their first intimate encounter to take place inside a moving carriage.

He dismounted in the inn's stable yard and stretched his back. Once he felt more limber, he moved to help Anabel out of the carriage.

Anabel looked around the inn yard and at the buildings on the high street beyond. "I know this town," she said.

"Do you?"

"Yes. They have a large fair here in spring. I was here with my family earlier in the year."

"Did you stay in this inn? Or would you prefer to go to another one?"

"I'm sure the inn is fine," she replied. "When we travel, we sleep in tents."

James's mouth fell open at the casual mention of her family's rustic accommodations. He could not picture a creature as lovely as Anabel sleeping on a pallet on the cold ground. She should never endure such discomfort again. Knowing how much she cared for her family, however, he opted not to linger on the topic.

"Let's move inside," he said, holding out his arm for her to take, "and you can tell me more about your adventures."

They walked into a small foyer. He could see the dining room to his right, and a sitting room opposite. A twinge in his back had him looking at the stairs, anticipating a comfortable mattress to stretch out on.

"Welcome," A man said as he approached. His clothing was plain but clean and well-pressed. "I'm Mr. Jenkins, the owner of this fine establishment. How may I help you this evening?"

"Yes," James replied. "We would like accommodations for the night."

"Of course. You're in luck, sir. I've got one room left for you and your wife."

James cleared his throat. The fantasies of kissing Anabel's soft skin and feeling her pressed against him flooded back into his mind. He took a deep breath and mentally chastised himself. "Sir," he began.

"We'll take it," Anabel said before he could continue. Her hand looped around his left bicep and gave a small squeeze. He met her pleading gaze.

He nodded to Jenkins. "Yes, we'll take it. Please have our things sent up, along with some water. And see that my man is cared for, if you will."

"Of course, sir," Jenkins replied with a smile. They completed the transaction and Jenkins handed James the key. A maid led them up to the room.

After the door closed and they were alone, James looked at Anabel with disapprobation. "That was not well done of you."

She looked at him with wide eyes, her breathing rapid and her cheeks pink. "I'm sorry. I wanted to move us into the room as soon as possible. I'm tired and worn out from our journey."

"You could have allowed me a moment to request a cot from the man." He leaned forward and studied her face, trying to hide his smirk. "In fact, I might do that now."

"No!" Anabel said, flinging herself into his arms. "Please," she said, her voice lower and breathier than a moment before. "I want to share a bed with you, James. I don't want to delay our passion out of some misguided sense of propriety. If you care for me, and I care for you, and we plan to wed, why can't we share some of our passion now?"

Her words were enough to drive him mad. He growled and pulled her close, grinding his hardening length against her belly. "You want to share our passion?"

She tilted her head back, staring up at him with wide eyes. "Yes, please," she breathed, licking her lips in what was surely an involuntary movement.

The sensual movement of her tongue made his patience snap. He surged forward, taking her mouth with his own in a brutal, claiming kiss. A soft moan came from her throat as she melted into him, wrapping her arms around his neck. James slid his hands down to her firm backside. He palmed one of the cheeks through the layers of her dress and squeezed as he plundered her mouth.

Anabel suddenly giggled and squirmed in his arms. James pulled back and looked at her in question. His hand remained where it was, but he stopped squeezing.

"I'm so sorry," she said as she panted to catch her breath. "I'm afraid I'm a little ticklish."

"Oh, are you?" James asked, thinking of ways he could tease her as he prepared her for lovemaking.

"Yes. I knew I was ticklish on my side and my feet, but I never knew my bottom could also be a sensitive area."

"Have many people touched you here?" he asked, gliding his hand over her rear.

"No, no one," she breathed. Her gaze softened as his other hand feathered along her collar bone.

"Never?" He kissed along the creamy skin of her neck.

"N-no." She gasped when nipped at the soft flesh. "I was not often alone in the last five years, and my cousin Ferris kept away any boys who showed an interest in me."

"I'll need to have a chat with him," James said, his lips traveling a path back to hers. "He may have been your protector, but I am taking that role now." He took her mouth in another deep kiss.

He was ready to shed their clothes right there when a knock sounded on the door. "Begging your pardon, sir. I have your water and some fresh towels for you."

James reluctantly pulled away from Anabel. "This is not over," he said, lightly patting her rear before he stepped away entirely.

Anabel moved to the window. James opened the door and let the maid and the footman in the room.

After the servants left, James closed the door and rested his head against it. Anabel was more passionate than he would have expected from a débutante. She might be an innocent, but she was a willing student. He was excited to be her teacher.

Anabel felt hot and uncomfortable as she sat across from James in the dining room. He'd insisted they clean up and go downstairs to eat. She'd made a light protest, but James had informed her there would be no more intimacy if she did not keep up her strength. She'd started to argue, but then her stomach had growled. They'd laughed together and begun washing.

Despite his threat, James seemed to be unable to stop touching her. As she'd stood before the mirror at the wash-stand, he'd feathered his fingers along her neck. He'd placed a soft kiss on the juncture between her neck and her shoulders before leading her out of the room. He'd held her hand under the table and rubbed the skin between her thumb and forefinger. The intimacy of the touch had been enough to make her sigh.

Anabel felt flushed all over. Her nipples were pressing against the soft muslin of her chemise, and the throbbing in her core had returned. She also struggled to keep the guard up in her mind. Losing focus might let the door be pushed open again, but these feelings were all-consuming. She wasn't sure if she wanted to push him away or climb into his lap. Inciting his passions back in the room had been a mistake.

"James, please," she said, not sure if she wanted him to stop or continue.

He stilled his hand. "I'll take care of you, Anabel. But I need you to trust me."

"I do. I just don't understand what I'm feeling. It's all so new."

"Just feel it. The understanding will come later."

She closed her eyes and breathed deeply, letting the sensations flow through her. It was not a new exercise for her. Her grandmother had counseled her to do the same thing to help keep her powers in check. Her magic was tied to her emotions. Anger made them uncontrollable. What would pleasure do?

She was pleased to see the door in her mind was still locked and barred. James squeezed her hand, and Anabel shuddered. She watched the door closely, but it seemed to be holding firm.

"Anabel?" he asked, once more rubbing his thumb along the back of her hand.

Opening her eyes, she gazed at James in wonder. She felt stronger than ever and allowed her fear to be pushed aside in favor of more pleasant sensations.

Before she could dwell on them for too long, a plate was set before her. The fare was simple—chicken with roasted root vegetables—but it was seasoned beautifully. The chicken skin was nicely browned, and rosemary and sage mingled with the other aromas. Taking up her fork, she cut off a small piece and raised it to her mouth. The flavors exploded along her tongue, and she moaned in appreciation.

She looked up and saw that James, rather than eating his own meal, was staring at her curiously.

"What is it?" she asked, dabbing the corners of her mouth with her napkin.

"I associate that sound with your pleasure. Hearing it in response to something other than my actions has made me a little jealous."

"You're jealous of the chicken?" she asked with a laugh.

He laughed as well, breaking the tension. "Not jealous, exactly. Let's just say you are not the only one struggling with patience."

Anabel smiled at him before returning to her plate.

They tucked in to their meals, and only when they had both set their forks down did the conversation continue.

"I suppose there are things we need to discuss with regard to our pending marriage," James said as he wiped his mouth.

"We've been discussing this all day," Anabel replied. "What else is there to talk about?"

"We've discussed superficial things, yes, but there are bigger decisions to be made."

"Such as?"

"For one thing, where will we live? I have a townhouse. It's not grand or in a fashionable part of town. However, I believe you would like to be closer to your brother, would you not?"

Anabel paused. The idea of their marriage had been an abstract thing until that moment. She'd put off considering it until after they reached her family. She had no preference about where she wanted to live. She'd been focused on getting through the day for the past six weeks.

No. Not just then. She hadn't given any thought to the future for a very long time. She'd always assumed she would reside with her family. Before James, she'd had no dreams of a husband or children. She'd only half-heartedly agreed to help Suraya with the apothecary because she wanted to support her friend. Anabel did have a knack for managing business affairs, but she'd never expected to do it for a living.

"In truth, I'm not sure what I want," she finally said. "I am afraid to go back to London. I fear the ruin of my reputation and all who associate with me. Even as a married woman, most people will treat me with suspicion if they think I am a..." She looked around the room. "You know."

"I do," James replied. "And, if may be so bold, I believe fear is what exacerbates your struggle. You have said that these episodes happen when you're afraid. If we can work through your fear, that might remove much of the concern."

"It cannot be that easy."

"Why not?"

"Because nothing in life is. You know this as well, James. You were born into a well-to-do family who have only improved their fortunes, but you still struggle. Life is about struggle."

"Yes, because struggle makes us who we are. It shapes us. Working through your fear will not be easy. There will be challenges, but I will stay at your side as you face them." He grabbed her hand once more, his touch gentle this time. "That is what marriage is to me, Anabel. It's a partnership."

His words sounded too good to be true. Anabel had trouble trusting anyone outside of her family, but she couldn't deny the pull toward James. Her intuition told her he was someone to rely on, just as she'd felt she could trust Eleanor the previous night. The long-term implications terrified her. She was already starting to rethink her agreement to their marriage.

She closed her eyes and breathed in and out slowly. She was not going to let fear keep her from what she wanted, at least not tonight. She would deal with the rest later.

"James," she said as she opened her eyes and pinned him with her gaze.

"Yes?"

"I trust you."

His smile was devastating. "Good."

"Please take me upstairs and show me what else you want from a marriage," she said, letting her need show on her face. She might not be ready for long-term plans, but she knew she wanted desperately to lay with this man. The rest would be sorted out later.

As he led her up the stairs, Anabel's heart pounded in anticipation of their lovemaking. She passed a lovely flower arrangement and idly trailed her fingers along the soft petals as she passed. She failed to notice when the vase tipped over gently, as if someone had lain it on its side. Nor did she notice the buds trailing after her one by one.

Back in their room, James locked the door and turned toward Anabel. Her face and bosom were rosy, and he could see a faint outline of her pert nipples straining against the fabric of her dress. She was holding something back from him, and they had not settled the question of where they would live. An honorable man might refuse to share a bed with her until these things had been decided, but James didn't feel honorable in that moment.

He wanted her. The day had been a long tease for him. He couldn't wait to feel her lush body against him without any garments between them. He shucked his coat and laid it across the back of a chair before he pulled her roughly against his body.

"You asked me to show you what I want from marriage," he said, then he placed a hard, quick kiss on her lips. "I want everything, Anabel. I don't want you to hold anything back from me. I know that's difficult for you, but I have faith."

"What would I hold back? I have no experience to understand what could even be held back."

"You'll understand soon."

Before she could ask another question, he kissed her deeply. When his lungs begged for air, he pulled back and looked at Anabel's dazed face. "Turn around," he said gruffly as he helped her move within the cage of his arms. He unfastened the buttons of her dress and then pushed the garment to the floor. Then he loosened her stays. As he lifted the undergarment over her head and dropped it to the floor, Anabel turned in his arms. Her body was covered in a muslin chemise, the fabric so thin he could see her nipples. He started massaging the tender flesh of her breast before pinching the tight buds between his thumb and forefinger. Anabel closed her eyes and gasped.

"Keep your eyes on me," he commanded, and she immediately complied. He ghosted his mouth over hers before he let it travel down her neck, over her collarbone, and then finally to the pert nipple. He sucked it into his mouth, using the fabric to heighten her sensation. He looked up and saw her lips were parted as she writhed under his ministrations.

"Let me see all of you."

She allowed him to remove her chemise. Her stockings came next, and then she was fully naked. She wiggled, rubbing her thighs together.

"Bloody hell," he said. "You are so beautiful." James wished he could take more time with her, but for now he wanted to show her pleasure. The kind he meant to provide her every day for the rest of their lives.

"Sit down on the bed," he commanded. She settled in the middle of the bed with her legs stretched out in front of her. James tugged her down, so her bottom was perched on the edge of the mattress. She reached out, but he shook his head. Once she was seated, he pushed on her torso to encourage her to lay back. The minute she was in position, he knelt in front of her and picked up one of her feet, placing it on his shoulder.

"James?" she asked, uncertainty lacing her tone.

"Trust me, Anabel. You will enjoy this."

He held her gaze as he nipped at her inner thigh. She squealed lightly, making him smile as he gave the other leg the same treatment. Then he let his tongue trail along her sensitive flesh, until his mouth hovered just above her core. He held himself there, letting her feel the warmth of his breath as he trailed a finger though the soft skin of her sex. She was wet and ready, and his mouth watered. Still, he had no intention of rushing this.

"Have you ever touched yourself before?" he asked as he lightly toyed with her folds.

She flushed and pressed her lips together.

"Tell me, Anabel. Don't hold back."

"Yes," she croaked out as he grazed the bundle of nerves at the top of her sex.

"Good," he said with a smile. He moved his finger until it was poised at her entrance and then slowly slid the digit into her tight channel. She gasped at the intrusion, and he couldn't hold himself back. He lapped at the flesh, letting his tongue caress her clitoris. He continued the soft kitten licks as he felt her frustration building. She was wriggling her hips, trying to get him to give her more pressure.

Chuckling low to himself, James decided to stop playing around. Releasing his restraint, he pumped his fingers in and out of her body while sucking her pearl into his mouth. It took only a few minutes before her hips lifted, and she cried out in rapture as her quim squeezed his fingers. He gentled his motions, but continued to move, drawing out her pleasure.

When her torso finally fell back to the mattress, he withdrew his fingers and continued placing soft licks on her outer lips.

"Please," she cried. "I cannot take much more."

She would be surprised when she learned how much she could take. But for now, he acquiesced. He met her eyes as he raised his hand to his mouth and licked her cream from his fingers.

"Delicious," he said as he stepped to the side of the bed.

"I've never...I...what was that?"

"That would be your climax, love. Have you never achieved one?"

"I thought I had, but never as intense as that."

He smiled as he stepped to the basin and washed his hands. Grabbing a towel, he gently cleaned her folds before encouraging her to climb under the covers.

"But you haven't had your climax," she protested sleepily.

He knew she had read books—those not meant for young ladies—which described the sex act. They were all focused on a man's pleasure, so it made sense that she would not consider the evening complete until he had found his release. James intended to teach her the multitude of ways a couple could find pleasure, but he could wait until she knew a little more before dipping his pen in her ink, as the saying went.

"It will keep," he replied as he tucked her in.

She looked like she wanted to protest again, but her exhaustion was evident. She was asleep within minutes. James moved to the corner and freed his cock. He replayed her enthusiastic reaction as he took himself in hand. It only took a few pumps before he spilled his release into the towel.

James stripped down and curled up next to Anabel. With any luck, he would fall asleep before his cock hardened again.

Chapter 13

Anabel awoke feeling warmer and more relaxed than ever before in her life. She replayed the evening's activities in her mind. James had not found his own release, and that frustrated her. While he'd given her great pleasure with his mouth, she wanted more. She wanted to lie with him truly.

She stretched her legs, then realized James was curled around her. His front was pressed to her back, and she could feel his member against her buttocks, hard and ready. Maybe she could convince him to complete her ruination this morning.

Her mind was whirling when his hold tightened.

"Whatever you're planning, it won't work," he said before he lightly nipped her neck.

"What would make you think I'm planning something?"

"I can feel you thinking," he replied with a laugh.

Ridiculous man. She rolled over in his arms and faced him. When she saw his passion-laden gaze, she wriggled closer to him and hooked one of her legs over his thigh.

"Show me something else you'd like to do in our marriage bed." She began to tilt her hips, but he put a firm hand on her thigh, halting her movement.

"Minx." He placed a quick peck on her lips. "We don't have time for dalliances this morning. We need to be on the road soon."

He leapt out of bed before she could protest and pulled on his pantaloons. Anabel sat up, holding the sheet to her chest. She looked around the room and noticed the petals and stems scattered on the carpet.

"Did you bring me flowers?" she asked. The buds looked ragged. The stems were all pointing in the same direction, and the flowers had all lost petals. If she didn't know better, she would think someone had shoved them under the door.

"I'm sorry to say I didn't think that far ahead. I will procure some for you today. Do you have a favorite?" His back was to the door as he used the mirror of the washstand to tie his cravat.

"James," she said. He looked back at her, and she gestured toward the flowers strewn across the floor.

He finally looked down and saw what concerned her. "How strange," he said, kneeling to look at them. "Did you gain an admirer last night? I've never heard of a person pushing flowers under a door."

Then Anabel recognized them. It was the bright arrangement she'd seen in the hallway last night. She'd touched the buds gently before entering their room. She tried to think of everything else she'd touched the night before. Her plate and fork, a water cup and a teacup. What if James opened the door and found broken pottery?

She was suddenly very keen to leave. She jumped out of bed and dressed in a hurry.

"What is it?" James asked.

"The flowers, James. I touched them. They followed me here. I must have let down my mental shields when we were...when you were...." Her inability to finish a sentence irked her.

"Giving you pleasure," he added helpfully.

"Yes, that. I've told you my power flares when I'm angry. It must also do so when I am," she paused. "You know."

"Experiencing pleasure."

She tried to button up her dress and grunted. Normally she had no trouble doing so, but panic made her power harder to control.

James took over, his touch gentle. "Don't worry, love. We will take care of this. A ruined flower arrangement is not so bad. I can tell the owner that we broke the vase by accident and compensate him for the loss."

"But what if other things are broken? What other strange occurrences happened last night? They could be looking for me even now."

"Breathe, darling." He wrapped his arms around her. "Let's not borrow trouble. We don't know that anything else happened, and, even if it did, we can handle it. No one is going to immediately suspect a witch."

"Are you sure?" she asked, her voice trembling. She breathed slowly in an effort to banish the tears rising behind her eyes.

"I am. I'll help you." He gently lifted her chin, and she met his eyes. "Cry if it will help you get these frustrations out, but don't cry out of despair. We will face this together."

Anabel nodded, and he released her. Silently they finished dressing and packing up their things. They collected all the stems they could find, and Anabel held the ruined bouquet while James opened the door.

There were no broken dishes sitting outside their door. She walked out into the hall and found the vase sitting on the table, unbroken. She picked up the flowers that were strewn along the carpet before approaching the table. She deliberated before she dropped the flowers to the table. She could not recreate the lovely arrangement, but she could remove the suspicion of anything supernatural occurring.

They deposited their bags in the foyer before moving into the dining room for their breakfast. James asked the kitchen to pack a basket, and Anabel requested her cup of hot water. The room was empty—the hour too late for the working class and too early for the gentry. The scene was quite domestic, and Anabel relaxed, daydreaming about what life might be like with James as her husband.

James rode alongside the carriage while Anabel read. The sky was dark ahead, and they might need to stop soon to wait out the storm.

After he'd calmed her down, Anabel had been more open with him than before. He'd proved himself, although she likely hadn't meant to test him. The incident had shown him, however, how dangerous an unintentional use of her powers could be. He could not say why this had made him understand the gravity of the situation, and not when she smashed a teacup against a wall without touching it. He chalked it up to lust on his part that he'd downplayed the first event.

Learning about Anabel's magic lifted many of his concerns. He found he no longer cared that she might have drawn him in with her abilities. Whatever force had brought them together, he was thankful for the intervention. He would need to help her master her abilities, however, if they were to avoid scandal.

While the innkeeper would likely think nothing of the flowers, servants and neighbors would be another matter. He would need trustworthy staff who would not tell tales about their mistress. Anabel could overcome her struggles, but there might be mishaps along the way. He did not want to continue to feed the rumors in town that she was a witch, especially after she became Lady Anabel Marley.

He smiled at the thought of her married name. He liked the sound of his surname attached to hers. She would still be Lady Anabel. Though their children would not be in the direct line, they would be closely related to a dukedom. His father would have to accept that connection, or James would separate from the man. He was surprised to realize he had no concerns about that. James was ready to make a stand.

He looked through the open window of the carriage. Anabel was leaning against the opposite side, fast asleep. He smiled. She was usually guarded, and he enjoyed the way she relaxed with him. He was proud to earn her trust and vowed to do everything in his power to keep it.

He returned his thoughts to her problem. He hoped that her grandmother would have some tips to help her grandchild better control herself. Perhaps she could teach James what signs to look for and what tips to use when Anabel became overly anxious.

A crack of thunder pulled him from his thoughts, and Anabel awoke with a cry.

"It's all right, love," he called through the window. "There's a storm up ahead, but we'll be fine. I see a farmhouse just up the road. We'll ask if we can take shelter, or if they can direct us somewhere safe."

She was obviously groggy and simply nodded her head. James rode ahead to speak with Taylor. This section of the road was dead center between towns and not usually a place for travelers to stop. However, there would be a public house if there was a town nearby.

The house was in disrepair, but there were signs of habitation, including two horses grazing in a field nearby. However, he began to doubt his plan as they came nearer.

"I don't like it, sir," Taylor said when they were almost to the drive of the house. "I got a bad feeling."

"As do I," he responded. "Perhaps we should drive ahead instead and try our luck with the storm."

No sooner had he spoken those words than a spear of lightning hit a tree roughly half a mile away. The boom of thunder spooked their horses. James was able to get his mount under control quickly, and then moved to help Taylor calm the team. The tree caught on fire, and James watched in horror as half of the upper branches came crashing to the ground, thoroughly blocking the road. The rain had not reached this area yet, so there was nothing to douse the flames as they spread through the underbrush.

"There's nothing for it now," he muttered. He still didn't like what was happening and couldn't shake the foreboding feeling as he dismounted. He handed the reins to Taylor, instructing the man to watch the carriage and horses while James inquired at the house.

"What's happening?" Anabel asked, now fully awake. "Are we still planning to stop here? I don't like the feeling of this place."

"Stay in the carriage," he warned her. "I'm going to see if they can help." He looked back over his shoulder at Taylor. "If anything appears amiss, leave my mount and drive away. Head back south to the nearest town. I will meet you there."

"No!" Anabel protested. She jumped down before he could stop her. "I'm coming with you."

"You certainly are not," he scolded. "I have no idea what is inside that house, but I agree that there's a strange feeling about this place. I refuse to put you in danger."

She moved closer to him so she could whisper her next reply. "I can help you. My ability may seem like a parlor trick, but it is useful for situations like this. I can disarm an opponent. I can also use my secondary ability to help feel out the resident of the house."

"Secondary ability?" James asked with a lift of his brow.

"Yes," she sighed. "It's not as well developed, but I can feel the energy of people and places. When I said I don't like the feeling of this place, I was referring to its energy. It feels..." she paused, "I think stale is the best word. I believe this house has been abandoned for some time."

"Then why are there horses in the pasture?"

"That's the question, isn't it? I can help you determine if the person who answers that door is trustworthy."

"We are going to discuss this secondary ability when we stop for the night. I need to understand all you can do if I'm to protect you."

Her face soured. "I am perfectly capable of protecting myself."

"I would like to protect you just the same."

She huffed at his words, but he had no time to dawdle. He wasn't sure if the fire would spread closer. He looked back at Taylor. The man was watching the fire, but when he felt James's gaze, he nodded in understanding.

"Let's get this over with," James said as he reached for Anabel's hand. He secured it in the crook of his arm, more for his own comfort than hers, and walked up the drive.

Anabel had described the feeling of this house as stale, but that was an inadequate word to describe what she was experiencing. The home had an ominous cast to it. The closer they approached, the more her instincts urged her to run. Something in the house was trying to pull the life force from everything around it.

"James—" Before she could plead with him to turn back, the door opened. A pale man with stringy blond hair stood there. His posture was stooped, making him seem shorter than his long limbs suggested. Even from several paces away, Anabel could smell the man needed a bath. What struck her the most, however, was his energy. He was the thing pulling the life force from everything around him.

Most people would not understand what this man was doing. They might feel fatigued after spending time in his presence. But Anabel understood, and it sickened her. The ability to pull energy from others without contact was not natural. Her grandmother had explained that their abilities were gifts to help balance the world. Those who used their gifts for personal gain corrupted their souls. It was 'dark magic.' Anabel had never encountered dark magic before, but she knew that was what was emanating from the man before them.

"Can I help you?"

Anabel knew that voice. It was the one that had been taunting her for weeks. She wanted to run, and she tried to keep James from moving forward.

"Let's turn back," Anabel said, before James could respond to the man.

"We can't," James whispered. "We need help." They continued their slow approach. "Hello there," he said. "We ran into a mishap on the road. Can you direct us to the nearest inn or public house so we could take shelter?"

"You can stay here," the man responded. His voice was gravelly.

"Er, no, thank you. If you can just point us the right direction, we'll take no more of your time."

"Storm's going to be bad." The old man pointed to the sky, and they were caught in a sudden downpour, as if the man had made the rain come.

Anabel wanted to run as fast and far as she could to escape whatever was about to happen, but she was soaked. It was a spring rain, but the air was chilly. She was shivering in no time.

The man held the door open. "Nice and dry in here. Have your man bring the horses round to the stables. He can stay with them."

Before James could even turn to speak with the coachman, the vehicle rolled past them.

James responded dazedly. "Of course, Taylor. We'll join you after the rain has stopped and the roads dry out."

They turned back to the house, and the ominous man beckoned. Anabel tried to pull her arm free, but James held her fast. He was stronger than her, and she couldn't make him stop or free herself from his grip. In a moment, they were at the door.

"Who are you?" she asked, staring at the pale man.

"Call me Merlin," he replied, grinning at her with his rotting teeth.

"Merlin?" she asked in disbelief. "You're the one who's been speaking in my mind, aren't you?"

"I am. Welcome to my home."

He pushed them toward a sitting room where a small fire burned. The house was covered in dust, the furniture at least a hundred years old.

"Have a seat," Merlin said as he gestured toward a moldering settee. James still held Anabel's arm as he moved them in the direction Merlin had pointed. Anabel was horrified to see he was looking straight ahead, his eyes wide. His movements were stiff, as if he were a puppet on a string. He sat down awkwardly and pulled her down beside him.

Anabel turned from James toward their host. "What did you do to him?"

"Now, don't you worry your pretty head about that. I'm not doing him any harm. Just a little obedience spell is all."

"A spell?" she asked, feigning ignorance.

"Don't be coy, dear. You know all about spells, don't you? You don't use them, but your grandmother wouldn't let you go out in the world unarmed."

"What do you know of my grandmother?" Her heartbeat sped up.

"I know all about Mrs. Hana Moon. We have history."

"Funny, I don't recall her ever mentioning you."

His laugh was a dry, croaky sound that set her teeth on edge. She had a hard time placing his age. He didn't look old enough to be a contemporary of her grandmother's, but he did not look young. His age seemed frozen in time somehow. She suspected the dark magic was keeping him alive.

"Unraveled my secret, did you?" he asked, giving her a knowing look.

"How do you mean?"

"Your mind is as wide open as the land. I can read your thoughts from a mile away."

"And you knew who I was connected to?"

"I've been tracking Mrs. Moon for a long time. She thinks she's hiding her brood doing that damn traveling, but she's only free because we allow it."

"Who is we? Do you work for the Crown?"

He barked another loud, dry laugh. "Who I work for has nothing to do with the Crown. But don't worry about that. We have important things to discuss."

His tone became menacing, and Anabel couldn't fight the shiver that ran through her. "What could we possibly have to discuss?"

"You're going to let me replace your soul with mine. This vessel is dying, but I can move on to a new one. You are the perfect vessel."

"How is that even possible?"

"Anything's possible with the right spell," he replied with a shrug.

She scoffed. "If you've been watching me, you should know that I'm not very powerful. All I can do are fancy parlor tricks." She raised her hand toward a book sitting a table just out of her reach, but the item stayed where it was. She grunted as she tried a few more times before giving up.

Merlin laughed again. "This house has magical dampeners. The only one that can use magic here is me. Besides, that paltry magic is not your power. You haven't begun to tap your full power. But you don't need to worry. I know how you fear it. I can release you."

"And what would I get in exchange?"

"Safe passage for your man, and a guarantee I won't harm any of your family, including that hoity-toity brother of yours."

Anabel furrowed her brow. "Why do you need to negotiate with me at all? Why can't you just take it like you steal life force?"

"The soul is a funny thing. I can't just replace my soul with yours. You must accept the bargain."

She swallowed. "What happens to my soul then?"

"The same as any disembodied soul. You'll go to heaven or hell. Doesn't matter to me."

Fire rose up within her. "I won't be handing over my body. We'll find a way to get out of here."

"Suit yourself," he replied. "I'll give you a few days, then see if you've changed your mind."

With a wave of his hand, the room shimmered and the elegant, but decaying surroundings fell away. They weren't in the sitting room anymore. They were sitting on a hard wooden bench, a wall of packed earth behind them. The fire was gone, and she shivered in the cold air. James sat as still as a statue. Anabel slumped forward and let her tears flow.

Chapter 14

James felt like he was underwater as he listened to the soft sounds of Anabel's sobs. He'd heard everything, and he longed to comfort her.

Merlin, he thought with a dry laugh. What a ridiculous name. The man was delusional. The thought of that vile man replacing Anabel's soul with his own was repugnant. James had to believe there was no way the man could accomplish his goal.

He tried to turn to no avail. The man had spelled his body, but his mind was still free. He choked down his frustration and tried moving again, which only managed to give him a headache.

"Oh, James," Anabel said, her head dropping to his shoulder. "I wish you could talk with me. I am so afraid. What are we going to do?"

I'm right here, love! He yelled, but nothing seemed to get through.

"He's ridiculous if he thinks I'm powerful."

She began pacing in the small room. James was relieved to see her, although his vision was like looking through a dirty window.

Anabel wrung her hands. "That's not entirely true," she said in a whisper as she leaned toward him. She touched his arm as she looked into his eyes. James longed to pull her into his chest and soothe her worries.

"My secondary ability," she continued in a whisper. "I feel the energy of a thing and I can share my life force. I've done it with plants, and sometimes I can pull energy from them. But I've never used it with people. It always felt wrong."

This revelation explained some of what Merlin must be thinking. *That must be why he wants to use your body,* he thought.

"Did you say something?" She straightened up and removed her hand from his arm.

You heard me? He marveled at the thought.

She didn't seem to hear him the second time. "Of course he can't talk," she muttered to herself. "He's under some kind of trance. At least he's unaware of the danger we're in."

She sat down and held his hand.

I am very aware, love. I just can't tell you.

Anabel sat up, keeping hold of his hand. "I can hear you," she said, slowly looking down at their joined hands. "I must need to touch you to make it work."

The tension in his head dissipated. *You are incredible,* he said, trying to convey with his thoughts what his body could not. He felt her responding smile, like sunshine on his skin.

"I think you are flattering me a little."

It may be flattery, but it is still true.

"You are quite charming," she replied with a laugh. "Now, if I only knew how to free you from this trance."

Even if you cannot, I'm thankful we have a way to communicate.

"As am I."

What did you mean when you said that man was speaking to you in your mind?

"I..." she breathed a shuddering sigh. "I thought I was going mad. I heard this voice telling me I was going to hurt everyone I loved. It's been going on for weeks. Every time something bad happened, he told me to run to him. I was hoping my gran would know how to get rid of it. I had no idea there was a real person behind it."

James sighed. *I wish I could have taken some of this burden from you.*

"You did, by being with me. But I was afraid to tell you about it."

Please don't ever be afraid to confide in me. He tried to grip her hand, but he could not. In lieu of physically comforting her, he decided to lay his heart on the line. *I have no idea what will happen, but I must tell you, Anabel, that I love you. I know it is early, but I've felt a strong pull to you from the moment we met. Please don't let that vile man take your soul. I would rather perish a thousand times than be the reason you gave up your life.*

"James," she said, her voice watery. "I think...I think I love you too. I don't want to lose you." She moved to stand before him but held on to his hand. "Can you see me?"

A little. My vision is clouded.

"Oh, I wish I could remove that blasted spell! If I could use my power, perhaps I could draw it out of you."

As she spoke, his vision cleared, but then the room went dark.

"James! You just blinked!"

He wrenched his eyes open to see her lips parted and her hand touching her chest. *Some of the effects fell away as you spoke. You can draw this from me.*

"But how? My magic is being blocked by the house."

I have no notion of how, but I believe it will work. Please try again.

"All right," she replied in a shaky tone. She placed both of her hands in his listless grip and closed her eyes as she breathed slowly.

Anabel was silent for several minutes while she worked her magic. Control came back slowly, part by part. His nostrils flared as he smelled her unique scent, infused with jasmine and orange blossoms. The corners of his mouth lifted once he realized the intervention was working.

A tingling sensation ran through his body as he was released from the spell. It seemed to radiate to his hands last. The moment he could control his fingers, he pulled her to him.

"You did it, love!" He embraced her firmly. "You truly are incredible!"

She opened her mouth, likely to say some diminishing remark, but he was having none of it. He cupped her face and looked into her eyes.

"I'm not just flattering you." Then, before she could say a word, he captured her mouth in a searing kiss. The kiss was brief but intense, and when he was finished, he met her gaze once more. "I love you," he said, overjoyed that he could say the words out loud.

Before Anabel could say anything, the door to their prison opened with a bang. Merlin stood before them, a thunderous look on his face.

"So," he said, his tone dripping with disdain. "The little witch has realized she can do more than parlor tricks? It's time we raised the stakes."

Before James could put himself in front of Anabel, an invisible force grasped his neck and squeezed. He fell to his knees as he struggled for breath. Before the blackness took him, Anabel knelt at his side and cried out his name.

The moment James started to go down, Anabel fell to her knees and cradled his head in her lap. The skin around his lips turned blue as he struggled for breath. She held her own breath as she watched him struggle for a moment before passing out. Blessedly, his color returned as his breathing evened out.

She looked upon the man who called himself Merlin. "What did you do?"

Merlin shrugged. "I'm not all bluster. I can do much to your man. I can tear him apart limb by limb with a wave of my hand. You're not dealing with a novice."

Anabel's fear was replaced by fury. "Oh yes, I forgot. I'm dealing with the oldest wizard in all of Britain," she said in a mocking tone. "Do you have Excalibur lying around somewhere as well?"

The man punched the air in front of him. Anabel saw the black tendrils of his power touch her, and she repelled them with a thought.

Merlin cried out in frustration. "You might be able to protect yourself, but you can't keep me from killing your man. I'll let him live for now. You can have more time to think over my proposal, but let me leave you with another reminder."

He waved his hand, and the left sleeve of James's jacket burst into flame. Anabel screamed as the fire blazed a narrow path down his arm. The flames were doused almost as quickly as they came. The fabric of his sleeve fell away, revealing the angry cut on his arm. It looked as if he'd been sliced by a knife, though there was no blood, just a scalded gash along his skin.

James was still mercifully unconscious, although his brow was furrowed and his breathing shallow. He groaned as his body started to writhe.

"What is this?" she asked, pointing to the wound.

"Just a little curse. The cut is superficial, but it will never heal. He will feel the agony of that wound for the rest of his life. Of course, he won't live much longer, so it doesn't matter. If you agree to my terms, I'll lift the curse. If not, I will add more wounds. If I give him enough, he won't be able to live through the pain, though it is a slow, torturous death. I enjoy watching people die from hundreds of shallow cuts. The essence draining from their body is delicious."

"You monster." She directed all of her will at him. Merlin's eyes widened comically as he flew away from the door.

The door to the cell was open. If James had been awake, Anabel would have grabbed his hand and run, but she couldn't leave him. He groaned and the wound seemed to pulsate, as if it had a heartbeat of its own.

Still, they had to attempt an escape. She tried to get him on his feet, but his body was heavy. Every time she jostled him, it seemed to multiply his pain. Before she could even get his torso lifted, Merlin yelled.

"You bitch!" He lifted his hand, and a gust of air slammed the door shut.

She arranged James's head in her lap and softly ran her fingers along his brow, trying to comfort him. Perhaps she could remove some of his pain. She placed her hands on either side of the wound and directed her will toward the cut, trying to pull the curse from his body.

Her efforts were for naught. The more she tried to draw the pain from his body, the more he screamed in agony. Tears sprang to Anabel's eyes, and she finally pulled her hand away and let out a defeated sob as she considered their circumstances. She'd been able to free him from the obedience spell, but this was something else entirely.

Hanging her head, she gave in to her despair. What was she going to do now? She was so caught up in self-pity, it took a moment for her to realize that someone was calling her name from the small high window near the door of their enclosure.

"Bel!" the voice called again, in a hurried whisper. "Are you sure she's in there? She isn't responding."

"She's in there," another voice said. "I can feel her."

Anabel blinked, too stunned to believe this was happening. "Raya?" she called out tentatively. "Ferris?"

They sunshine tones of Suraya's voice moved closer to the window. "Yes! We've come to rescue you."

"Rescue me?" Anabel asked in bewilderment. "How did you even know I was here?"

"Gran had a vision," Ferris replied in his no-nonsense tone. "She knew you were in trouble somewhere along the Great North Road and sent us to find you."

"And the vision led you to this house?"

"That was me," Suraya replied. "I can always sense you when you're nearby. We have a special bond, you and I."

Despite everything, Anabel had to smile at her friend's words. But what if this was another trick of Merlin's?

"How do I really know it is you? Tell me something only Suraya would know."

"With Ferris here?" she asked incredulously.

"Yes," Anabel insisted.

Anabel could see Suraya's tawny skin and dark hair as she leaned closer to the window as she spoke.

"When we were seventeen, we dressed like men so we could visit Covent Garden," Suraya finally said.

"You what?!" Ferris shouted.

"Shush," Raya chastised him. "It was years ago, and we only got as far as a pub at the entrance of the Garden."

"Still, that's no place for young women to—" Ferris's voice cut off abruptly.

"Raya?" Anabel whispered as loud as she dared. "Are you both well?"

"Yes," Suraya said as calmly as she could. "I had to stop Ferris. I don't need a lecture right now. We need to get you out of here."

"I can't make the door budge. It's locked from the outside."

"The wizard has spelled it somehow," Ferris said. "Only he can move it."

"I think I can get you out another way," Suraya said.

"How?"

"Step back as far as you can."

"I have someone in here with me."

"Can you move him?" Ferris asked.

"Not easily. He's heavy."

Ferris gave a dry laugh. "Since when does something being heavy keep you from moving it?"

"The wizard put some sort of damper on my magic. I can't..." She realized the difference. "I can't control something without touching it right now."

"Let's work together, then," Suraya said. "I will send a thick vine through the floor of your cellar. You touch the ground and make the soil pile up by the door."

"All right," she replied. "Please be careful. Merlin is very powerful."

Suraya laughed dryly. "What a wretch to call himself 'Merlin.' He is not some great wizard. He's a parasite, stealing life from unwilling victims."

"Move quickly," Anabel pleaded. "He could be back any minute."

"He won't be back," Ferris said. "Not for a while. Whenever he uses his powers, he must lay down for several hours to regain his strength."

"Also, I put a sleeping draught in his tea," Suraya said. "He should sleep until at least tomorrow morning."

"How'd you manage that?" Ferris asked incredulously.

"His servants aren't the least bit loyal," she replied with a laugh. "It took just a few coins, and she was ready to do as I asked."

"I need to keep a better eye on you," Ferris mumbled.

A weight lifted from Anabel's shoulders. She was no longer alone.

When he started coming out of the fog, James noticed two things. First, his arm was in agony, like he was being scratched repeatedly by a sharp knife in the same spot. Second, Anabel was talking to someone.

He bit his tongue to keep himself from crying out as another sharp pain ran along his arm. "Anabel?" he called as he tried sitting up.

"James! You're awake!" Anabel cried, wrapping her arms around him.

"Who's James?" a male voice asked.

James panicked, thinking Merlin was back, but the so-called wizard's voice was deep and raspy. This man sounded young, perhaps a few years younger than James himself.

"He's the person in here with me." Anabel sounded like she was speaking to her brother.

There was no response for a moment, but then the man said, "We'll discuss this after we get you out."

"Yes, we will," Anabel replied, not at all cowed.

"Enough." The sharp command had come from a woman. Her soft, melodic voice was soothing, but she put enough force behind it to quiet both Anabel and the man.

"Right," Anabel said in response. "James, can you stand? We need to move back. Suraya is going to help us escape."

"Suraya? Your friend?"

"You told him about me? He must be special. We have so much to catch up on, Bel." Suraya's voice, which had been so stern just a moment ago, now bubbled with excitement.

"We will as soon as you get us out. Please hurry. I know you said you gave him a sleeping draught, but I don't trust that man. He could be stronger than your potion. Let's get out of here as soon as we can."

"Of course," Suraya said, her seriousness having returned. "Stand back."

Anabel helped James up, and they moved as far back into the cellar as they could. Anabel knelt and touched the dirt floor with her hand. Nothing happened for a long moment, but then a rumbling sound came from beneath them. The ground shook, and James had to reach out for the wall to stay upright. Suddenly, a large vine sprouted from the floor, like the beanstalk in the old fairytale. Soil piled up, making room for the thick vine, but then rolled away from them toward the door.

The stalk punched through the wall of the cellar, just below the ceiling, and tilted up. A weak light flooded into the room. The rumbling stopped and Anabel stood. The opening was just big enough for them to climb through. The soil blocked the door, which would keep anyone from Merlin's household from entering the cellar as they made their escape.

Anabel grabbed James's hand and pulled him toward the vine. "Can you climb with your injured arm?"

"Yes. It hurts, but I can move it."

"You go first, and I'll follow you."

He shook his head in protest. "Absolutely not. I must insist you go first."

"James!" Despite their circumstances, she'd never looked more breathtaking than when she was frustrated.

"Anabel, give me this, please. You are obviously powerful and don't need my help to escape. Let me feel I have at least some part in this rescue."

She assessed him, nodded in agreement, and turned back to the vine.

"Are you able to get out?" the man spoke from just outside their escape hatch.

"Yes," Anabel replied as she lifted her skirts tied them together at her waist. Her stockings and drawers were visible, but she would be able to climb the vine unencumbered.

"Quickly," the man said again. "I agree with you, Bel. I don't want to take the chance the wizard awakens before we've fled."

Anabel began ascending the vine. It was not a very far climb, and the vine extended several feet above the surface, allowing her to easily step down to solid ground.

"James. It's your turn now."

James grabbed onto the vine with his good arm. He started to reach with his injured one but cried out in agony as the pain flared up.

The man's face appeared then in the hole to the surface. "Can you ascend with your uninjured arm? I'll help you as soon as you are within reach."

James nodded and started his climb, keeping his wounded arm tucked in close to his body. The climb was difficult with just one hand, but he was able to make it. As soon as he could, the other man grabbed under James's shoulders and hauled him clear of the opening. Once he was on steady ground again, James lay for a moment, crying out in both pain and relief.

"Thank you," he said to the other man as he rose.

"Of course. I would never leave anyone to the mercy of that maniac."

James held out his uninjured hand. "I'm grateful, nevertheless. I am Sir James Marley."

The man took his hand and shook. "Ferris Moon."

His new companion looked strong, but his body was wiry and still filling out. He appeared to be slightly older that Anabel. The man had beige skin, with a head of thick, curling black hair and a well-trimmed beard. His handshake was strong, revealing several thick calluses on his palm. He spoke with a slight Scottish burr.

James recalled Anabel's mention of her cousin Ferris the night before. "Are you one of Anabel's family?"

"Aye," Mr. Moon replied. He eyed James warily but said nothing more.

James turned to Anabel. "Are you well, love?"

She started to nod, but her eyes welled up with tears and she flung herself at him.

James caught her and held her with his good arm. "It's all right, love. I've got you."

"I was so worried, James! I have no idea what he's done to your arm or if we can remove the curse. What if it gets worse the further away you get from him? Or what if he can use it to find you?"

"I can help with that," the young woman said as she held out two small pouches. They had a strong, though not unpleasant, scent.

James's pouch had a leather cord attached so it could be worn around the neck. Anabel slipped hers over her head immediately, but James hesitated.

"Thank you, Miss Moon. What is it?"

"It's a charm bag with a piece of onyx and some herbs for protection. It will conceal you from Merlin's sight." She pulled up a similar pouch worn on her person. "I made one for each of us. I never go out unprepared. Also, I'm not Miss Moon. My name is Miss Kashef, but I would prefer it if you would call me Suraya."

"Thank you, Miss Kashef," James said as he slipped the talisman over his head. "Please forgive me, but it would not be proper for me to call you by your given name."

"But it is proper to refer to Lady Anabel in such familiar terms?" Mr. Moon chimed in.

"Ferris!" Anabel scolded. "Sir James and I are engaged. And don't call me Lady Anabel. You've never used my title."

"Engaged?" Mr. Moon asked, turning his full attention to Anabel. "When did this happen? Why aren't you in London planning a fancy society wedding?"

"I will tell you all later, but first, let's get as far away as we can from that horrid man."

"Right," Mr. Moon conceded. He started to walk toward the edge of the wood that surrounded the property, but James stopped him.

"Wait, please. We must rescue my coachman. I don't know if my carriage is intact, but we cannot leave Taylor."

"That's settled, then," Miss Kashef said as she breezed past them. Capturing Anabel's arm in her own, she calmly walked to the stables. James and Mr. Moon had no choice but to follow in their wake.

Chapter 15

"Ferris is trying to scare away your knight," Suraya said as they walked toward the stables.

"Pardon?"

"Our self-elected big brother and constant thorn in our sides, Ferris, is trying to intimidate Sir James. A man who's also your betrothed? When did that happen? I leave you alone for six weeks and you're practically married when I see you again. I knew I should have accompanied you to London."

Anabel smiled. "This was a sudden development." She laid her head on Raya's shoulder. "I'm so glad to see you. I have missed you."

Suraya patted Anabel's head. "I've missed you too. I worried about you from the moment you left."

"And I have been longing to return, most especially when I heard a voice in my head. I thought I would be bound for an asylum if I could not get back to the family."

Raya turned to Anabel, her eyes wide. "You've been hearing voices?"

"Not voices," Anabel replied, shaking her head. "One voice, and now I know it was Merlin. He was trying to lure me to him, apparently because he wished to threaten my life sooner."

"Merlin threatened your life?" Suraya grabbed her arms.

"In a sense. I can tell you more once we are on the road."

They reached the stables, and Anabel was relieved to see the horses happily munching on some oats. She was also glad to see that the rot of the main house had not extended to the stables.

Her relief was short-lived, however. Mr. Taylor was nowhere to be seen.

"Taylor!" James called into the room. "Are you in here? We must depart quickly."

The room was silent, other than the sounds coming from the animals. They all waited for Mr. Taylor to respond, and had the room not been so quiet, they would not have heard the soft snoring coming from the final stall on the right-hand side.

James ran to the stall and reached for the door with his injured arm. He cried in pain, pulling his arm back toward his body.

"Raya," Anabel said. "Do you have anything that will help his pain?"

"I have my pain relief tonic."

"Thank goodness," Anabel said. "Do you think Gran will be able to remove the curse from his arm?"

Suraya stared at James, considering. "If she can't, she can get us to someone who can. She has many connections. She'll make it right."

The tension melted from Anabel's body, and she embraced the other woman tightly. "Thank you for coming to my rescue," she said with tears in her eyes.

Ferris assisted James in pulling Taylor from the stall. The man was so still one would think he was dead, were it not for the soft sounds of his breathing. James tried shaking him, but nothing roused the man.

"I have no idea what they've done to him," James said. "Help me get him into the coach. I can drive."

Ferris moved quickly, helping James get Taylor settled and harnessing the horses to the carriage. James gestured toward the door of the coach.

"Ladies, if you please. Mr. Moon, would you mind riding next to me for a time? A second set of eyes would be helpful."

"Sorry, chap," Ferris replied, turning toward the exit. "We have our own transport."

James stared at the other man for a moment. "Oh, yes, of course. Where is it? I'm happy to deliver you there. Perhaps we can reconnect at a safer location."

"It's in the opposite direction. We can get there ourselves."

"Splendid. Where should we meet, then?"

Ferris gave James a considering look. Anabel felt as though she was watching a game of shuttlecock as her gaze bounced between the two men.

"There's a house about five miles away. Follow the main road until you see a drive lined with four large oak trees. The drive leads to a small cottage. You'll find safety there."

James gave a curt nod and reached out his hand. They shook briefly before James moved to climb into the driver's seat.

"Let's go," Ferris said, gesturing to Suraya and Anabel.

"Anabel, can you look after Taylor?"

The two men spoke at the same time and then froze before glaring at one another.

"I'm taking my cousin with me," Ferris said, baring his teeth.

"Anabel is not leaving my care."

"And how helpful your care has been!" Ferris yelled. "You've done nothing but put my cousin in danger. She'll be safer with me."

"She's my betrothed, and I will keep her safe."

"Why're you traveling alone with her, then?" Ferris's nostrils flared before he launched himself at James. "You've compromised her!"

Without thinking, Anabel threw her hands out. She'd never deliberately tried a move so bold before, but something in her abilities had been unlocked today. Ferris froze mere inches from James.

James seemed not at all fazed by her display of power.

"Bel, release me," Ferris grunted. It took a moment to decipher his words, as he had spoken without moving his lips.

"Not until you vow you will not harm James."

They were silent for a long moment before Ferris conceded. "Fine," he groaned, and Anabel released her hold. His movement resumed, and he fell to the hay-covered ground. He pushed himself back up and turned away from James as quickly as he could.

Suraya gave him a warning look, which he ignored. Raya had turned to give Anabel a hug when a bellowing from the house made them all pause.

"M-Merlin is awake," Anabel said, swallowing as her mouth went dry.

"Impossible!" Suraya protested.

The door to the house flew open, and Merlin stomped outside, followed by two burly footmen. "Get in the carriage," James commanded, his manner suddenly that of the disciplined naval officer he had been.

Suraya and Anabel clambered into the coach and Ferris mounted the driver's seat with James. The second the door was closed, James snapped the reins and yelled for the horses to hurry. Thankfully, the team seemed in good shape and maintained a fast pace as the carriage raced away from the house.

They came to the main road and stopped abruptly.

"Raya!" Ferris called. "We need you to clear the road."

Suraya and Anabel stepped out of the coach and saw the felled tree limb from earlier, now charred and black from the flames. Holding her hand out, Suraya strained to move the heavy limb out of the way.

"It reeks of his magic," she said with a grunt.

Anabel placed her hand on her friend's shoulder, lending her strength.

The remaining branches on the tree bent in a graceful arc to touch the broken limb. They wrapped around the fallen bough before moving it out of the road.

Anabel stood in awe, but her reverence was soon interrupted by thundering hoof beats coming from behind them. They threw themselves back into the carriage and James flicked the reins and yelled to the team. Anabel and Suraya sat on their knees, looking out the back window.

"Can you slow his progress?" Anabel asked, when it appeared that they were not going to escape the evil man's grasp.

"I'm running out of energy, Bel. I can only do so much in a day."

Anabel realized that the same was not true for herself. Somehow, despite all the magic she'd done, she still felt healthy and vigorous. She placed a hand on Raya's shoulder again and concentrated on sharing her energy. Raya's confidence returned and the tree released the burned limb to crash spectacularly to the ground. Vines shot up and wrapped around the limb to anchor it and expand the obstruction.

"That should slow them," Suraya said with a satisfied smile. She collapsed on the bench opposite.

Anabel reached out to her friend.

"Now," Suraya said, squeezing her friend's hand, "you must explain how you ended up engaged."

Despite their dire circumstances, Anabel smiled as she relayed the events of the last several days to Suraya, happy to be back with her friend.

James searched for the house Mr. Moon had described. He hoped they would reach it soon, as the horses could only maintain a breakneck speed for so long.

"Are you sure we will be safe at this house you described?" he asked Moon. "Merlin won't pursue us there?"

"It's protected," the other man replied in a clipped tone. "The wizard can't find it."

"How do you know that?"

"Because no one can find it unless I want them to."

James glanced at the other man warily. "That's possible?"

"I can conceal my location from everyone, even the most powerful of magic wielders."

James wasn't sure how to respond. He looked back toward the road, watching the horses closely. He recalled the moments before their frantic escape, when Moon had been heading in the opposite direction. "Where were your horses? I don't think we could retrieve them safely right now."

"We didn't have horses."

"No? Then how were you planning to escape with Anabel?"

"I had a perfectly safe method of travel."

"I'll care for her," James protested.

"Be that as it may, you are not capable of protecting her the way we are. Our grandmother told us about her vision. That man wants to take over my cousin's body. I refuse to let that happen. I have ways to prevent that, as do others in my family. You have no way to fight against that maniac and no idea what you're up against."

James was put off by the man's censure. Mr. Moon could be no older than five and twenty, but he lectured James as if he were his grandfather. "You are right," he conceded. "I have no idea what I'm up against. I will do anything I can for Anabel, but I know when to ask for help. However, I am not leaving her side."

They rode the rest of the way in silence, the only sound the thundering of the horse's hooves. The sky was darkening. In the rush of their escape, he'd taken no notice of the weather, but there was no trace of the rain that had been pouring down on them when they first entered Merlin's house. When they'd left the stables, the sky was lit up with the colors of an early sunset. Now that they had been traveling for an hour, the sky was nearly full dark.

"Not much further now," Moon said. He pointed toward a spot a half mile away, where there were indeed four large oaks framing the driveway. Beyond the trees, however, the drive looked more like a path for the local citizenry that had fallen into disrepair. "Turn here," Moon instructed, as James guided the team to the drive. As they passed through the gates, James felt a sickness in his stomach and a warning sounding in his head telling him to leave this place.

"It will pass shortly," Moon said somewhat sympathetically. "The property has magical wards. The wards warn any passing person not to tread this path. It will make them feel progressively more ill as they proceed up the drive. Only a handful of non-magical people have ever made it to house still conscious. Having me with you will help reduce the effects."

"This is reduced?" James asked, choking down the urge to cast up his accounts. "I'd hate to see the spell at full strength."

"The wards are powerful. I'm sure Raya can give you something for your nausea when we're inside."

James swallowed and breathed deeply, trying to settle his stomach. Just as he thought he could take no more, they came upon a modest brick cottage set on a pretty lawn.

"There are stables in the back," Moon advised. "Drive around and I'll help you tend to the horses."

"What is this place?" James asked as they approached the stable.

"A stronghold of my family's." The younger man's face sobered. "I give you my word that you and Anabel will be safe, and I will not try to separate you again."

James nodded at Mr. Moon as he pulled into the stables. They quickly dismounted and moved to tend to the horses. The carriage remained still, and James feared something had happened to Anabel. He opened the door to see Anabel sleeping soundly on one side and Taylor still unconscious on the other. Miss Kashef smiled, placing one finger on her lips to silence him.

"She gave me some of her energy when I was blocking the road," Miss Kashef said in a whisper. "She said it didn't drain her, but she fell asleep no more than ten minutes later."

"I am sure the shock of the day is getting to her," James replied. "I hate to wake her, but I would like to get her inside." He made to step inside the carriage, but the moment he braced his injured arm again the door frame, a fiery pain shot up the limb. He screamed and fell back.

"James?" Anabel's sweet voice called to him, a beacon in the fog of pain. She moved closer, and he regretted awakening her. His guilt was washed away as she placed her cool fingers on his cheek. The pain receded into the background. He turned his head to nuzzle against her palm, grateful for the support.

He only allowed himself a moment of tenderness before he used his right arm to raise himself to a sitting position. He met Anabel's worried gaze and did his best to give her a reassuring smile. Her fingers lightly rested on his left hand. "I'm well," he said. "Thank you for drawing some of the pain from me."

She gasped and stared down at her hand in wonder. "I didn't. At least, I didn't mean to. I just wanted to help you."

"It seems like you've tripled your power since we were last together," Miss Kashef said, smiling at her friend.

"It does," Mr. Moon agreed. "We should get inside the house so we can talk further."

"Yes, let's do that," James agreed. He tried to get up using his good arm, but his center of gravity was off. He fell back on his rear, nearly crushing his hand in the process.

Mr. Moon came over and held out a hand to James. Between the two of them, they were able to haul him to his feet.

They started to leave the barn when James suddenly remembered his coachman. "Taylor," he said, looking toward the coach.

"Here, sir," Taylor replied, moving around from the far side of the vehicle. "I'm afraid your injury awoke both myself and the lady."

"I'm sorry for the rude awakening," James replied. "Are you well?"

Taylor shrugged. "As well as I can be. I'm not sure what happened. As soon as I got to the stable and tended to the horses, I felt a strong urge to go lay in one of the stalls. I couldn't ignore it."

"I'll fill you in later," James said. "Come, let's get inside the house and we can discuss more."

Taylor followed James as the group moved from the stables to the safety of the cottage.

Anabel took in her surroundings with awe. She knew her family had a few properties throughout the country. Although they usually preferred to sleep on the road, family members occasionally used these houses when they needed a break from traveling. Anabel had not visited one of the houses before, as they were all in less populated areas. The remote locations, she'd been told, were to help conceal the family and their abilities.

From the outside, it appeared to be a squat but sturdy two-story brick cottage with perhaps three small rooms on each floor. Anabel was worried they would feel cramped in the little house, but as she walked in, she was taken aback by how spacious it felt. It wasn't as large as her brother's cavernous London home, but the interior was at least two times larger than the exterior suggested. The rooms felt warm, as if they all had fires in their hearths and no drafty corners.

"Isn't it lovely?" Suraya asked as she looked around. "I'd never been to one of these until a few days ago. Someone enchanted this place to always be comfortable for the occupants. It grows or shrinks to contain the perfect amount of space, and it is always comfortably warm or cool, depending on the season."

"Impressive," Anabel replied.

"Your family is incredibly talented," James noted as he looked around the room.

"Aye." Taylor echoed his employer's sentiment, a look of pure shock on his face.

It occurred to Anabel that Taylor had not been informed of the abilities possessed by her family. Her heart began to pound as she anticipated his reaction.

Meeting James's eyes, she tried to convey her concern without speaking the words. He looked confused, so Anabel reached out and grabbed James's right hand. Staring into his eyes, she tried to convey her thoughts.

I'm worried about Mr. Taylor. He isn't aware of what I or my family can do.

James's face relaxed, and he gave her smile as he replied. *I've known Taylor for a very long time, and he isn't ruffled by much. But perhaps it would be best if I spoke with him first.*

Thank you, Anabel replied, relaxing her expression.

James released her hand and turned to his coachman. "Taylor, perhaps you and I should speak. I'm sure you have some questions about today's events."

"Aye, that I do," Taylor responded, looking furtively around the room.

Suraya gave the pair a dazzling smile. "That sounds lovely. Why don't you all settle in the sitting room while I retrieve some tea? Anabel, can you and Ferris provide some music to help us all relax?"

"Of course," Anabel said, immediately understanding her friend's meaning. Unlike with James, Anabel did not need to touch Suraya to know what the other woman was thinking. One winter at the family home in Scotland, Ferris had taught Anabel a song meant to relax the listener. It didn't alter their thoughts or actions, only removed tension from their body. It was a good plan on Suraya's part. Taylor might be more willing to hear what James had to say if he was less upset.

The sitting room was as spacious as the foyer had been. Anabel was still amazed by the magic all around them. She moved to the pianoforte set against a wall and settled onto the seat. Ferris took his place at her back, ready to turn the pages for her, although they both knew the song by heart.

The sheet music in front of her was exactly the music she needed. She gave Ferris a curious glance. He simply shrugged as if to say *what else would you expect from a magical house?*

Anabel began playing. The song was slow but light, threading a string of joyful magic throughout the room. She knew from experience the music would make Mr. Taylor feel more relaxed.

As she worked through the first verse, Ferris leaned over her shoulder to turn the page. "Do you want to know what they're talking about?"

"No," Anabel hissed back. "And stop listening in. That is a private conversation. The only reason I agreed to come in here and play was because I thought this song would help Mr. Taylor feel more comfortable."

Ferris huffed. "He's feeling quite comfortable now. So much so that he is trying to convince his employer to leave this place immediately and leave you to the mercy of the madman."

"What?" Anabel cried as she played a sour note. Lifting her hands from the keys, she inspected her cousin, trying to understand his words.

Her break in playing had paused James's conversation with Taylor. Ferris's gaze bounced between Anabel and the two men on the settee.

"I'm sorry," Anabel said. "I'm a bit more nervous than I realized."

"Of course, my lady," Taylor replied. His expression reminded Anabel of the wary looks she'd received from Mary and the chambermaid back in London.

"Here we are," Suraya said, breezing through the door. She settled the tea tray on the table before the settee and sat across from the two men. Without asking, she poured each of them a drink and set the cup before them. "Drink up, Mr. Taylor. I know you've had a trying day. We'll find you somewhere comfortable to rest so you can recover your strength."

"Now see here, miss," Taylor protested, even as he lifted the cup to his lips. He looked down as it hovered just below his mouth. "I don't—"

"Take your tea, Mr. Taylor," Suraya said as she lifted her hand and mimed the action. Taylor followed, as if a puppet on a string. The movement was eerily similar to how James had acted when under Merlin's spell. Anabel did not like it at all. They should be protecting Taylor, not enchanting him.

James stood, watching frantically as Taylor drained his cup in one long draw. Once he was finished, he set the cup of tea on the table and gave James a puzzled look.

"Why are ye' standing, sir?"

Taylor certainly seemed more relaxed than before. The wariness was gone from his tone and his gaze.

"Just needed to stretch my legs," James responded. Without another word, he walked to the window, peering out at the night sky. He had not touched his tea.

Ferris approached the coachman. "Come, Mr. Taylor," he said, extending his hand. "I'll show you to a room where you can rest."

"That sounds lovely, lad," Taylor replied as he reached up to clasp Ferris's hand.

The minute they were out of the room, James glared at Suraya. "What did you do to my coachman, and are you planning to do that to me as well?"

Anabel watched the interaction between the man she loved and the woman she thought of as a sister. Anabel had no idea if she could trust Suraya any longer. Did she know her family at all?

James fumed as Miss Kashef approached him. She moved cautiously, as if in the presence of a dangerous animal, and James supposed his manner was like that of an untamed beast. He was furious. Even when he and his men had been fending off attacks on their ship, he'd never felt more anger.

He looked to Anabel to see her reaction and was gratified to see she was giving her friend a side-long glance.

"Sir James," Miss Kashef began.

"No!" He knew he was being too loud and not behaving like a gentleman, but he couldn't stop himself. The memory of being held in Merlin's thrall was too fresh. The fact that this woman had the same power terrified him.

"I won't hurt you," Miss Kashef said. She was poised on the balls of her feet, as if she wanted to move forward but dared not. "I can explain what just happened if you will please just sit down."

"Did you bewitch my tea as well?"

She opened her mouth but hesitated for a moment. "I didn't put the same potion in your cup. It does contain a few drops of a tincture to help relieve pain, which Anabel asked me to provide for your arm."

"Then how did you enchant Taylor? You poured both cups from the same pot."

"I added a drop of the potion to the cup before I poured the tea. It was only a small amount. I saw how nervous he was, and I wanted to put him at his ease."

James scoffed. Taylor had had no desire to drink his tea before she made him. "Bewitching a person is bad form. It's why witches were persecuted in the first place."

Miss Kashef looked at him with exasperation. "That is not the entirety of the story, as I'm sure you know. The massacre of witches and magical practitioners had a multitude of causes. Yes, careless spell casters were part of it, but so was the persecution of women, no matter their magic."

"Is that why you did it? Are you trying to get revenge for something men did to you?"

Miss Kashef stomped her foot. "You and Anabel are perfect for each other! You're both suspicious of everyone and everything. You'll never be happy because you'll always be waiting for the next bad thing."

"Now wait a minute!" Anabel said, finally moving to James's side. "You don't know what we went through today. Don't make assumptions based on our behavior after having been abducted and imprisoned." She stopped and looked at James. "We are grateful for your help, but you must make some allowances."

"I don't understand why you're so upset!" Miss Kashef said, her posture tense. "All I did was make sure that Mr. Taylor drank the tea so he would be relaxed and not go around yelling about witches."

"They're upset about the relaxation spell?" Ferris asked as he returned to the room. "Mr. Taylor is resting in one of the rooms upstairs. He'll be in a much better mood when he awakes, and that wouldn't be the case if he hadn't drunk his tea. Given the thoughts he had upon entering the house, he would be running down the lane looking to tell the next house about the witches nearby. We would have had a mob at our gate by morning."

"How can you know that?" James asked.

Anabel sighed. "Ferris knows things about a person just by looking at them. His ability has proven highly accurate, so the family heeds his warnings.

"I thought your talent was hiding things?" James said.

"I have both powers," Ferris said with a shrug.

"And you saw Taylor running from the house?"

"Not exactly, but I could sense his fear from the moment he stepped out of the coach. His desire to run increased the longer he remained in our presence."

"How did you know about this?" Anabel asked, turning to Miss Kashef.

"I didn't."

"But you said you spelled him so he wouldn't go talking of witches."

"That wasn't a premonition," Miss Kashef replied, her voice melancholy. "'Twas based on previous experience. I've had it happen to me. I didn't want to take the chance that it would happen today and put us all in danger."

Anabel moved tentatively toward her friend. "I'm sorry for assuming the worst," she said, tears in her eyes. "I wasn't thinking." She looked at James and Ferris. "Why don't we all sit down and talk some more?"

James begrudgingly followed her to the sitting area. He retook his spot on the settee and pulled Anabel down beside him.

"I think it would be helpful to share a little more information about what happened today," he said. "Merlin used me to get us inside the house. He took over my free will before I realized there might be danger. It was terrifying to see him threaten Anabel and be unable to stop him." He threaded his fingers with Anabel's and squeezed her hand. "He made me his puppet. So, when I saw what you did to Taylor, I came to the worst possible conclusion."

"I had no intention of taking away anyone's free will," Miss Kashef said.

"But you did," James replied. "Taylor was not given the choice whether to drink the tea."

Miss Kashef burst into tears. Anabel moved to the young woman's side and soothed her with rhythmic pats on the back.

"I'm so sorry," she choked out. Ferris handed her a handkerchief, which she used to dab her eyes.

"I think we are all exhausted," Ferris said. "Why don't we all get some rest and reconnect in the morning? We'll be safe here for the night."

"Are you going to contact Gran?" Anabel asked as she slowed her patting.

"It can wait 'til morning," Ferris said. "She knows we're safe. The rest will hold."

James nodded in agreement. "Where will Anabel and I sleep?"

"You think to share a room with her under my family's roof?" Ferris gave him a dry chuckle. "There are plenty of rooms in this house. We can each take one."

"Anabel, can you join me in my room for a time?" Miss Kashef asked. "I want to catch up with you."

Ferris rolled his eyes. "You write each other every other week. What else could there possibly be to catch up on?"

James didn't like being separated from Anabel, but he'd expected this once they caught up with her family. He had expected it from a wise old grandmother, however, and not from an obnoxious brother type. Regardless, he would obey the orders, for now.

He followed the three others up the stairs, trying to ignore the nervous pit in his stomach as he replayed his time under Merlin's thrall.

Chapter 16

Anabel shut the door to Suraya's room and was taken aback. The room was decorated lavishly, the walls covered in colorful Turkish rugs. There were small candles surrounded by glass chimneys to protect the flame, and the partially opened wardrobe was filled to the brim with clothing unique to Suraya's signature style.

Suraya settled on the bed and smiled. "Isn't it beautiful? The house provided this room for me yesterday. It's exactly what I would have picked for myself."

"This magic is truly amazing," Anabel replied, lightly touching one of the rugs on the wall. The quality was astonishing. "I haven't seen rugs this fine, even in my brother's London house."

"I have," Suraya replied. "At a market many years ago, a merchant was selling these rugs. He said there were newer weaving methods being used, which resulted in a tighter weave and finer texture. I desperately wanted one of my own. I suppose the house found that memory and decorated my room with them."

Anabel didn't respond, but the word *amazing* floated in her mind as she ran a hand through the short fibers of the carpet. What kind of room would the house give her? She couldn't think of any possessions, but she did want to share a room with James. She wasn't sure how the house would interpret that.

"I'm sorry for upsetting James." Suraya sat on the bed, her finger tracing a pattern on the cover.

"Let's not discuss it further." Anabel replied. She was weary and didn't relish the thought of more arguing. "What did you want to discuss?" They'd spoken briefly in the carriage, but exhaustion had gotten the better of her. She had so much energy when she was helping Suraya, but the moment they had been free she had fallen into a deep sleep.

"Well, you told me how you'd ended up engaged," Suraya said, "but not how you felt about it. Do you want to marry Sir James?"

"I do," Anabel replied immediately. Every time she said it, she felt more certain that this was her path.

"So, you won't be coming back to us after all." Suraya looked away.

"Raya," Anabel said, moving to the bed. "When I left, my intention was to help Isaac find a wife and then return to the family. Can you forgive me for changing our plans?"

Suraya clasped Anabel's hand. "Of course I can. I'll miss you terribly, but I understand. I've been thinking of leaving the family as well."

"Truly?"

"I've grown weary of the traveling life. I know Gran and Fiona enjoy it, but I want to be settled. I want a room like this, though it probably wouldn't be as grand."

"Are you still planning to start your apothecary?"

"I would like to. Do you think maybe you and Sir James could help me find a space for it? I've been storing extra ingredients for my inventory. I may have to start with a smaller space or perhaps partner with another merchant before I can open my own shop, but I believe I could do it."

"We would be happy to help you!" Anabel was overjoyed. "I'm sure you could stay with us. James has many contacts in London that can help you."

"Do you know that for sure?"

Anabel laughed. "In truth I haven't confirmed it. But I feel it to be true. His family's company supplies several shops in London and the surrounding areas. He'll be able to help you. I know it."

Suraya hugged Anabel. "Thank you. I would appreciate the assistance. Although, you should probably discuss this with him before promising anything."

"James will help," Anabel replied with certainty.

Suraya yawned, and the action spurred a yawn in Anabel as well.

"We should sleep," Suraya said.

"Agreed. Do you know where my room is?"

"I believe it's the room next to mine. Ferris is down the hall on the other side of the stairs, and James will likely be there as well."

Of course, James would be far away, in a room next to Anabel's overbearing cousin. She supposed she would not be seeing James again this evening. When she'd awoken that morning, she'd been hoping he would continue to show her the things he wanted from a marriage. She was eager to continue learning how a husband could please his wife, and how she could please him in return. Now that was not to be. At least for this evening, she would need to cool her ardor.

She gave Raya a hug and entered the darkened hallway. Touching the next closest door, she felt a soft hum. The energy of the house was so strong it felt nearly alive, but it was not malevolent. Anabel pushed the door open, curious as to what she would.

She gasped as she took in the neat surroundings. The room was a balance of masculine and feminine decor. It had a lovely dressing table and a pile of books on the nightstand. But it also had a table with a decanter of brandy and a sitting area by the fire with leather armchairs.

The most exciting feature of the room was not what was there, but who.

"Anabel," James said. "I don't understand. Ferris said your room was on the other side of the hall, and I wouldn't be able to see you tonight."

Anabel smiled at him. "I believe the house disagrees with my cousin."

James couldn't believe his good fortune. He had resigned himself to not seeing Anabel until the morning, but there she was, in this strange room. He now understood the feminine elements in the decor. The room was cozy and not overly spacious. It contained elements he would pick if he were preparing a room for the two of them to share.

He advanced and held her wide-eyed gaze as he leaned around her and locked the door. The click reverberated through the room. Anabel shuddered but gave him a seductive smile as she looked up.

After the day they'd had, James had no patience left. He pressed her against the wood, pinning her hands above her head with one hand as he caressed her face with the other.

"I don't care what happens tomorrow, or the next day, as long as I'm with you. As of this moment, I consider you my wife. As soon as I can, I'll carry you off to Scotland to make it official. But for tonight, consider me your husband. I intend to show you what a good husband does for his wife."

Anabel released a shaky breath as his hand stroked along her throat. James was on edge. He had been gentle so far, not wanting to scare her away with his darker desires, but he could hold back no longer.

"Tell me if anything I do tonight frightens you."

"Why would I be afraid?" she asked, her eyes challenging him.

"Well, for one thing, you're unfamiliar with the sex act. I know you've read some books, but there are things you can only learn by experience. And I prefer some things that not all men do."

"What kind of things?" Her voice was shaky.

James took her mouth with his, pulling her in for a brief, but intense, kiss. Drawing back, he saw a multitude of emotions pass across her face. Excitement. Fear. Lust. Curiosity. He wanted to show her so much, but he needed to pace himself.

Dropping his head, he bypassed her mouth and dragged his lips along her throat. He tilted her chin up, giving himself more access to her delectable skin, and then nibbled along her neck, enjoying her sound of pleasure.

"I like to be in control," he said as he pulled back and met her gaze.

She smiled at him. "I already knew that."

"It means something different here. When we're alone in our bedroom, I would like you to obey me."

Anabel crinkled her nose. She tried to pull her hands free, but he held them fast to the door. He was taking a risk, but he couldn't continue until she understood the dynamic he wanted.

"What do you mean, obey you? I'm not a child, James."

He almost laughed at her petulant expression. Her ardor had cooled, but her previous behavior had hinted that she would enjoy what he wanted if she gave it a chance.

James pressed his hips into hers as he kept her pinned to the door. "Let me make one thing clear. I don't think of you as a child, Anabel. I know you are a woman." He thrust his hips, letting her feel his erection. "A passionate." *Thrust.* "Sensual." *Thrust.* "Independent woman." *Thrust.* His free hand grabbed her breast, kneading the soft flesh through the layers of her dress.

"James," she whispered.

"I know, darling. I'll take care of you. We've had a very trying day. Let me take your mind off it for a while."

He felt the moment she yielded to him. James freed her arms and surged forward, kissing her fiercely. Anabel's soft mouth played with his, their lips molding together and breaking apart in a sensuous dance. He dipped his tongue in and tasted hers before nibbling on her lower lip. Anabel moaned once more and James grabbed her thigh, hoisting her up so her core met his own.

Pinning her with his hips, he tugged her skirts out of the way so that only his pants and the thin fabric of her drawers were between them. Feeling the heat of her sex through their clothing, he ground against her, and Anabel gave him another enticing whimper.

James pulled down the bodice of her dress just enough to free one of her breasts from her stays. As he continued grinding against her, he leaned down and pulled a swollen nipple into his mouth, sucking deeply. Anabel grew more frantic, writhing against him. She was nearly at her peak already, and he smiled against her soft flesh. Keeping her pinned with his hips, he reached between the slit in her drawers. He found her wet and hot, ready for his cock, but he wanted her needier. His fingers dipped into the slick channel briefly, and then circled her clitoris, rubbing in time with her movements.

Anabel called out his name as he rubbed her. She pulled back and gazed at him in wonder.

"Come for me." As if she had been waiting for his permission, Anabel shattered under his ministrations. Her fevered cries made his cock impossibly hard, and James couldn't wait to sink into her welcoming heat.

Anabel stared at James as she came down from her orgasm. She was still unsure about his insistence on control in the bedroom, but so far, she had no complaints.

"Let's remove these clothes," James said as he released her, letting her feet fall to the ground. His voice was thick with arousal. Anabel allowed her gaze to drift down to the bulge in his pants.

She'd wanted to reciprocate the pleasure he'd given her the previous night, if only she hadn't been so tired. She smiled now and palmed the hard flesh over his trousers, marveling at how he felt.

"I want to see you," she whispered as she continued to massage his length.

"Say please," James replied, his voice a delicious growl that made her knees weak.

"Please."

"Please, what?"

"Please can I see you?"

"See what? I'm right here."

She scowled at his teasing. "This," she replied, giving him a firm squeeze.

"It's called a cock. Say the word, and you can see it."

Anabel shuddered at his commanding tone. "Please, may I see your cock?"

James tossed his head back and groaned at her words. "Yes, darling," he replied.

Together they unbuttoned the fall. As the fabric fell away, his member seemed to jump into her hand, free from its confinement. Anabel looked down in fascination at the appendage. It was thick and much longer than she'd expected. The skin was velvety smooth, and the muscle underneath was warm. She couldn't resist the urge to wrap her hand around it, gliding her hand along the shaft.

James hissed then stilled her hand. "Another time, love, I will let you explore to your heart's content. But for now, I need you to stop. I'm not nearly done with you."

He moved so quickly that Anabel didn't realize what was happening until she was lying on her back. James had removed his coat before she'd arrived, and he quickly shed his waistcoat and shirtsleeves. His muscles were defined, and there was a sprinkling of light brown hair all over his upper torso that narrowed a trail leading to his erection. She bit her lip as she took her first good look at him, unsure how he would fit inside her.

James smiled at her. "Don't worry. I plan on making this as pleasurable as possible."

He first removed her stockings, then her drawers. He seemed content to leave her skirts rucked up around her waist for the time being. When she was naked from the waist down, he knelt and pulled her forward so that her bottom sat on the edge of the mattress. The pleasure he had given her the night before flashed through her mind, and Anabel felt her face heat as she recalled that sinfully decadent experience.

He moved his head closer to the juncture of her thighs, so she felt his hot breath on her core, but before he touched her with his tongue, she stopped him.

"Wait."

"What is it?" he asked. The bristles from his cheek rubbed her leg and she had to focus to keep from giggling.

"I don't want this to end like last night. I want you inside me, James. Please."

He gave her a devilish smirk. "Since you asked so nicely, I'll oblige. But first I'm going to make you climax once more. I want you to be ready for me."

Anabel opened her mouth to respond that she *was* ready, but he dropped his head and latched on to her clitoris before she could utter a word. Her mouth widened in surprise as pleasure shot up through her body.

James worked her over thoroughly, alternating between licking and sucking her sensitive bud and pinching it with his fingers. He only teased her for a short while, though, before sucking her pearl into his mouth while his fingers slid inside her body. It was tight, and a little uncomfortable at first, but then he touched something inside of her while he continued the suction on her clitoris. The orgasm took Anabel by surprise—the feeling so intense she could only scream as the pleasure overtook her body. Gradually, the feeling subsided, but James continued pumping his fingers in and out of her body.

"You're so beautiful," James said as he looked down at her sex. His eyes were glazed over, and Anabel wished she could see what he was seeing. "You're taking two of my fingers. Do you think you can take another?"

"Three?" She croaked out.

James chuckled before looking back down at her sex. He added the third digit, his thumb pressing on her clitoris as he continued pumping his hand in and out of her channel.

Anabel couldn't speak. She could only feel. Then James once more latched his mouth onto her bud. Her head flew back as she came to completion again, unsure how to handle all this pleasure. Everything went dark, and when she opened her eyes, James was hovering over her.

"Are you all right, love?"

"Yes," Anabel moaned.

"You're not sore? Don't lie to me if you are."

She paused before answering him. Despite three orgasms, she still yearned for more. She wanted to join their bodies together. Her climaxes only made her more ready. There was no pain that she could recognize.

"Please," she said as she wrapped her arms around his neck. "I need you inside of me. I'm not sore. Please, James."

James nipped at the skin of her forearm. "I love hearing you beg."

He thrust his hips forward just a little and Anabel finally felt the flesh of his member pressing against her entrance. She wrapped her legs around his torso, tilting her body up and encouraging him to slide in a little more.

"Stay still," he growled in that delicious voice, and Anabel realized that she'd been writhing her hips against him. She immediately stopped.

James sat back on his knees and pulled her legs away from his body, spreading them wide. He then cupped her buttocks in his hands, holding her still as he pressed his length against her. He slid in slowly, a fraction at a time. She felt a pinch of discomfort and winced involuntarily.

"It'll be over in a moment, sweet," James said as he filled her. At last, he was fully seated, and Anabel took a moment to understand what she was feeling. She was full, slightly sore, and desperate for what came next. Despite James's hold she was wriggling again. He slid a hand to her thigh to stop her movement.

"I'm in control," he reminded her. He withdrew his manhood, and Anabel nearly cried at the sudden feeling of emptiness. Before she could say anything, he thrust his entire length inside of her. She keened as he began thrusting in earnest.

As he continued pumping his hips, his hand came to her clitoris once again, rubbing it in tight circles. Unbelievably, Anabel felt another orgasm growing. She panted as his movements became frantic.

All at once, the climax took her, more intense than the last three combined. She felt like she was underwater. His grip on her thighs became punishing as James sought his own climax. He yelled out almost violently as his orgasm overtook him. Pumping hard and fast into her body, he filled her with his seed.

Chapter 17

J ames collapsed on the bed next to Anabel, spent from his exertions and the stupefying orgasm. Panting, he pulled her into his embrace and nuzzled against her neck.

They were silent for several moments, and James thought Anabel was asleep. But she surprised him by speaking into the quiet a moment later.

"That was…" she trailed off, seemingly unsure of what words to use to describe their love making.

"Spectacular," he suggested. He propped himself up with his elbow to look at her.

She smiled. "Yes, that's exactly the word. Spectacular." She stretched, and her smile changed to a pout. "But if that's how every night is going to be after we're wed, I need to build up my stamina. I'm exhausted."

James smiled ruefully at her. "Did I hurt you? I tried to hold myself back, but I can be aggressive in the bedroom."

Anabel cupped his face. "You didn't hurt me. I loved every minute of it. I'm just not used to so much vigorous activity." She gave him a soft peck on his lips, which he returned. "I'm sure you and I can work together to build up my endurance."

James grinned and loomed over her, planting a kiss at the base of her throat. "Oh, I have so much to show you."

"I'm looking forward to it." She yawned as he kissed and nibbled at her neck. "But for now I'm exhausted," she repeated.

James stopped teasing and pulled back. "Apologies, darling. You are just so delectable. After this adventure, I plan to find a nice, quiet house away from everyone else and spend a month loving and pleasuring you so thoroughly that you'll have no strength for anything else."

The smile she gave him was brilliant. "I can't wait."

Reluctantly, James pulled himself away from her and walked over to the washstand. The room—which had been so tidy when he first entered—was a complete mess. Items had been pulled from drawers. Several garments from the open wardrobe were strewn across the floor. And the brandy decanter was laying on its side, the crystal stopper thankfully keeping it from spilling.

"Something about your abilities has changed," he observed as he wet a small cloth.

"What?" she asked, taking in the scene around them. "Oh no." He saw the minute her panic began to overtake her. "I didn't even touch any of these things. How did I move them?"

James knelt on the bed, giving her a gentle kiss. "Easy, love. You mentioned earlier that something was unlocked within you today. Perhaps that's why things you didn't touch are being affected." He ran a hand up the inside of her thigh. "This is going to be cold," he warned, before he ran the cloth along the sensitive lips of her sex.

Anabel shivered. Once she was cleaned up, he tossed the cloth to the floor and wrapped her in his arms once more. The bed cover had been kicked down during their love making, and he pulled it up over their bodies.

"How is your arm?" she asked, her finger hovering over the jagged line that still marked his skin.

James paused, blinking rapidly. The cut still stung, but he could move it without thinking about the pain he'd felt earlier.

Anabel laughed nervously when he didn't reply. "Considering how much you just used it, I hope you weren't in pain."

"No, no pain," he replied, looking back to her. "You must have removed it from me."

She blushed. "Surely not. I'm sure it was Raya's tea that did the trick."

He shook his head. "It was you. Your powers have improved vastly today."

Anabel sucked in a sharp breath. "I'm afraid of what that means."

He smiled at her. "We'll deal with the ramifications tomorrow. We're in a magical house. What better place is there to figure out your powers?"

"Oh, Lord," she said, trying to sit up. He held her fast. "Do you think Ferris heard us?"

James chuckled as he wrapped her in his arms again. "If he did, we'll deal with it. I was serious about going to Scotland. We're far enough north we may as well continue our journey. Then we can make our union official, and your impertinent cousin won't have any reason to complain."

"Oh, he doesn't need a reason," Anabel quipped.

James grinned, pulling her as close as possible. The only light in the room had been from the fire in the hearth, but even that had muted. The fire spilled warmth throughout the room, but it felt as if the house were dimming some light source. He wasn't going to complain. The house had brought Anabel to him—a gift that endeared the domicile to him.

"Sleep," he commanded.

Anabel briefly relaxed in his arms, but her peace did not last. "We're going to sleep naked again?"

James ground his hips against her thigh, letting her feel his semi-hardness. "Yes, and if you keep trying to get out of bed, I'll be forced to make you climax for a fifth time. Perhaps then you'll be exhausted enough to sleep."

The threat seemed effective, and she melted once more. "As tempting as that sounds, I'm not sure I could take another climax," she said with a yawn.

"Then prove it," he replied with a smirk. "Go to sleep."

She relaxed by degrees, until he heard her soft breathing.

Once she was comfortably sleeping, James spoke into the quiet of the room. "Thank you," he said, wanting to voice his appreciation to the house. Satisfied, he sunk into his pillow and drifted off to sleep.

As soon as the light of the early morning sun filtered into their room, Anabel awoke. Despite the late night and the enthusiastic love making, she felt refreshed.

Though she was awake, she was not ready to leave the bed. She knew she should get dressed soon, but the moment she left her bed she would have to deal with the messy room and, even worse, a nosy cousin who'd appointed himself her guardian. Hopefully the house had muffled the noise from the night before. They had not been quiet in the least.

She studied James. He looked softer when he slept. Not younger, but less worried about the burdens he carried. He had grand plans for his business. How might she fit into his life?

She had no desire to be a part of the *haute ton*. She would much rather have a life and family with James. She pictured what her life could be. She would help James with the management of his business. They would live in a modest townhome with two beautiful children. Several vignettes flashed in her mind, such as going on a family walk in the park, and snuggling up next to a cozy fire and reading a book together.

She felt a change in James's breathing as he came awake and met his sleepy gaze.

"I just had the loveliest images run through my head," he said, his voice thick.

"Oh?" she asked. "What did you see?"

"I saw you working alongside me in the office, then walking together in Hyde Park with two children who had your chestnut hair, and then you and I reading by a fire."

Anabel was astonished for a moment before she realized she had been touching him. "I must have sent you those images as I thought of them."

He gave her a warm smile and pulled her closer. "You were thinking of our future?"

"Yes," she confessed in a whisper. "I have never really known what I wanted for myself," she continued. "But I think spending my life by your side would be quite pleasant."

James didn't reply but instead took her mouth with his own. He started by giving her sweet and soft pecks but quickly switched to hard and passionate kisses. Anabel could hardly keep her wits about her as he molded their lips together.

He reached down and pulled her leg over his hip and ground against her, his cock already thick and hard. His rod nudged against her sex, and she shuddered in pleasure.

Tearing his mouth from hers, he looked down, watching as the head of his erection slid against her sex until she was wet enough that he could enter her welcoming body. Anabel stared at him while he filled her completely.

As he was preparing to thrust, a knock sounded on the door.

"James!" Ferris called from outside the room. "Time to wake up. We've much to do today."

Anabel tried to pull away, but James held her close as he slowly pumped in and out of her body. The pace was torturous. She parted her lips to cry out in both pleasure and frustration, but he clamped his hand over her mouth, shushing her.

"James!" Ferris called again.

"I'm awake," James replied. He continued that maddeningly slow rhythm. "I'll be out shortly. I need to get dressed."

"Very well," Ferris replied. "I'll go awaken the girls and Taylor."

The room went quiet, and James picked up the pace of his thrusts. The position hit a new place inside Anabel's body, and she groaned softly.

Their breathing got faster, but, aside from the soft creaking of the bed, the room was quiet. James pinched her nipple as he drove deeper.

Anabel approached the precipice, but before she could reach her climax, she heard another knock on the door.

"Anabel!" Ferris called again.

A moment of panic overtook her. Did he know that she slept in James's room? Before she could respond, she heard Suraya speaking.

"She's probably still sleeping. Leave her be. She had a trying day yesterday."

"We don't have time for that," Ferris complained before he knocked again. "Anabel! Time to get up! James is getting himself ready. You should as well so we can have breakfast together."

She realized that, as far as Ferris could tell, he was knocking on the door to two different rooms. James continued his movement while she considered what to say.

"Bel!" Ferris called again with a much louder knock.

"I'm up!" She yelled, her voice croaky.

James was relentless. His hand slid from down to her clitoris, and he rubbed it in those tight circles she enjoyed so much.

"Come on, slugabed!" Ferris yelled. "Get dressed."

Anabel's mouth fell open as her orgasm barreled toward her.

"Don't be rude," James whispered in that deliciously commanding voice. "Tell your cousin you're on your way." He kept his mouth at her ear, thrusting as fast as he could while rubbing and pinching her clit. "Tell him you're coming," he ordered her.

She hadn't realized that she'd been holding her climax back. As soon as James commanded her, she let it go, and pleasure rushed through her body. "I'm coming!" she managed to call back, her voice reedy. She wasn't even sure if Ferris was at the door any longer.

As her climax waned, James found his own. He buried his head against her shoulder as he grunted out his release. Anabel let out a shaky breath as he slipped out of her body.

James smiled at her as he pulled away. "Did I say I was taking you away for a month? Make that two months. Or perhaps more, because I don't think I will ever get enough of pleasuring you."

He gave her a rakish grin as he turned to dress. Anabel took a moment to appreciate his firm backside before she moved to get dressed as well. She was looking forward to their escape as much as he was.

❦

James stretched as he took in the space around them. He'd forgotten about the state of the room after their lovemaking. He was fairly certain their morning session had led to more chaos. Items from one side of the room had moved to the other. The brandy decanter had rolled off the table and onto the thick rug below. It hadn't broken, but the stopper had fallen out, and half of the bottle's contents had spilled onto the carpet.

He heard rustling as Anabel rose from the bed and took in the scene.

"Oh my," she said in a low voice as she looked around at the mess.

"We'll manage it, love," James assured her as he looked around for his clothing. "Let's get dressed first."

He found his garments and dressed quickly before turning to her. Anabel was standing naked at the foot of the bed. Her face was screwed up in concentration while her hands moved through the air in front of her. She moved like a conductor leading an orchestra. She was putting things to right. Although he'd already seen her powers a few times, what she was doing now was more advanced.

Within a moment, the room was tidy once more. Anabel turned to James and gave him a broad smile. "It's never been that easy before."

James couldn't stop himself. Crossing the room, he pulled her into his arms and gave her a passionate kiss. She melted in his embrace and started to wrap her arms around his neck, but he stepped out of her reach. Anabel furrowed her brow at his hot and cold actions.

"Sorry, darling," he replied to her silent question. "If I continue touching you while you're unclothed, I won't be able to stop myself from taking you. We'll continue once we are alone again."

She gingerly touched her lips. "Then why did you kiss me?"

"I can't help myself when I see how amazing you are. I am the luckiest man in the world because you chose me."

She blushed so prettily that he had to turn away. "Please get dressed. I'm easily distracted at the moment."

He heard her giggle and move toward the wardrobe. "All right," she said as she threw the doors open. "Why don't you head downstairs to eat? I'll be along shortly."

James moved toward the door, averting his gaze. When he reached it, however, he turned back. "Anabel," he called.

She slid a chemise over her body. "Yes?"

"Remember that I love you."

She gave him a brilliant smile, and James had to pull himself away so he didn't linger. He stepped into the hall.

He was on the same side of the hall as Ferris's room. It was impossible for he and Anabel to have had adjoining rooms, let alone the same room. If he hadn't believed in magic before, he certainly did now.

Descending the stairs, he followed the sound of voices to a small, well-appointed dining room. Ferris, Taylor, and Miss Kashef were all sitting around the table. The furniture and tableware were well made, though not ornate. Against the far wall stood a buffet with several breakfast options.

"Good morning, Sir James," Miss Kashef said as he entered the room.

"Good morning," he replied, heading to the buffet. "Whom do I have to thank for this delicious looking feast?"

"It were here when we arrived," Taylor replied, seeming more amazed by the circumstances than wary of them.

"Yes," Miss Kashef replied. "A few women from the village come here to help with tasks. I informed them of our company last night, so they prepared some extra fare for us."

"I wonder where they are?" Taylor asked. The man seemed like he was still in a trance. James did not like it, even if he understood the necessity.

"They had their own homes to care for," Ferris replied. "They'll be back to clean after we've gone."

James brought his plate to the table, watching as Taylor processed the information. James appreciated them helping his driver feel more comfortable, but it seemed like the man might not be buying the story. "Taylor," he said as he took his seat. "Perhaps you could head to the stables and check on the horses?"

The man seemed happy to have something to do. "Aye, Sir James."

He was out of the room a moment later. Once they heard the door close, Ferris pointed to James. "Taylor needs to take your coach back to London today."

"I told you, I am not leaving Anabel," James protested.

"I didn't say you'd be going with the coach. Just Taylor."

"Why does he need to go? Don't we need him to continue our journey?"

"We'll travel another way," Miss Kashef said.

"Oh, I hate traveling by portal," Anabel said as she entered the room.

"Portal?" James asked.

"There are magical gates that allow you to cross great distances in mere minutes. It's very handy, but the experience can be"—she seemed to be looking for the right word—"unsettling."

"The discomfort only lasts a moment," Ferris argued. "And it's the quickest way to get to Gran. Taylor can't come with us."

"How will we get back to London then?" James asked, more than a little confused by everything.

"There are other portals you can take," Miss Kashef responded. "You'll be back home in no time."

"I still don't like sending Taylor home. How am I to explain this to him?"

"Don't send him to London," Anabel said, grabbing his hand under the table. "Send him to Gretna Green and tell him we'll join him in two days' time."

"Gretna Green?" Ferris said, looking between them.

"Oh, do stop, Ferris," Miss Kashef said. "They're betrothed, and she's a lady of quality. If they return to London unmarried, it'll ruin her reputation and be a stain on the rest of the family."

Ferris gave a pinched expression, but wisely did not reply.

"What should I tell Taylor we are doing for the next two days?" James asked Anabel as he raised her hand to his lips and kissed the back of her wrist.

"You can tell him the truth," she replied with a grin. "We are going to see my family. They are not far from here."

"We're at least 30 miles from York still."

"By road, yes. But the path we are taking is much shorter. And perhaps you shouldn't tell him we're going to York, exactly."

James smiled at her as she squeezed his hand. "Very wise, darling." He walked to the sideboard, made her a plate, and placed it in front of her.

"Now eat up," he said in his most commanding voice. "You're going to need your strength for the coming days."

A glow passed across Anabel's cheeks when he emphasized the word coming. James chuckled before sitting next to her again. In two days, she would be his wife. He couldn't wait.

<h1 style="text-align:center">Chapter 18</h1>

It had been easy to send Taylor off to Gretna Green. He was almost too compliant, and Anabel suspected that was a lingering effect of the potion Suraya had given him. She agreed with James about her friend bewitching Taylor, even if it had been for the best.

Suraya, she knew, would want to keep the peace. Her unusual abilities had been the reason she was chased out of her village as a child. After one of the town leaders learned about her magic, an angry mob had appeared at her family's house, insisting she needed to be killed. Her uncle had smuggled her out, taken her to Beirut, and paid a ship's captain to take her to England.

Even though she had been very young, Suraya clearly recalled the terror she felt throughout the entire ordeal. Anabel understood why she would go to extreme lengths to prevent an event like that from happening again, but that didn't mean she had to like it.

"Anabel?" James's voice pulled her from her reverie. They were in a wooded area. The gate before them was comprised of two trees with interlocking branches, sometimes referred to as a 'fairy gate'. The portals usually did not work for those without magical abilities, but there had been exceptions throughout history. Those instances had led to many of the fairy tales told throughout the kingdom.

"How does this work?" James asked.

"It will only take you to a place you've been before," Ferris replied. "But if you are entering with someone else, you can use them as your target instead."

"So, I don't need to know where I'm going as long as I focus on Anabel?" James asked.

"Exactly. Direct all your attention to her. In your mind, say you want to go where she goes. Make sure to keep that thought in mind, or you will get lost in the portal."

"What happens then?"

"If we're very lucky, we might find you in a few years," Anabel responded. She held out a hand for him, and he clasped it tightly. "Just keep your concentration on me. The journey is only a few minutes. And whatever you do, do not let go of my hand."

The gate was alarmingly close to Merlin's house. Anabel looked at her cousin. "This is how you were planning for us to escape yesterday, wasn't it?"

"Yes," Ferris replied. "We should get going soon. We are expected."

"And we don't want the wizard to find us," James added.

"He can't. I've protected the area."

"But you can't erase the magical signature of the gate," Anabel protested. "He could sense it if he tried. What's to stop him from following us?"

Suraya placed a hand on Anabel's shoulder. "I'll take care of that, Bel."

Anabel turned. "What? How?"

Suraya took a deep breath. "After you all pass through, I'll compel the trees to disconnect and close the gate for future travel."

"What?" Anabel grabbed her friend's hand. "No! I don't want you to stay behind, Raya. It's dangerous."

"I'll be fine," Suraya replied. "I've taken precautions. He won't be able to find me. Ferris spelled my charm bag to give it extra power. Merlin can't see me."

Anabel felt no better about the plan. "I don't like this."

Suraya opened her mouth but stopped abruptly as they heard a shrill voice behind them. "Come on you lazy fools! They're here somewhere. I feel them."

Anabel's heart sped up. Merlin had found them, and he was close.

"Time to go," Ferris said, grabbing her hand.

"No!" Anabel hissed as she broke free. She turned back to her friend. "Raya, please come with us. You can destroy the gate from the other side."

"No. We need that one to remain. This is the only way to make sure he can't follow you."

The sickly form of Merlin came into view. He was looking right at them, but did not seem to be able to see them.

"What happens when we leave you?" James asked. "Does Ferris's magic stop once he is no longer here?"

"No," Ferris interjected. "It'll last for about a day after I am gone. Suraya will be safe."

"I've taken precautions, Bel," her friend assured her. "Please, go. We don't have time."

As if to punctuate her statement, the air around them shimmered. Merlin raised his hand, his brow furrowed in concentration. "The gate is somewhere nearby. They must be escaping." He turned to his accomplices. "As soon as I get this wall down, slit their throats."

The larger man grumbled but said nothing else.

"Bel," Ferris urged. "Come on, we must go. Suraya will be fine. Trust us."

Tears sprang to Anabel's eyes, and she grabbed her friend in a tight hug. "Please take care."

"I will," Suraya assured her.

The ground shook, knocking Anabel down. The air shimmered and a change came over the area. She felt the moment the magical wall dropped.

Merlin met her gaze, clearly seeing her.

He stepped towards Anabel but stopped, looking at her companions. "What interesting company you keep, girl." He pointed to Suraya's stiff body, her face blazing with anger. "This one is far more powerful than she is letting on." He turned and pinned Ferris in the same way. "And this one, well...those were some impressive protection spells, lad. I ought to possess your body. I'd like to be a randy youth again."

"You cannae take us!" Ferris cried, his Scottish brogue thickening.

"Watch me, boy!" Merlin's hands curled into fists. Ferris and Suraya fell to their knees, clutching at their throats. "Get the other man!" Merlin commanded his henchmen.

He eyed James warily. "How do I know he ain't going to hit me with some sorcery?"

"He's no witch," Merlin replied. "He's just an idiot besotted by one."

"James, run!" Anabel pleaded, but he only moved closer to her. Picking up a large branch, he placed his back to Anabel and faced their attackers.

"I'm not leaving you," he insisted. Anabel groaned at his need to be chivalrous. Looking at the two burly men and the unnaturally strong wizard, she had no idea what to do.

"You've got this, love," James said in a low whisper. His confidence in her abilities warmed her heart. She recalled her lessons with Uncle Fergus. She imagined the magic around them as strings and saw the strands stretching from each of Merlin's hands. Furrowing her brow, she cut the threads.

With ragged breaths and coughing both Ferris and Suraya began gasping in great mouthfuls of air.

"You are just full of surprises, aren't you?" Merlin sneered. "I don't need them. You are obviously the most powerful one here." He tried to choke her as well. Anabel saw the string of his magic as it was hurled at her throat and gently waved it away.

Merlin yelled and ran toward her and James. Before he could reach them, however, Anabel held up her hands and froze him in place.

"Raya? Can you help with this?"

"Of course," her friend said, her voice still thick and hoarse. She pointed at the ground at Merlin's feet, and thick, heavy vines sprang up, covering his legs.

Anabel looked around for his cohorts. Ferris was grappling with one of them while the other was trying to sneak up behind Raya. She found two rocks nearby and used her magic to hurl them at each of the men's heads. Twin thuds sounded as they both fell unconscious to the forest floor.

"Go!" Suraya yelled as she turned back to Merlin.

Anabel hesitated. She didn't want to leave her closest friend in so much danger.

James gently tugged on her arm and moved in the direction of the gate. "She says she can do this, Anabel. We should trust her."

"He's right," Ferris concurred.

Anabel nodded at her friend. "Be safe," she whispered.

"I will," Suraya whispered back, nearly inaudible.

Anabel took one last look at Merlin, whose body was nearly encased in vines.

Reluctantly, she walked towards the gate.

James frowned. He regretted leaving like this. He knew Anabel was worried about Miss Kashef, but the young woman seemed confident, and Ferris had agreed. James could only try to soothe Anabel's concerns while going along with the plan.

Holding fast to Anabel's hand, he stepped under the tree branches and found himself in a place made of color and light. He was in a tunnel. The walls were shimmering like water on a sunny day.

He could feel Anabel's hand in his, but he could not see her. The experience was disorienting, and James rubbed his forehead with his free hand to try to stave off the oncoming headache.

James. He heard Anabel's voice in his head. *Stay focused on me. I'll guide you.*

James nodded before realizing she likely couldn't see him either. *Tell me what to do*, he replied mentally.

Just keep hold of my hand and continue walking forward.

The walls around him appeared to move faster than his pace, adding to his bewilderment. Closing his eyes, he relied on his connection to Anabel instead. "I will always go where you go," he said, picturing her face in his mind.

Then you'll come through this fine.

Her voice soothed him. Despite the reassurances that the trip would only last a few minutes, it felt like hours. Anabel encouraged him as they walked, explaining how her family would love him.

"Not if Ferris speaks with them first," he replied.

Anabel laughed, and the clear sound warmed him from the inside. He focused on his love until the air changed around him. Cautiously, James opened his eyes to see an unfamiliar wooded area. He blinked to adjust his eyes to the daylight. The sun was just as high in the sky as it had been earlier.

"How long were we in there?" he asked, surprised to find his voice groggy.

"No more than five minutes," Ferris replied coolly.

"It felt much longer," James replied.

"Here, take this," Anabel said, pressing something into his palm.

James closed his hand over a smooth item wrapped in wax paper. "Another magical remedy?" he asked with a smile. His eyes had finally adjusted, and seeing the face of his beloved went a long way toward improving his mood.

"Ginger candy," she replied with a smile. "Good for stomach upsets."

James ate the candy, wincing at the spicy flavor. The oils from the ginger made his mouth tingle, but the sensation grounded him further. He finished the sweet and breathed deeply.

This wood differed from the one they'd been in when they entered the portal. That had had thick, seemingly never-ending trees, but this wood was sparse. He could easily see the land beyond—rolling hills covered in heather with a few rocky outcroppings. Though James had never visited this part of the country, he'd heard enough about it to recognize the landscape as Yorkshire.

"Let's go," Ferris said. "We've a few miles before we arrive at the fair."

The man's brogue was thicker, and his posture was stiff. James wanted to put the younger man at ease but recognized the show of pride. "Lead the way," he said, choosing action over reassuring words.

Anabel turned to look back at the gate. "I hope Suraya is all right."

"We'll see her soon," Ferris said. "I'm sure she's fine."

Anabel wrung her hands. James pulled her in for a hug and breathed in her scent. "Your friend is strong. She will be well."

"How can you be sure?"

"I have to believe it. She has survived many trials, as you described to me. She can handle this one."

"Thank you," Anabel whispered into his neck. He held her for a moment longer before releasing her.

Ferris was looking back at them, a mixture of frustration and sympathy on his face. "I'm worried about her too," he told Anabel as they started to walk again. "But she'll be fine."

Anabel nodded, but did not reply.

They came upon a road that ran down the center of the valley between two hills. After following it for several minutes, they heard the trotting of horse hooves, following by the clattering of a wagon.

"Well, look what the cat dragged in!" a woman called from behind them. They all turned to see the driver of the wagon slowing down as she approached them.

"Fi!" Anabel exclaimed, a broad smile spreading on her face.

Ferris rolled his eyes as the driver stopped the wagon.

Anabel ran to the woman as she disembarked from the driver's seat. The two embraced in a friendly hug. "Oh, Fiona, I'm so worried."

"What about?"

"Suraya," Anabel said. "She stayed behind to disable the gate so we wouldn't be followed."

"Who was following you?"

"A horrible man," Anabel replied.

"Aren't they all?" Fiona replied. "I'm sure she'll be fine. She's got a lot of power, that one. I dinnae ken what happened, but she'll get herself out, whatever it is." The woman released Anabel and turned to face James. "I suppose you're the man we seen with our Bel here."

Her accent was thick, and it took James a moment to understand her. "You've seen me?"

"Aye. In Gran's crystal ball." The woman gave him a cheeky smile.

The woman was shorter than Anabel but appeared to be closer to James's own age. She wore an old-fashioned white blouse with long sleeves and a long brown skirt. Her curly red hair was tied back loosely at her neck, the long strands falling over her shoulders. Her eyes were the same deep brown as Anabel's. In fact, if you looked past the hair, the two women could be sisters.

"James," Anabel said, "this is my cousin, Fiona Moon. She's Ferris's older sister. Fi, this is my betrothed, Sir James Marley."

James looked at Ferris with wide eyes.

"I know," Ferris said. "I would not believe we're siblings either."

James took in the man with fresh eyes. He certainly didn't look like his sister at first glance. Where she was fair-skinned, his skin was golden. Where she had red hair, his was black. But he also had the same eyes. The eyes tied this family together.

James turned back to the newcomer. "It is nice to meet you, Miss Moon."

"Ach, no. Call me Fiona, or Fi for short. None of that 'miss' stuff."

James nodded, unsure of what to say. She was different from anyone he'd ever met. He wasn't sure what to expect when he met the rest of Anabel's family.

They rode the rest of the way in Fiona's wagon.

James stayed close to Anabel's side, taking in the buzz of activity around them. He didn't seem put off by all the noise, thankfully, but he silently observed the family. Anabel pulled him aside before they reached the tents.

"My Gran's name is Hana. I'm sure you'll meet her in a minute. That's my uncle Fergus." She pointed to a tall, bulky man with olive-toned skin and thick, curly, black hair. "He's Gran's oldest, and father of Fiona and Ferris. My aunts Effie and Elspeth are around here somewhere. They're twins."

"Are they the parents of all the young people?" James asked, watching as two of the younger cousins sparred with wooden swords.

"Yes. Fergus's wife Ada is probably with Effie. They're close." She pointed to a man who was clearly not related by blood, with pale skin and ginger hair. "Elspeth's husband Callum is over there, watching the boys. Those are two of his sons, Wee Callum and Ewan." His sons had reddish-brown hair, but their skin was closer to that of Ferris. "My other uncle, Bruce, and his wife, Muriel, are in Scotland, looking after the family property, but their children Moira and Wallace are here. Then there's Finella, she's Ferris and Fiona's younger sister. Elspeth and Callum have three other children, Ailis, Beitris, and Doug. And Effie has twin boys, Ian and Shug. That's everyone."

James looked at the group. "It may take me a while to remember everyone's name," he finally said.

Anabel laughed and pulled him along. "Don't worry. No one will take offense."

The crowd parted as they approached, and Gran appeared before them. She was a short woman, with olive skin and black hair streaked with grey. Though she was in her late sixties, her face had few wrinkles and lines. She wore a serviceable blue dress with two brightly colored shawls, one tied at the waist and the other around her shoulders.

"Gran," Anabel said as the woman made her way toward them.

"C'mere, me girl. Give us a hug." Anabel happily stepped into her grandmother's warm embrace, breathing in the sweet scent of orange-blossom water.

"All right, me girl. Lemme see this lad of yours," Gran said as she stepped back from the embrace. She looked up at James, who was more than a foot taller than her. "You're a fine strapping specimen, aren't you?"

James laughed. "It's nice to meet you, Mrs. Moon."

"Nae, son. Call me Gran." She paused, assessing James. "An you're a knight. Earned your honors at Trafalgar."

"How did you know..." James began to ask, but Gran cut him off.

"You may as well get used to it, boy. I have the sight, you see. It's a right pain in my arse, it is."

She walked toward a set of chairs set up behind the tent, where someone had placed a pot of tea and three cups on the table.

"Sit." She gestured, and James and Anabel sat obediently.

Gran poured them each a cup of the dark, heavy tea she preferred, then sat back in her chair. They were quiet for a moment, holding their cups but not imbibing.

"Gran," Anabel said, "I need to tell you—"

"Not now, girl. You ken I cannae talk 'til we have our tea." She gestured to the cups in their hands. "Drink up, so I can read your future."

"Read our future?" James asked Anabel in a low murmur.

"I've learned it's better not to argue," she replied.

They drank while Gran watched. No one spoke, although the noise around them returned to normal. Anabel enjoyed the late afternoon sun on her skin and the warm feeling of safety surrounding her.

"Gran," she began as soon as she finished her tea.

"She's all right," Gran replied, anticipating Anabel's question.

"She is?"

"Aye, you'll see," she replied, holding out her hand. "She'll be back afore soon. Now, gimme your cup."

Anabel handed over the empty cup, and Gran peered at the dregs in the bottom, turning it to and fro to interpret the patterns she saw.

"You've had a trial, haven't you?"

Anabel nodded. Merlin popped into her mind, but also all the torments that had driven her from the city. She thought of the struggles on her journey, both before and after she had met up with James. Although James had been a bright spot.

"I see you've started tae see that even in a bad situation, some good can come of it," Gran said, watching Anabel closely.

Anabel didn't trust herself to reply, so she only nodded.

Gran turned the cup more. "I see you come back seeking safety. Your family will always help you, but you must learn tae handle some things on your own. You have more strength than you know."

She smiled. This didn't feel like a normal tea leaf reading. Gran was using the leaves as a prop while she gave Anabel a pep talk.

Gran's tone became more serious. "You have a battle ahead of you. Twill feel like you have no allies, even among those you trust most. You must trust your instincts above all else, even if it means someone you depend on is lying."

Anabel frowned. "Can you see what the battle is?"

Gran didn't respond right away. She continued turning and tilting the cup, lifting it high enough that Anabel was afraid it might spill. "Nae," the older woman finally replied. "It's been hidden from me."

"That sounds ominous," James commented.

"I have the sight, lad, but that doesn't always show me everything. Life would be boring if we always ken what's coming, aye?"

Gran placed Anabel's cup on the table and motioned for James to give her his. Once she had it in hand, she held it up and started turning it. Suddenly, she dropped the cup.

"What is it?" Anabel asked. "What did you see?"

Gran looked at them with wide eyes but did not say a word. She slowly shook her head, pinning her gaze on James.

"Gran?" Anabel asked, her panic rising.

James squeezed her hand lightly. The soothing touch helped calm her a bit. She glanced briefly at their joined hands before looking back up at Gran. The old woman had a perplexed look on her face. Anabel wasn't sure what to say. Her heart was racing as she tried to predict what Gran had seen.

"Mrs. Moon," James finally interjected. "What did you see? Am I in danger?"

"Aye," Gran replied, her voice shaky.

"What is it?" James asked, his voice frustratingly calm.

Gran shook her head. "I cannae tell you."

Anabel heard the words Gran wasn't saying. James was in danger, and if Gran couldn't tell him, then Fate was preventing her from doing so. Anabel swallowed thickly, blinking back tears.

Chapter 19

Anabel stood abruptly and walked away at a fast clip, obviously trying to put some distance between herself and her grandmother. James watched until she was no longer in sight.

"I'm not sure I want to know what you saw," he said, turning back to Mrs. Moon. "But I believe I need to if I'm to help your granddaughter."

Mrs. Moon stared at him with those deep brown eyes. "You truly love her. I can see. You would dae anything for her."

"Anything," he echoed.

"Then I think the best thing you can dae is leave, Sir James."

James was momentarily taken aback. "Leave? I can't leave. I have a duty to care for Anabel. I won't leave her side."

Mrs. Moon's eyes filled with tears that threatened to spill over the rim. "Then you," she paused, taking a gulp of air. "You'll most likely die."

James had been looking in the direction Anabel had gone, but his head whipped back to look at her. "I'm going to die?"

"I believe so."

"When? Tell me what you saw."

"I cannae say. Not that I dinnae want tae, mind you. I'm physically unable. Take it up with the Fates."

James scoffed. He had a hard time believing some ancient Greek deities were truly meddling in his life.

Mrs. Moon scowled at him. "If you dinnae believe that, then believe this. If you stay, what's chasing Anabel will come after you. Anabel will try tae save you afore saving herself and put her own life in danger."

James stood from his chair. He wanted to argue, but he couldn't deny the truth of the old woman's words. He bent down, picked up his cup, and placed it on the table with a small *thunk*. "I control my own destiny," he said. "I will keep my future wife safe."

He turned and walked after Anabel, hoping to catch up with her.

He hadn't gone more than a few yards when Ferris joined him. "You should have gone back to London when I suggested it."

James rounded on the younger man. "I don't have time for you to gloat, Ferris. I've told you I'm not leaving Anabel's side."

He turned before Ferris could reply, continuing his pursuit of Anabel.

"But what if she asks you to?"

He stopped mid-stride but refused to look back. Ferris's steps were muffled in the soft grass as he approached.

"If Anabel asked you to go, would you?"

"Not if I thought she was being coerced into it."

"Come now, James. Think about what you're saying. Gran said Anabel would try to save you. It didn't sound like Gran believed Anabel would be successful. What if she had to live with the knowledge she'd caused your death?"

"Why are you all so sure I'm going to die? Because of what your grandmother saw in a cluster of wet tea leaves?"

"Gran has the sight. She's the most powerful among us. If she says something is going to happen, it will. There's no stopping it."

"Well," James said, jaw clenched. "There's a first time for every-thing."

He stormed away from Ferris, but he couldn't shake his anxious thoughts. Would he truly die if he continued on this course? Who would tell his parents? More to the point, how would his father react? Would Edward even grieve James knowing his son died in pursuit of the woman he'd been told to let go?

He continued walking until the noise of the fair faded and he was on a side street of the town. He begrudgingly admitted Ferris was right. He should have just gone home to London.

The town still bustled, but the alley was peaceful compared to the cacophony of the fair. James leaned against one of the buildings and rested his head on the wall. He needed to find Anabel, but he was so weary. He wished he could return to the night before, when he had been warm and safe with Anabel in his arms.

The door of the public house on the other side of the alley opened suddenly. He shrunk into the shadows so the patrons wouldn't see him, wanting a moment of solitude.

Two men marched out in a fury. They were Merlin's hired men. Merlin's house was more than a day's ride from Yorkshire. How did they get here so fast?

Had Miss Kashef been able to get away from the men? Had Merlin bested her? Anabel's grandmother had said she was safe, but how could that be, with Merlin's men here?

"I hate it when he sends us through them portals," one man said. They were just outside the pub, watching the pedestrian traffic.

"Quit your jabbering. We need to find that gent she was traveling with. Boss says we need him to make the bitch do what he wants."

"And what do he want?"

The larger man smacked his companion's head with his broad hand. "That ain't for us to know. Let's go. We'll start at the fair and see if we can find him."

"I don't like the fair. It's so boring, and too many poor people. Ain't nothing in their pockets."

"We do this job, and we don't have to pick pockets no more."

The two continued their banter as they walked away from the pub. James stayed hidden in the shadows for several more moments before he peeked out to see if they'd gone. They were looking for him, and Merlin planned to use him as bait. Was this how he would die?

Anabel will try tae save you afore saving herself and put her own life in danger.

James shuddered. He was torn between running back to warn Anabel and leaving to prevent the vision from coming true. The thought of going pained him, but perhaps he would be better served to withdraw.

He couldn't go without at least sending Anabel a note. Spotting a merchant selling paper and writing utensils, he crossed the road, trying to ignore the sudden pain in his chest. He would write her a note, and then he would leave. If he wasn't there, she couldn't put her own life in danger. And when this was all over, they could start their life together.

Anabel tried to stop the shaking in her limbs as she stumbled away from the family tent. How could the world be so cruel as to bring her and James together just to tear them apart? Furthermore, why was Merlin pursuing her so doggedly? Even if she were as powerful as he claimed, she was not the only powerful witch in England. She wasn't even the most powerful witch in her family!

Although Gran said Suraya was safe, Anabel felt deep in her bones that her friend was not well. Something was amiss, and Anabel was the only one noticing it.

She found herself in a small grove of trees on the edge of the village green. Walking toward the healthiest one, she pressed a hand against its trunk, breathing deeply as she exchanged energy with it. She felt the bark on her skin and willed her weariness away.

"It's not kind tae give the tree your megrim," Fiona said as she entered the grove.

"I don't think it works that way."

"Did you learn how tae speak tae trees since we last met?"

Anabel lifted her head to peer at Fiona. "Life would probably be easier if I had. They know everything."

Fi laughed. "That they dae." She placed a comforting hand on Anabel's back. "I heard what Gran said. It upset your knight something fierce."

"Did she come out and say it, then? She was refusing to, though I don't understand why. The minute she dropped the cup, it was obvious she'd seen something bad."

Fiona shrugged. "Summat about the Fates. You'd think after all these years reading leaves, she'd have improved her delivery."

Anabel grinned wryly at her cousin. "Some things never change, I suppose." She moved to the edge of grove, watching the bustle of the fair. "Did you have a show today?" Fiona usually performed at least once a day while they were at a fair.

"Nae. The town didn't hire me this year."

"But why? Your shows are always such a draw."

"The gossip going 'round is they have a new preacher who's been talking about 'the dangers of temptation from loose women,' whatever that means." Fiona scoffed at the statement. "Not sure who he thinks is loose. I've got stronger muscles than some men." Fiona slapped her taut stomach.

"I suppose he's referring to a different type of loose."

Fiona's mouth formed an exaggerated 'O'. "He's been talking about my cunny? The rogue!"

Anabel laughed despite her misery. "Not your cunny in particular, I believe. Unless you have some history with the man."

Fiona scrunched up her face. "He's not my type."

"Have you seen him?"

"Nae, but he's a man of the cloth, so he cannae be my type." Fiona's face turned dreamy, and she stared up at the sky. "I'd prefer a handsome knight anyhow," she said, grinning mischievously.

"Maybe if he transfers his affections to you…" A sob choked her throat. "What it he dies, Fi?" She broke down, unable to control her tears. Fiona pulled Anabel into her arms.

"Hush, dear. What Gran saw may not come tae pass."

"But Ferris says whatever Gran sees always happens."

"Ferris is a young lad and knows naught of the world. He hasn't seen enough tae understand how things work."

"Have you ever seen something she predicted not come true?"

"Aye. Sometimes fate is changed, and the future Gran saw is nae more."

"What do you mean by that?"

Fiona pulled back. "Gran's predictions are like warnings. If you heed the warning, that's usually enough tae change the course. If you dinnae, then things will play out as they will."

"How do know if we've changed the course?"

"I suppose when Sir James does not end up dead."

A lump formed in Anabel's throat. She closed her eyes, trying to stem the flood of tears running down her face.

Fiona pulled Anabel back into her arms and let her cry. Anabel was so grateful for Fiona at that moment. She'd been like an older sister all these years.

When her eyes started to dry, Anabel looked up and noticed the light had faded. She watched the early stars dotting the sky for a long moment before disentangling herself from her cousin.

"Thank you, Fi."

"Anytime, love. That's what family does."

They watched as the torches were lit at the fair. Nighttime didn't stop fair activity. The fairs were often busier at night, with more attractions and shows. Many locals were only able to join the festivities after work.

The smell of pasties wafted their way, and Anabel's stomach grumbled. She hadn't eaten since breakfast that morning.

Fiona tugged her toward the activity. "C'mon, let's get you fed before you eat me."

Anabel laughed, but didn't argue. They purchased two of the delicious meat pies, eating them as they walked back to the family tent. She slowed her steps as they got closer, afraid to see James. She hoped her family was treating him well.

They walked up and Fergus approached. "We were wondering where you'd gone off tae."

Anabel hung her head. "I didn't take Gran's news very well."

"No, you didnae although, I cannae say I blame you. It's never good news tae hear that someone you love is destined tae die."

Anabel winced. Fergus was not known for his subtlety. "Where is he?" she asked tentatively.

"He ran off not long after you did. We thought he'd caught up with you, but a boy delivered a letter with your name on it just now, saying it was from a fine gentleman."

Anabel turned his words over in her mind and struggled to make sense of the tumult of emotions roaring through her. The pasty tasted like ash in her mouth. Fergus handed her the letter, and she numbly gave him the pasty in exchange. He took a bite and stepped away to give her some privacy.

Anabel took the letter to a lamp-lit seating area in the main tent. She plopped down on a brightly colored cushion and opened the letter.

> *Anabel*
> *, Your grandmother shared some of her unhappy vision with me. She told me you would put yourself in greater danger trying to save me. I said I would never leave your side, but I can't put you in that position. I love you too much to make you carry such a burden. I will continue to Gretna Green and wait for you there at the Blue Horse Inn. Come to me when you are ready, love. I fear this battle is not over yet. I want so badly to fight by your side, but I want to fight for our future more. Your family will keep you safe and be there when you battle Merlin. Please carry my love with you. I cannot wait to call you my wife. And remember, you are stronger than you know. Trust yourself. Don't be afraid of what you can do. You have a gift, and you can overcome any odds.*
>
> *With all my love*
> *, J.M.*
>
> *P.S. Merlin may be closer than we realize. I saw his men in town, and they discussed traveling via portal. Please be careful and stay safe.*

Anabel wiped fresh tears from her cheeks. She hadn't thought she'd be able to cry anymore that night, but she had been wrong.

James was gone. She longed to go after him, but, if what he said was true, Merlin would be here soon. She ran out of the tent, winding around to find Gran sitting in the same spot.

"We need to talk," she said by way of greeting.

Anabel sat opposite Gran at the table and shared her encounter with Merlin.

James engaged a boy to deliver his letter and took a seat in the pub, waiting for the child to return. He'd offered double for the boy to confirm he'd delivered the letter to the right tent.

The pub was the same one he'd seen Merlin's henchmen exit earlier that day. He wasn't sure if they would return, but he kept to the shadows just in case. As soon as the boy confirmed he had delivered the letter, James would be off. A hired horse was waiting for him at a nearby inn. He didn't want to ride at night, but he needed to escape Merlin's machinations.

The door opened, and James caught sight of the child. The boy showed him his empty pockets and held out his hands. James fished out the requisite coins and deposited them in the boy's hand.

James's vision swam. He blinked several times until the boy came back in view. He was exhausted, and he thought momentarily to take a room at the inn before embarking. He dismissed that thought, however, not wanting to delay any more.

"Thank you, lad," he said, picking up his tankard of weak ale and draining it. He'd had some cheese and bread but couldn't muster up an appetite for anything else.

The child nodded and walked off. James left a few coins on his table and moved toward the exit. The room was blazing, and he couldn't wait to be back in the cool air of the night.

He stepped outside and breathed. The evening was humid, but the wind from the moors seemed to be slowly pushing out the heat.

James felt a bit lightheaded, but, before he could ponder the reason for it, the ground was pulled out from under him. He fell hard onto the stone pavement.

Had someone at the pub poisoned his drink? He'd had nowhere near enough ale to impair him this much. He tried to push himself up from the ground, but his arms wobbled and he couldn't rise.

"Well, look what we have here," came a deep, craggy voice. James saw shoes and managed to crane his neck to see one of Merlin's men looming over him.

"You shoulda killed us when you had the chance," the man said, sneering.

James wanted to put the impertinent man in his place, but he couldn't move. He felt alarmingly like he had when Merlin had first placed him under a spell.

A deep fear overtook him as he thought of Miss Kashef. She'd subdued Merlin and his men. If they had escaped the trap, what had happened to her?

"What should we do with him now, Tim?" the other asked.

"Get him in the alley. The bitch will be along in a bit."

The men pick him up by his arms and legs, allowing his body to dangle between them. Annoyingly, his head bumped against the wall of the smelly, cramped space between the two buildings.

"Bill, you cod's head!" Tim yelled. "Boss said not to hurt him."

"I don't do it on purpose!" Bill replied. He released one of James's arms as he used his own hand to emphasize his point. James's left side listed toward the ground. His arm dragged, and something sharp poked his hand and caught on his sleeve. A rather large chunk of glass was nestled in the cuff. He felt a modicum of relief to have a weapon.

His captors dropped him halfway down the alley. "Sit him up," Tim said. "Make it look like he's our mate and can't hold his drink. We don't want no nosy townspeople coming along and thinking we done killed him."

"I don't like this," Bill said. "We already done everything the boss hired us for. Why do we have to follow this bitch around now?"

"Did you suddenly grow a bloody conscience?" Tim yelled. "I seen you slit a man's throat and laugh while his blood sprayed on your face. Why's this job a problem?"

"I don't like killing on someone else's orders!" Bill hollered back. "I got me own code, and I don't like taking orders."

The sound of Tim's boisterous chuckles filled the silent alleyway. "You got a code, do you? Brother, you ain't no more moral than a whore in church! And in case you forgot, you take orders from me."

"Maybe I don't no more."

James watched the drama with rapt attention. He couldn't do much else, and perhaps Bill's mistrust of Merlin might work out in James's favor. He felt a *thunk*, and, from the corner of his eye, he saw Tim press Bill against the brick. Bill's breath came out in squeaks, as if Tim were pressing a hand against his throat.

"You listen to me," Tim said. "You take orders from me, or I'll slit you from neck to navel and strangle you with your own innards. Understand?"

Bill must have confirmed his understanding, because Tim continued. "Right now, I'm saying we work for this madman because we're getting paid to. He's gonna make us rich, and then you can take your earnings and go off and live by your code for the rest of your life. But until we do that, you listen to what I tell you."

He stepped back, and Bill fell to the ground, his body shaking with hacking coughs.

Footsteps echoed in the alley way, and a woman's skirts came into view. "Oh dear. Did you two have a disagreement?"

The voice sounded strangely familiar.

"We got him for you," Tim said.

"I know," she replied. "But you couldn't do it without my help. Why does he keep you two around if he has to do all the work in the end?"

Tim grunted under his breath but made no other reply. The woman walked over to Bill. A slender hand reached down and lifted the man's chin up. "Stand up, William."

Bill stood before the woman, still wheezing.

"You poor thing," she said. "Did your brother hurt you?"

"I'm all right," he replied, his voice croaky. He tried to take a step backward, but he was only able to lift his foot.

"You're all right?" she asked. "Are you sure?"

"Aye," Bill replied.

"That's quite a relief."

James heard a sickening crack and then Bill's body collapsed to the ground. His lifeless eyes stared at James, his neck at an unnatural angle. James's stomach turned, but he did not cast up his accounts.

"Oi!" Tim yelled. "What'd you do that for?!" Despite his bluster, James heard a thickness in the man's voice.

"Oh, spare me," she replied. "Were you not just threatening to take his life by your own hand? I've saved you some work."

"But he were me brother," Tim protested. James didn't think that would garner much sympathy from the woman.

"And you'll be joining him soon if you don't shut your mouth!" she yelled.

"But we needed him to carry the gent."

"Sir James can walk just fine on his own. Can't you?"

James felt his body obey her command. Rising to his full height, he finally saw the woman. She wore a dark cloak, the hood drawn. His body moved toward her. James roared internally at the evil hag.

"Insulting me? The fair Lady Anabel wouldn't take too kindly to that."

James hated that she could hear his thoughts in addition to being able to control his body. He stopped a few feet away but continued to yell at the woman in his mind.

"Curse me all you like. Nothing you say will affect me in the least." She moved toward him, the light of the moon illuminating her form. James stopped cursing the moment her face emerged from the shadows. He was being controlled by Miss Kashef.

Chapter 20

Anabel sat back after she had relayed everything to her grandmother. Fiona, Fergus, and several of their other relatives had crowded around the table as she spoke. When she'd finished, the area around the tent was quieter than she'd ever before experienced.

"Crivvens," Fergus finally said, and the entire family breathed a sigh of relief at the broken silence.

Anabel laughed, in spite of her worry. "Crivvens indeed."

"My vision said someone wanted tae steal your body, but I couldn't see who. I never thought it'd be Merlin. I thought that mangled old bug was dead," Gran said.

"He was telling the truth when he said you knew him?"

"Aye. Me mum fought him when Fergus was a wee one."

"What happened?"

Gran's face went blank for a moment. "I thought she'd killed him."

"It seems not." Anabel sighed deeply. She'd like to hear more of this story, when her life wasn't in danger. "So, what are we going to do? James is gone," she paused, swallowing thickly before continuing, "s-so he won't be a distraction. How do I keep that madman from taking my body? Is there some trick that will help me defeat him?"

"Nae," Gran replied. "Tis my fight."

"What will you do? He's trying to take my body."

Gran opened her mouth, but a wave of noise coming through the tent stopped her. Before they could ask, the crowd parted, and Anabel saw Suraya.

"Raya?" Anabel asked. She could hardly believe her eyes.

"It's me," Suraya replied, her eyes brimming with tears.

Anabel flew from her spot and embraced her friend. "I've been so worried! I didn't want to leave you."

"I know," Suraya responded. "But I'm all right. I got away from those men."

"What happened?"

"I buried them in roots so thick they will perish before they ever get free."

Anabel furrowed her brow. That didn't sound like her friend.

"C'mere, me girl," Gran said as she levered herself up from her chair.

Anabel stepped aside so Gran could hug Suraya. She had only told Gran some of contents of her letter during their conversation. She thought of sharing James's warning, but intuition told her not to.

Stepping away from the crowd, Anabel saw Ferris watching the procession with a frown.

"What are you thinking?" Anabel asked as she approached him.

"I don't know," Ferris replied. "Something feels off."

"I was thinking the same thing."

They both waited in silence as the family gave Suraya hugs and encouragement. Suraya may not have been their blood, but in many ways she was closer to the family than Anabel had ever been. Perhaps it was her father's title or having grown up apart from everyone, but Anabel had never fit in the way Suraya had. She'd never begrudged Raya's place, but she now recognized that she'd agreed to return when Isaac asked because she felt like an outcast even among her own family.

The well-wishers dispersed, and Suraya spotted Anabel and Ferris and walked in their direction. The closer Raya got, the more certain Anabel was that her friend was concealing something. She wished she could discuss more with Ferris, but there was no time. An idea came to her, and she hoped it would work.

Anabel extended her hands to both of them. Suraya readily clasped her hand, but Ferris was tentative. He was the least tactile of her cousins, and she worried that he wouldn't play along, but, thankfully, he grabbed her hand after a moment.

"I'm so grateful you're all right," Anabel said as she squeezed then released their hands. "Today has been awful." She pulled Ferris into a stiff hug. Placing a hand on his neck, she spoke to his mind, as she'd done with James the day before.

Don't say anything, she instructed him.

This is a new ability, Ferris replied. Not wanting to make the hug awkward, she pulled away but held his gaze for a moment longer. Ferris responded with an inquisitive look.

Anabel turned from Ferris to Suraya, pulling her friend into a hug as well. She was tempted to use her abilities to learn more but didn't want to chance it. She deliberately kept her touch light as she embraced Raya.

"Where's James?" Suraya asked as she pulled away.

"He's gone," Anabel replied, the thickness in her throat returning.

"Gone? But he said he wasn't going to leave your side?"

"I guess he lied." The letter was tucked into Anabel's pocket, and she was glad she'd decided not to reveal its contents.

"I'm so sorry," Suraya said. She squeezed Anabel's shoulder.

"It's fine," Anabel responded. She looked up at the sky as she pondered her next move.

"I'm famished," Ferris said. "Let's go grab a bite before we bed down for the night. It's been a long day, and we could all use some rest."

It was as good a plan as any other, so Anabel followed them to a nearby stall and grabbed a fresh meat pasty. She didn't taste a bite of her food. She still had no appetite, but she needed to keep up her strength.

The fair was going strong, but a fire had been set up with a few blankets spread on the ground nearby for family members to rest. The three of them settled down on one. Fiona walked over and started speaking, but Anabel didn't hear what she said. The stress of the day was getting to her. She was still unsure of what was happening with Suraya, but she needed to rest for the battle with Merlin.

Stretching out on the blanket, Anabel looked up at the stars.

"Poor lass," Fiona said. "Rest your weary head. We'll keep an eye on you."

Anabel might have nodded as her eyes drifted close. The blanket was warm and cozy, thanks to Fergus. It only took a few moments for sleep to overtake her.

James came to in a dark, dank place. It appeared he was in another cellar, although this time Merlin—or rather, Miss Kashef—had left a guard with him. Tim sat in the corner across from James, his eyes closed.

James turned to get a better look at the man. Tim stirred, and James quickly refocused on the wall he'd been staring at when he'd awoken.

As he looked at the rotting boards holding the shape of the cellar, he realized he'd been able to move his head. He slowly wiggled the fingers on his left hand, which was out of Tim's sight.

His limbs were working. He had no idea how the spell had worn off, but he was grateful for the freedom to move. He squeezed his hand in a tight fist and felt the weight of something foreign. He recalled the piece of glass which had been caught in his cuff. The shard could be used as a weapon. The question now was how to best use it.

"I know you're awake," Tim said. He walked into James's line of sight then stretched, his long arms reaching the low ceiling of the cellar. James caught sight of a wicked-looking knife sheathed at the man's belt.

He dared not twitch. He could only hope the man hadn't seen him move his head.

Tim dropped his arms and looked at James. "Well, ain't you a sad sack," he said with a sneer. "Can't even move to piss. If you shite your pants, I ain't changing you. I didn't sign up to be a nursemaid to some goldfinch."

James held as still as possible while he contemplated his next move. Sometimes the most strategic thing a man could do was wait for the right moment.

Tim kept talking. "That bitch killed me brother. I'd like to gut her something fierce. Don't know where she gets off giving us orders. Boss says to follow her, and I do, and now I don't got Bill no more. I promised me mum I'd take care of him."

You have a funny way of caring for your brother, James thought.

"I'm gonna get that bitch back. Soon as I has my money, I'm gonna put her to bed with a mattock and tuck her up with a spade."

The fact that Tim seemed to think Miss Kashef was in league with Merlin was interesting. She'd seemed so sincere when she'd been helping James and Anabel escape. Although she'd spelled Taylor, she had seemed truly contrite. Had it all been an act? Had she always been working with the wizard, or was this a new development?

"I need to figure out where the boss went. If he ain't around, I don't get my money. I bet that bitch don't have it. Maybe instead of killing her, I'll put her to work to make her repay me. I bet a pretty little thing like her would make a lot of coin on her back."

Merlin was missing, but before he left, he'd told his men to obey Miss Kashef? There was something here James wasn't seeing. He reviewed everything he'd heard in the last several minutes. A little risk was needed to gather more information.

"Do you know who she is?" he asked.

Tim turned so swiftly he bumped his head on the ceiling, A shower of dirt fell over him.

"Did you talk?" Tim asked, approaching more closely. "You ain't supposed to talk. She said that potion would hold you for days."

"It appears she gave me the wrong dose," James replied. He kept the rest of his body still, only stared at the wall.

Tim unsheathed his knife and pointed it at James. "Don't try no tricks now."

"It's not a trick," James replied. "I can't move anything else, but I can talk. Quite frankly, it's a relief."

"Why?" Tim asked. He still held his knife aloft, but his posture was less aggressive and more questioning.

"Why is it a relief?" James replied. "Because I can tell you when I need to piss rather than soiling myself."

Tim chuckled, then seemed to realize James was his opposition and hardened his face. "I ain't holding your prick for you."

"Well, I suppose it's a good thing I don't need to relieve myself at the moment, isn't it?" James was partly lying. Talking about it had brought on the urge. He needed to get out of this room soon, but for the moment, he feigned helplessness.

Tim sheathed his knife. "Figures that bitch would be too stupid to give you the right dose. Suppose I should tie you up so's you don't get control of your limbs back and try to attack me."

"Is there rope in here?"

Tim scowled, and James silently cheered. It would help him tremendously if he wasn't bound.

"Look," James continued, "I don't know what potion she gave me, but I can't move anything other than my face. It's rather boring."

"It ain't my job to entertain you."

"Of course not. I was just asking out of curiosity. Have you ever met that woman before today?"

Tim stared at him for a long moment before he shrugged. "I suppose it don't matter," he muttered to himself. "No, I ain't never seen her before. She helps the lot of you escape and traps me in vines, and when I come to again, she's standing over me. I tried to attack her, but she held me off like the boss do. Then I see's the boss behind her, telling me to follow her orders. Then he scuttles off, and she tells us to get moving."

James tempered his elation with the reminder that Tim expected James to be dead shortly. "Did she try to make you do something you haven't done before?"

"No," Tim said, obviously perplexed. "She talks just like the boss, 'cept she sounds like a bitch." He looked at James curiously. "Why're you asking? She helped you get out yesterday. You never seen her before?"

"Never," James replied, biting his tongue to suppress the urge to nod. "Supposedly my betrothed knows her, but now I am questioning everything I've been told."

"Ya gonna marry the hoity-toity wench ya was with yesterday?"

"That was the plan. Now I'm not sure, since her actions have put me under the control of murderers, thieves, and witches."

Tim's posture stiffened. "I might be a murderer, but I ain't no thief. That were Bill's job." He swallowed thickly and then stomped the packed earth floor.

"I beg your pardon," James replied. "I was referring to the wizard that wants to steal my lady's body.

Tim scoffed. "He's supposed to be some great wizard, but all I sees him do is sleep. I didn't know he could take over someone else's body. That's a neat trick."

"Sure," James said, "a very neat trick, as long as you aren't waking up married to the body he inhabits."

Tim put his back to James and stared at the narrow door to their enclosure. "I'm gonna take a piss," he said with a grunt. "Don't go nowhere." He snorted as he exited the room. "Not like he can move anyhow."

The door was open. James made himself wait another minute to ensure he was truly alone. He fished the piece of glass out of his cuff and palmed it, running a finger along the sharpened edge. It wasn't as fine a weapon as Tim's knife, but it should serve his purpose.

As soon as he finished his countdown, he hurried to the door and peered out. They appeared to be on a small farm stead. The house in the near distance was much humbler than Merlin's dilapidated manor house. James listened but could not place Tim's location.

He hesitated for a moment longer. He would have preferred to know where Tim was, but this opportunity was too good to pass up. He dashed out the door and into the open field.

Once free, he hid behind a stack of hay and looked up to the stars to orient himself, keeping an ear out for Tim. Once James had a clearer idea of which direction to head in, he hurried with all speed.

His progress came to an abrupt halt, however, as Tim stepped into his path.

"Where do you think you're going?"

Anabel awakened with a start. She was lying in the same place, but she'd been covered by another blanket. Fiona and Suraya slept next to her, each under their own blankets.

She tried to recall recent events through the fog in her mind. The day's activities had wrapped up. Some vendors had already packed up, but there would be one more day of festivities. Many other vendors had done as the Moon family and bunked down for the night.

Blinking groggily, she realized Ferris had woken her. He had a hand on her shoulder and shook her gently.

She opened her mouth, but he put a finger to his lips. She nodded.

Ferris helped her to her feet and led her to the main tent. Gran usually slept there, but she was back at the table, smoking her pipe.

"Gran?" she asked, not quite understanding what was happening.

"I had a vision, dear one. It's time."

"Time?"

"Your battle with the wizard will be tonight."

"My battle? I thought you said you were going to handle him."

"I thought that too, but I've seen how the Fates mean tae play this. You'll be the one tae defeat him. If I fight, I'll meet me death."

Sourly, Anabel thought it was a convenient excuse for Gran to avoid having to do anything, but she nodded. "What do I need to do? Can I do anything to prepare?"

"I dinnae ken, child. I wish I could see more, but the vision is cloudy. All I can say is you must trust your instincts. They'll not steer you wrong."

Anabel's breath caught in her throat. Gran's words mirrored what James had said. She wished he was here. She would love to have him hold her until the battle came.

She didn't realize Ferris had left until he returned, carrying a kettle of hot water. He placed it on the table next to Gran.

"I'll make you some tea," Gran said.

She didn't want tea, but arguing would be useless. Gran made everyone tea when they were about to face a challenge.

Gran pulled her box of herbs from beneath her chair. Inside were two dozen small bags of assorted ingredients. None were labeled, and only Gran and Suraya would be able to identify them. Gran pulled out eight or so bags, taking a pinch from one and a dash from another and placing them in Anabel's cup. When she was satisfied with the blend, she poured hot water over it and pushed the cup toward her granddaughter.

Anabel breathed in the fragrant steam.

"Drink while it's hot," Gran said.

"I'll burn my tongue."

"The heat will stoke your internal fires." Gran replied with a scowl. "Go on then."

Anabel took a tentative sip, giving a silent thanks the liquid was not scorching. Under her grandmother's watchful eye, she drank every drop, then handed the empty cup back to the old woman.

"What now?"

"The tea will guide you," Gran replied. "Good luck, love."

That was an odd thing to say, but no sooner had she formed that thought than her vision grew fuzzy at the edges. Things around her took on a red cast, and she felt drawn to look back toward where she'd been sleeping. She obeyed the urge. Everything and everyone around her was obscured, except for a small pinpoint of light. Entranced, Anabel walked toward it.

As she got closer, the light took on shape and form, becoming the one clear spot in her vision. She approached until the light was the only thing she could see. She blinked a few times to clear her sight. When she opened her eyes again, the fuzziness was gone, and everything was thrown into full relief. The light had gone, but in its place rested her best friend.

Suraya's eyes were closed, but she shifted restlessly in her sleep. Anabel had a sensation, almost like memory, of the light that had illuminated her vision only moments ago. This time, the light was not blinding. She saw a person lying in the same position, but it was not Suraya's body. Lying on the blanket next to Fiona was none other than the man who called himself Merlin.

Anabel stumbled backward at the realization from her tea-induced vision. Merlin had possessed her friend's body.

Ferris caught her as she stumbled, holding her up. "It's true then?" He whispered in her ear.

Anabel nodded. "How did you know?"

He shook his head. "I didn't. I had a suspicion. I could see something was off, like she was fighting something inside. I didn't know for sure until you realized it just now."

"What do we do?"

"Let's start by getting Fi away." He knelt by his sister's side as he had a short while ago for Anabel. Fiona did not respond as quietly.

"What?!" Fiona cried. "Why are you waking me? It's still night."

"Hush, Fi!" Ferris replied. "You're loud enough to wake the dead."

Anabel held her breath. Fiona had been loud. Maybe not enough to literally wake the dead, but certainly enough to wake the dangerous sorcerer lying next to her.

"Dinnae lecture me," Fiona replied, not moderating her tone in the slightest. "If you dinnae want me to make so much noise, you shouldn't have awakened me."

Anabel was inclined to agree with Fiona, but it was too late now. She never took her eyes from Suraya's prone body, so she saw when the wizard awoke. He sat up stiffly, like a corpse rising from the grave.

Anabel was ashamed that she hadn't noticed sooner. The way the body moved was so different from Suraya. Had she been so grateful her friend appeared unharmed that she'd missed obvious signs?

The wizard turned Suraya's head to look at Anabel. "You know, don't you?" he asked in her friend's voice.

"Yes," Anabel replied, her voice so low she was unsure if he heard. He pushed the blanket off his legs and walked to Anabel. Fiona stopped ranting as she looked up curiously at their friend.

"What's she doing?" Fiona asked.

"That's not Suraya," Ferris replied.

Suraya was a few inches taller than Anabel, and she felt each fraction of the extra height as Merlin loomed in front of her.

"Well," he said. "I supposed we should get this over with before we awaken anyone else. This is only a temporary host. You're still the one I need."

He locked Suraya's arms around Anabel's shoulders. "Let's start with a little persuasion," he said, and heat bubbled under the surface of her skin. She looked at her family, silently begging for help but also worried for their safety.

"Don't worry about them," Merlin said, his gazed fixed on her. "Do as I ask, and no one else will be harmed."

Anabel screamed her agony as she fell to her knees in front of her friend's possessed body. How would she win a battle against this evil man?

Chapter 21

"I'm leaving," James said, glaring at Tim. "Don't try to stop me, or I'll be forced to hurt you."

Tim laughed loudly. "What do a cod's head like you know about fighting? I could wipe the floor with you."

James squared his shoulders. He may have been an officer, but he'd traded his fair share of blows while serving. Fighting had been a good way to pass time between engagements, and the skills James had learned during those brawls would come in handy now.

James feinted right, and Tim took the bait, diving in that direction. James landed a solid blow to his vulnerable stomach. Tim groaned but didn't lose his footing. He spun, landing a hit of his own.

James resisted the urge to curl up. He stepped back slightly and watched his opponent. They circled each other, and Tim unsheathed his knife. He held the handle in his palm, the blade pointing backward. It was not what James had expected. Rather than wielding the knife like a sword, Tim was preparing to stab him.

He had to get the knife out of Tim's hand. The glass shard, his only weapon at present, was a poor match for Tim's blade. James would only get one shot, so he had to make it a good one.

Tim twisted his wrist and charged, the blade pointing toward James. The angle was awkward. The man's elbow was tucked in to his body, his forearm was rigid, and his wrist was parallel to the ground.

James saw his opportunity as if it were in slow motion. He spun away from Tim's blade and swiped the glass along Tim's forearm. Blood welled up along the wound. The cut was deep and surely stung. Tim cried out and reflexively opened his palm, dropping the knife.

Quick as a flash, James grabbed the weapon. He kept the shard of glass in his other hand, not willing to leave the other man with any means of defense.

"Think you got the best of me, do you?"

"I wouldn't say that," James replied, panting as he tried to calm his racing heart. He held the knife like a sword.

"You got lucky with that swipe. I've won fights with beastlier men than you with wounds worse than this."

"I'm sure that's true, but it doesn't mean you'll be able to best me."

James kept his voice even as he circled his opponent. Tim was protecting his torso well, not leaving any openings. If James lunged, Tim would try to wrest the knife from his grip. He had to be strategic. He had all the weapons, but Tim was a formidable opponent.

"You won't be the first swell I've killed. Likely not the last." The man's overconfidence could work in James's favor, but he had to keep him talking.

"What makes you so sure I'm an easy opponent?"

Tim's laugh was dry and wheezing. "You're all the same, ya nobs. With your fancy threads and fine words. Not one of you would survive a day of my life. You don't even know how to change clothes. Got to have a manservant to take off your pants."

The more he boasted, the more Tim's guard relaxed, changing his posture to lend credence to his words.

"What makes you think I'm a nob? What if I told you I'm the grandson of a London shopkeeper?"

"I'd not believe ya for a second! You got fancy clothes and fancier words!" He feinted, making James step back. "Let's stop this jabbering now. I'm getting me knife back, and then I'm gonna kill you with it."

He lunged again, but James was ready. As soon as the man was within spitting distance, James saw an opening at his torso and took it, plunging the knife deep into his gut. At the same time, he slashed the sharpened glass across Tim's face, leaving a long cut across his cheek and right eye.

Tim tried to retaliate, but his obscured vision and pain made him sloppy. James pulled the knife out of his torso and drove his knee into the man's groin for good measure. It may not be gentlemanly, but it was a surefire way to fell a man.

He pushed Tim hard, and the man fell to the ground, one hand covering the wound in his side and the other over his groin.

James could gloat, or perhaps finish the man off, but an image of Anabel doubled over and crying out flashed in his head.

He ran, pocketing the glass shard and holding the knife at his side as he sped away. He had no idea how to get to Anabel, but he trusted that whatever instinct was driving him now would not fail him.

Sooner than he'd expected, he entered the town where he'd been abducted. He wasn't far from the fair. He ran through the alleys toward the village green.

It must have been well after midnight. The town was dark, but a full moon illuminated his path. He burst into the jumble of tents, heading toward the colorful tent where Anabel's family gathered.

When he finally stopped, he stared at the table where he'd had tea with Anabel's grandmother only that afternoon. The old woman sat there now, smoking from an ornately carved pipe.

Panting heavily, he walked toward her. "Did you," he paused, swallowing against his parched throat. "Was it you? Did you compel me to come here?"

She held out a cup, and he drank it without looking at the contents, saying a silent prayer of thanks when he realized it was water. When he finished, he looked down, expecting an answer.

"Nae," she replied as she took the cup from him and refilled it from a pitcher on the table. "She did that all on her own. I dinnae think she realizes how much she needs you."

"But what of your prophecy? Am I to die if I help her?"

"If I said yes, would you walk away?"

"No," he responded, not a trace of doubt in his voice.

"Then what does it matter? Go," she said, pointing toward spot near the center of the green. "She's about tae face a most fearsome foe and having you by her side will give her fortitude."

James turned and saw Anabel's back as she stood opposite another person. He couldn't make out who it was at this distance. He started to walk but was stopped by the old woman's grip on his arm.

"Wait," she said. "Give her this." She added more water to the cup and added a small pinch of milky powder. The substance disappeared when it hit the surface.

"What is that?"

Mrs. Moon held out the cup to him. "Make sure she drinks it all afore she faces down the wizard."

It was a strange request, but James took the cup with him as he marched across the green toward his love.

Through the fog of pain, Anabel heard someone screaming her name, but she struggled to focus on anything beyond her own physical agony. This pain must be what James experienced when his arm was cut by Merlin's eerie fire. Was her skin on fire? It didn't feel like it. The heat was bubbling up from inside her.

"Anabel!"

Her name was being called again, as if from a distance. It sounded like James. She wished he could have held her once more before she met her death. He called her name again, and she felt a hand on her back. The pain did not subside, but the hand gave her something else to focus on.

Her vision was blurry, but her other senses seemed to be working. A cup pressed against her lips. Water was poured into her mouth, and it was so refreshing she drank greedily, the liquid dousing the flames within her.

"It's working!" Was that Fiona? Anabel's head was tilted back, and more water was poured into her mouth. She drained the cup in a matter of seconds. The water—which she suspected had been enhanced—washed away her pain and cleared her mind.

"Are you all right?" James asked as he knelt at her side. His comforting hand still rested on her back.

"Yes," she replied, swallowing to clear her throat. It took her a moment to realize that James was truly back. She threw her arms around him, crying softly into chest.

"I have you," he soothed, rubbing her back gently.

"I'm so glad you came back!" she cried, unable to stem the flow of her tears.

The day's events had been a jumble, and it took her a moment to remember why he'd left. She pulled back to meet his loving gaze.

"Gran's vision," she whispered. "You can't be here. You'll die!"

"I don't care," he responded. "I would rather be with you. Not for all the world will I leave your side again."

"How touching." Suraya's voice came from behind Anabel, and James looked up at her friend warily.

"Anabel," he whispered. "I need to tell you something."

"I know," she responded. "The wizard has possessed Raya's body."

"He possessed her?" James sounded relieved and worried at the same time. "I thought she was in league with him."

A bitter laugh came from Suraya. "This pious little ninny wouldn't join forces with me! She was too worried about her dear friend's wellbeing to be of much use."

The coarse words were a relief. At least her friend hadn't done anything nefarious on purpose. Gently, she pushed against James, indicating she wished to stand. He took his place at her side as she stared at the wizard in Suraya's body.

"Release her, wizard. Your quarrel is with me."

"That may be, but I don't have another body to go into. I'm afraid I can't do as you ask until you agree to my terms. If you let me permanently inhabit your body, your dear friend will remain unharmed. If you fight me, I'll be forced to injure her. I won't kill her, of course. I'll just make things quite painful for her."

"Why?" James asked. "That would only create pain for yourself."

"That's where you're wrong, boy. I don't experience any physical sensations when I temporarily inhabit a body. I can make things quite unpleasant for Suraya and not feel a bit of it." His mouth twisted into a snarl. "Have you already forgotten how much pain I can cause?"

The wizard snapped his fingers, and fire licked down James's sleeve, slicing through the fabric. James cursed, but did not collapse to the ground.

James breathed slowly, but he seemed to manage much better than before. The fire subsided, and the scar on James's arm was once again a pink line that seemed to pulse with his heartbeat.

The wizard grimaced. "That should have injured you more than that." He snapped Suraya's fingers again, but nothing happened. "You bitch! Stop that!" he yelled, seemingly to no one in particular.

"Raya?" Anabel asked. "Are you still in there?"

Merlin either didn't hear or didn't care about Anabel's question. He continued to try to snap his fingers, but the motion became more difficult.

"Suraya!" Anabel said, turning to James. "She's still in there! She still has some control."

James smiled. "I believe you're right. She gave Merlin's men a potion which was supposed to have incapacitated me for days, but it wore off in a matter of hours. She may have purposely diluted the dosage."

"This is our chance! If we can get her to expel him, it could get rid of him!"

"Wouldn't he take over another body and try again?"

Anabel looked at him. "I don't know what else to do. I can't let him hurt her."

As if to prove her point, Merlin yelled. Suraya's hand moving to her throat, as if she were trying to choke herself. Anabel threw her hands out and used her magic to pin Suraya's arms to her sides.

"Do not harm her, Merlin. Suraya, be patient. We'll get you out of this."

Hurry. Anabel heard a weak voice in her head that sounded a lot like Suraya. She kept a strong hold on the wizard. How could she remove his filthy soul from her best friend's body?

By this time, the family had all gathered around her. She drew comfort and strength from them. Ferris was walking in a circle around the perimeter, preventing outsiders from entering with his magic. Any stranger looking their way would see the family sleeping around the dying embers of the fire.

Just as Ferris finished, another familiar voice, one Anabel never expected to hear this far north, cried out her name. He banged his fists against Ferris's invisible wall.

"Isaac?" she asked, bewildered as she looked at her brother who clearly did not see her.

"You know him?" Ferris asked.

"That's my brother!"

A murmur of "the duke" traveled through the group as they realized the identity of their new intruder.

Ferris waved his hand, and Isaac stumbled as if he was leaning against a door that had suddenly opened. He took a moment to gather his bearings before running toward Anabel.

"What are you doing here?" She asked him in astonishment.

"I was worried when Sir James didn't return with you after a day. I decided I would be better served to follow you myself than to hire another person."

"Hire?" Anabel said, trying to make sense of his words. She turned to James. "He hired you?"

James rubbed the back of his neck. "I told you he sent me."

"Yes, but not that he *hired* you!" She turned back to her brother. "How much did you pay him to retrieve your wayward sister?"

Isaac frowned at her. "Is now really the time for this conversation?" He looked over to Suraya. He breathed in deeply, his eyes widening as he took in her appearance. "Who is she, and why do you have her trapped?"

"That's Suraya," Anabel responded in a clipped tone. "She is currently possessed by the soul of an evil wizard. We need to get him out of her body without harming her."

Isaac took her outrageous words in stride. "I can help with that." He turned to Suraya, a cold anger overtaking his face. "Wizard, you WILL leave the body of this young woman!"

Anabel saw the repercussions of his actions as if they were playing out in slow motion. "Isaac, no," she whispered.

Suraya's body seized before collapsing. There was no time for Anabel to worry about her friend's wellbeing, however, as her own body seized, and a malevolent presence overtook her. Her last coherent thought was of James. She hoped he understood what was happening to her.

James watched in horror as Anabel fell again. At least she wasn't screaming in agony. Rather, she appeared to be asleep. Kneeling beside her, he took her into his arms and kissed her temple.

"What is this?" the Duke of Montgomery yelled, more concerned with James's behavior than his unconscious sister.

"To what are you referring, duke? The fact that your sister is likely now possessed by the soul of the man who was recently in Miss Kashef?"

"How absurd! That's not what just happened. Anabel fainted for another reason." He scoffed, as if there was nothing else of concern. "I am referring to the familiar way in which you are holding my sister!"

"They're betrothed, Your Grace," came the soft voice of Miss Kashef. She sounded weary, but much gentler than when she'd been possessed. James was ashamed of how readily he'd assumed she was in league with Merlin.

"I'm glad to see you are yourself again, Miss Kashef," he said, trying to convey his apology.

She smiled at him but said nothing more. Montgomery was looking at her with wide eyes and a slack jaw. In different circumstances, James might have laughed at the man's expression. Instead, he looked down at Anabel as she fidgeted in her sleep.

"What can we do for her?" he asked no one in particular. There were enough magically inclined people around them to fill an assembly room. Someone would know how to help Anabel.

"You can start by giving her to me," Montgomery said. "I will care for my sister."

"You may as well give it up now, chap," Ferris said, placing a hand on Montgomery's shoulder. "I've been trying to get him away from my cousin since yesterday. He won't leave her."

"Who are you?" Montgomery asked as he shrugged off Ferris's hand.

"We're your family, lad," said Ferris's father. He held out his hand to Montgomery. "Me name's Fergus. I'm brother to your ma, and da to that one there, Ferris," he said, pointing to his son. "Me girl Fiona's around here somewhere."

"Here, da," Fiona said, appearing at his side.

Montgomery looked warily at the assemblage around him. The resemblance was unmistakable. He was one of the Moon clan, though James suspected the duke had never met his extended family before.

"Ach, dinnae fuss with introductions now!" Mrs. Moon said, sidling up to Fergus. "We can deal with that later." Her face softened as she looked at Montgomery. "I'm your Gran, son, and right pleased I am to meet you. Later, I'll make you some tea and we'll talk, but for now, we need to get your sister to my bed so I can get that nasty wizard out of her."

The preponderance of new people silenced Montgomery, and he nodded slowly. Mrs. Moon touched James and pointed toward the largest tent. "Can you carry her over there, son?"

James stood, holding Anabel close. The duke, still looking uncomfortable, followed closely behind.

Mrs. Moon led them to a curtained-off area at the back of the tent. She gestured toward a soft looking bed. James laid Anabel down before kneeling and taking her hand.

"I think you need to move, Marley," Montgomery said, his tone hostile.

Rather than replying, James looked at Mrs. Moon.

"It's fine for you tae remain. You're helping tae anchor her. She's fighting a battle right now for control of her body."

"Control of her body?" Montgomery repeated. "Do you mean to say he's right, and that she's possessed now?"

"Aye," Mrs. Moon replied. "I'm glad tae meet you, son, but your coming in and throwing your power around like a hammer didn't help the situation. I think once we have Anabel back, you should spend some time with us and learn tae better control your abilities. Tis a powerful gift. You need tae learn tae wield it properly."

The duke chafed. "I know how to wield my power."

"Do you?" Mrs. Moon's tone raised. "Because what I saw was a young man with nae consideration for the situation, trying tae control things he had nae business controlling!"

"I had every consideration!" Montgomery replied. "I have to consider everything around me at all times."

"Enough!" James yelled.. They were arguing like barn cats. "Fight about this later. Right now, help Anabel."

Mrs. Moon looked chastened. "He's right. Fetch me that chair, lad, and set it here next to my bed."

Montgomery's eyes blazed, but he did as the woman asked. Once settled, she placed a hand on her granddaughter's forehead. Closing her eyes, she sang softly in a language James vaguely recognized, although he had no idea what her words meant.

"It's Arabic," Montgomery said after the singing concluded. "My mother used to sing that song to me when I was a child."

"I've heard the language before," James replied. "There are some sailors who speak it at the docks, but I've not heard it in a song before. It's beautiful."

"It is," the duke agreed. "My mother would rather that Anabel and I forget our Levantine roots, but sometimes even she calls upon them."

"You have Scottish roots as well, son," Mrs. Moon said. She continued gliding her fingers along Anabel's furrowed brow.

"Will she be all right?" James asked. "Can you get him out?"

"The bastard is holding on tight. I cannae pull him out. Anabel must expel him. All we can dae is provide her support."

"Why did he go into her in the first place?" Montgomery asked. "No offense, but there are nearly a dozen other people here with stronger magical abilities than my sister. She's told me what some of you can do. Why did he pick her?"

"Your sister is more powerful than she understands," Mrs. Moon replied. "As I've tried tae tell her afore, although I believe she started tae understand these last few days."

"So, because she can levitate objects, he wants to take over her body?" The duke was not at all convinced.

"Nae, son. Her power is not related tae objects at all. Did she not show you the energy exchange?"

"Energy exchange?" The duke looked at the woman with a frown. "No. I didn't know she had a secondary power."

"Tis not secondary. Tis the root. She influences the energy of things around her. Anything she touches holds a remnant of her energy, which is why objects sometimes follow her. It's why the wizard wants her, an' it's also why she will be able tae beat him."

James squeezed Anabel's hand. He hoped the old woman was right.

Chapter 22

Anabel wasn't sure what was happening to her physical body, but her mind was in the middle of the sea, being tossed about by the waves as she struggled to keep her head above water. Somehow, she understood that keeping herself from drowning was paramount for her survival. The presence of the wizard was all around her. He was the water tossing her around, trying to pull her under. She was so tired. It would feel so good to rest her arms and legs for a few moments...

No. She stiffened pulling her neck up just as her attention started to lull. She could not let Merlin drown her. He would take over and she would lose her life if she drowned. She recalled his words with clarity. She had to allow him to overtake her body. He couldn't steal her life, but he could exhaust her so much that she found surrender more appealing than fighting.

She would not let him win. Anabel took a deep breath and dove under the water. She had no idea which direction she could swim in to find a safe harbor, but she had to trust her instincts.

Under the surface, the ocean was entirely different. Though the waves on the surface were choppy, the water underneath was smooth as glass.

Anabel took pleasure in the tranquil waters, glad that Fiona had taught her to swim a few summers ago.

As she pictured the tranquil lake she'd visited with her cousin, the scene changed. Instead of swimming through an endless ocean, she was now in the warm waters of the lake. She saw the sunshine through the water and propelled herself toward the surface.

As soon as her head emerged, she breathed in the warm summer air and felt sunlight on her skin. The place was just as she remembered, with willow trees lining the bank and a small rocky outcropping to one side. She had sat on those smooth rocks with her cousins, and she swam to them now.

She pulled herself onto the rocks, surprised to see her gown was dry as a bone. She supposed swimming in a lake inside one's mind did not require the destroying of one's clothing.

Settling on the rock, she looked around the landscape. She felt intuitively that the wizard would be somewhere nearby. They were never far from each other here.

"You can come out now," she taunted.

"Obstinate child," came his low growling reply.

Anabel watched as a doorway appeared in the rock face. She knew the man who stepped through was Merlin, but he was not the Merlin she'd met the day before. This man was beautiful. There was a slight resemblance, but instead of stringy blond hair, this man had long, flowing locks the color of golden wheat. The man she'd met previously was wan and frail, with thin limbs and a hunched posture. This man was robust, head held high, and shoulders pulled back to put his muscular form on display.

"Is this your true form, then?"

"You can call it that," he replied, leaning against the rock in a casual posture. He wore an elaborate green velvet coat with gold trim over a white shirt trimmed with yards of lace, matching green breeches, stockings, and heeled shoes. He did not have a wig, but his hair was curled, and she could see powder coating the brilliant locks. She was no expert on fashion history, but she guessed he would have been very stylish a hundred years ago.

"Are you truly as old as you're presenting yourself? Or do you just have a fondness for the costumes of yesteryear?"

He sneered as he stepped away from the rock he'd been leaning on. "I don't appreciate your snide remarks, child." He smoothed his collar. "I am without age."

"Then, why do you need my body?"

"I wouldn't expect someone as ignorant as you to understand."

"I think we've established that I'm not what you expect."

"I certainly didn't expect you to be so irritating," he mumbled.

Anabel couldn't help but laugh. She observed the landscape. It was so vibrant that she felt she was truly back at the lake with her cousins. "Why did you bring us here?"

"If I were in control, 'we' would not be anywhere. I'd have your body, and you would be floating off to wherever disembodied souls go."

She took a moment to interpret his words. "So I'm in control."

"For now. But it's only a matter of time. I just need to catch you in a moment of weakness." He loomed over her, and the sky turned dark gray behind him. Lightning flashed off in the distance.

She couldn't bring herself to fear him at that moment. With a wave of her hand, the ominous clouds disappeared. She stood up and pushed Merlin out of her way.

"I'd imagine my family is trying to expel you from my body as we speak."

"Possibly, but nothing they do can remove me."

"And if I removed you? What then?"

"I would only leave if I willed it."

"Or if someone compels you," she replied, thinking of the way Isaac had pulled him from Suraya's body.

"That brother of yours got lucky. It won't happen again."

Anabel turned back to face him. "Humor me. If you were expelled, where would you go? Do you have this body to return to?"

He shuddered, as if appalled at her suggestion. "This form has been dying for years. Now that I've abandoned it, it will decay rapidly. There is no point in trying to reanimate a corpse."

"So, where would you go?"

"Into another host, I suppose. Preferably one less obstinate than you."

"Oh, I'm so sorry," she said mockingly. "Am I making it hard for you to take my life? How inconvenient of me!"

"As a matter of fact, yes. And I tire of waiting, girl." He placed his hand in front of him and pushed out.

Anabel felt the blow as if it had been physical. She flew across the lake's surface, landing on her back on the shore opposite the rock face. Her back hurt from her ungraceful landing, but she reminded herself she was in control here. With a thought, she removed the pain from her body and stood, facing the wizard on the rocks.

"Blackguard," she muttered. She needed to get rid of him or at least trap him somewhere he could do no harm. He moved in her direction, but she held out a hand and immobilized him. With her other hand, she opened the rock face. Instead of a doorway, the carved opening revealed a tiny cave. With a push, he flew back and landed on the floor. Anabel covered the opening, sealing the wizard inside the rocks. She sighed at the blissful peace that surrounded her.

"Not so fast," Merlin said in her mind. "I won't be contained so easily."

The wizard stood behind her. Intuitively, she realized she had to hold him mentally just as she had physically. There would be no trapping him in the recesses of her mind.

"Anabel, please, come back to me."

James's voice was a whisper on the wind. She desperately wanted to awaken and see his face. Only a week ago, she had been uncertain of this man. Now he was her everything.

"I'm in control here," she reminded herself. She looked up at Merlin, who glared at her with a clenched jaw.

An idea occurred to Anabel, and she decided to test the theory. "How did you push me?

"What do you mean?"

"I mean, I control what's happens." She faced him head-on. "So how did you push me?"

Merlin balled his hands into fists. "Do not presume to know my power, child." His words were seething, but he made no move to harm her.

"Push me again," she demanded.

He made no move toward her.

"Do it," she said, tapping her foot.

Exasperated, he thrust his hands out, sending a ball of visible energy her way. Anabel waved it away, just as she had changed the sky and the ocean.

"I'm in control here," she said again, her words filled with pride. "You are going to stay here, and I'm binding you, both physically and magically." She blinked, and he was wrapped in strips of white linen cloth, not unlike that used to wrap wounds.

"Well," she continued with a chuckle, "I suppose I'm not binding you physically since you have no physical form. How awful for you."

"Anabel." She heard James's whisper again.

"I'll be there soon, love," she whispered in response.

She threw one last look over her shoulder at the menacing wizard wrapped tightly in his bindings, before looking at the brilliant blue sky. She closed her eyes and pictured James.

James was huddled by Mrs. Moon's small bed. Anabel had been sleeping for the entire day, and James had refused to leave her side. Others came and went. Ferris assured him the tent was secure and no one outside the family would disturb them. Miss Kashef came by to apologize to Anabel for not holding the wizard better. She'd tucked a small leather satchel and a sprig of dried wildflowers in the bed with her friend before weeping over the prone body.

She'd also apologized to James for her part in his second capture. He wanted to forgive her but struggled to say the words. He knew she hadn't wanted to be a host for the wizard, but his experiences from the night before had made him bitter. James did, however, release her from any blame for Merlin taking over Anabel's body. The fault for that lay solely at the feet of James's constant companion in his vigil, the duke.

Montgomery sat in another chair at the end of the bed. His eyes were red-rimmed, and he stared miserably at his sister. James couldn't bring himself to comfort the other man. If he hadn't thrown his ability around, none of this would have happened.

James felt a bit unsettled at the thought of the duke's ability. The man could literally compel others to do as he wished. Well, most people. The duke's mind tricks had not worked on James. He wasn't sure why. Perhaps he should consult with Mrs. Moon about that, after Anabel awoke.

"Anabel," he groaned quietly, resting his forehead in his hand. He was exhausted but refused to sleep while his beloved battled.

"Sir James," Miss Kashef said as she approached. "I've brought you some tea."

James could smell the enticing brew but pushed the cup away. "I don't need tea, thank you. And please, just call me James."

She smiled at him. "Only if you call me Suraya."

He gave her a wan smile. "Very well, Suraya."

"Thank you, James," she replied, but still held the teacup out to him. "Please drink this. It was made with restorative herbs. They can't replace sleep, but they can chase away some of your exhaustion."

James smiled a bit more broadly as he took the cup from her. "Thank you, then, Suraya."

"You're welcome, James." She reached down and held Anabel's hand.

"What was it like, having the wizard in your body?"

"Different from what she's experiencing, I'm sure."

"What do you mean by that?"

"The entire time he possessed me, I was awake. I knew his ultimate goal was Anabel, so he would free me, eventually. Beyond that, I had very little control. I could see what was going on, but I could only make small changes to his actions."

"You don't think that's what Anabel is experiencing?"

"I don't. She's been unconscious all day. If the wizard were in control, he would have fled by now."

Was she right? He kissed Anabel's wrist.

"Suraya," the duke said, "would you bring me some tea as well? I could do with some restoration."

Though James could only see one side of her face, he saw the sneer she directed toward the nobleman. "If you want a cup of tea, Duke, I will show you where the kettle and herbs are, and you can fix one yourself."

"But you brought him tea," Montgomery argued.

"James didn't put Anabel in more danger by recklessly trying to control everything around him." She marched away before the man could reply.

The duke scowled. "I didn't put her in more danger."

"Are you certain of that?" James asked. Did the duke have even an inkling of his wrongdoing?

"Of course," Montgomery replied, raising his voice. "I did nothing but help that woman, and she has been rude to me ever since.

"She's right. You were trying to control everything." The voice came from the bed.

"You're awake!" James cried. He pulled her into his body. "I'm so glad you're back."

"James," Montgomery said, his tone wary. "We need to make sure that it is actually Anabel and not the wizard."

James pulled back but kept hold of her shoulders.

Her warm brown gaze seared him. This was Anabel. She was in control.

"Where is he?" James asked as he sat back up. He couldn't let her go entirely, though, so he gently rubbed his thumb along the back of her hand.

"He's still in me, but I have him bound for the moment."

"I'll get him out," the duke said.

"No!" Anabel and James cried in unison.

"I have him bound, Isaac," Anabel said. "That's enough for now. We need to find a better way to remove him. If you force him out, he will go into someone else. At least I have the ability to hold him."

"How?" Montgomery asked. "Levitating objects is all well and good, but that doesn't mean you have the strength to bind someone like that wizard."

"I can't explain it," Anabel replied. "I can only say that I have more strength than I realized. These last few days have shown me that."

"Oh, good. You're awake," Mrs. Moon said.

Anabel sat up as her grandmother approached. The old woman rested a hand on James's shoulder.

"Gran," Anabel said with a smile.

"Love," Mrs. Moon replied. "Excuse me, sir knight. Can you use some of that chivalry and allow me tae take your seat?"

"Of course." James got up and walked to the end of the bed, next to the duke.

"You managed tae subdue him?" she asked Anabel as she felt the younger woman's forehead.

"For now. I bound him."

"How'd you bind him?"

"It was very strange, Gran. I wanted to restrict him, so I wrapped him in white linen bandages."

"Like a mummy?" the duke asked.

Anabel smiled. "Not quite." She turned back to her grandmother. "I don't know how long it will hold, but if we expel him from me, he will try to find someone else." Tears flooded her eyes, and James saw his beautiful, brave love break under the stress of all she was carrying. "Will I have to live the rest of my life like this?"

Mrs. Moon stroked Anabel's hair. "Nae, my dear. Tis temporary. We just need the right spell tae banish him."

"Spell? I thought we didn't do spells."

"We dinnae do them often, but sometimes they are necessary when a great deal of magic is needed."

"What do I need to do?"

"Just keep the nasty wizard at bay. I'll let you know when the time is right."

Anabel nodded, and even though she'd been sleeping for most of the day, she looked exhausted. His own fatigue started to overwhelm him, despite the restorative tea Suraya had provided.

"Sir knight," Mrs. Moon said, turning to him. "Take off your shoes and have a lie down with me granddaughter. I think a nap would dae you both some good."

"You want him to share a bed with her?" Montgomery asked.

James had his own objection. "That's a rather small bed. I don't think there's room for me."

"Give it a try, lad. You might be surprised."

Anabel scooted to one side of the narrow bed. James toed off his boots. If her grandmother approved, he wasn't going to object.

Carefully, he climbed on. Once he laid down, it didn't feel cramped at all. It was not a large bed, by any means, but it seemed a comfortable size for two people.

"How is this possible?" he asked Anabel.

"It's Fergus's gift. He can make any sleeping arrangement feel luxurious, no matter how sparse."

"That's a rather specific gift."

"I'm sure there's a more general explanation for it, but I've only ever known him to do this."

"Remind me to thank him later." James curled one arm around Anabel's torso.

"Come on, lad," Mrs. Moon said, speaking to the duke. "It's time for us to have our tea an' talk." Montgomery muttered something, but he followed his grandmother out.

As soon as they were alone, James gave Anabel a tender but passionate, kiss. "I love you, darling."

"I love you too," she replied, her words immediately followed by a yawn. "But when this is over, I want to speak about Isaac hiring you to retrieve me."

James could only smile. He would be glad to have a trivial argument with her when this ordeal was over. "Sleep, love."

She closed her eyes. James sighed contentedly and did the same.

Anabel slept for a long while. As she came back to consciousness and looked around, she realized her body was still asleep. She was in her mind again, and the wizard was there.

The linen, which had been wrapped so tightly, was now loose. A few strands sagged in the middle, as if he had been picking at them.

The scenery had changed. They were inside a stone building, a chapel, though not one she could recall visiting. Why would she bring them here?

"I brought us here," she heard Merlin say.

"Did I say that out loud?"

"You didn't have to. I'm in your mind. Right now, your grandmother is preparing some foolish spell to banish me. It won't work."

"So you keep saying." Anabel stared at the bandages. That wouldn't do. With a thought, she tightened them. The Wizard lost his footing and awkwardly fell to a bench.

"I'll get you back for that, bitch."

"So you keep saying," she repeated. Looking around again. "Why did you bring us here?"

He eyed her warily. "I want to show you something."

"You want to show me something?"

"Yes, you nitwit! You think you have outsmarted me and the evil you perceive me to be, but you know *nothing* of evil."

She shivered at his words.

The room suddenly came to life, the candles flaring. The air smelled like there was a biting winter chill just outside the windows. She heard footsteps and turned toward the entrance to the church. Merlin entered, just as youthful and beautiful as the Merlin sitting next to Anabel.

"Can he see us?" she asked.

Merlin scoffed again. "Of course not. This is a memory."

Anabel ignored his slight and observed her surroundings. The other Merlin wore robes that identified him as a member of the clergy. He walked up to where she stood, then stopped, looking over her shoulder.

"My lord," Merlin said, bowing to the person he faced.

"Reverend," the unseen man said, and the sound sent a chill up Anabel's spine. The man's voice was cold, in tone, and in the feeling it evoked. She fought the urge to shiver. Part of her wanted to look upon the man, but her fear overwhelmed her. Instead, she kept her eyes on the Merlin that was.

"Sir, please, allow me to explain," the Merlin of memory said.

"The time for explanation has passed, Mervyn."

Mervyn, was that his real name?

"But if you would just allow me—"

"Silence!" the man yelled, and Reverend Mervyn froze.

"You disappoint me gravely, Mervyn. I entrusted you with a duty you did not complete. Now the brat has escaped to the north where she will find refuge among the Scots. It was your job to eradicate her line. Give me one good reason why I shouldn't smite you where you stand?"

"Your Excellency, I can make amends. I can find the child and wipe out the line before it begins."

Mervyn froze again, but this time the room around them also stopped. The flickering candles were now still. She looked at the Merlin by her side, but he was unmoving as well.

"What a disappointment he turned out to be," the unknown man said, as he walked into Anabel's line of sight. He was dressed in elaborate robes that marked him as a high-ranking member of the church. He looked straight at Anabel, and she knew he saw her. He was tall, with hair as dark as a raven's feathers. He looked as if he'd never seen a day of sunlight in his life.

She couldn't place his age. The lines around his dark eyes made him look about fifty years old, but something told her he was much, much older than that.

Inhaling a shaky breath, she asked, "who are you? How are you here?"

"It's funny I need to introduce myself at all. There was a time when my voice struck fear into the heart of your ancestors. Your family has been on the run for so long, you all have forgotten what you were running from."

"What do you mean?" Her family were travelers, but she'd never thought of them as running from anything.

"Ask your grandmother. Perhaps she can share some of the family lore." He looked at the Merlin frozen at her side. "You've done well against him, child. Perhaps he did me a favor by not killing your line. I might have had more success with you on the job."

"I would never work for someone like you," Anabel said through clenched teeth.

"You might change your mind someday. If not you, perhaps another of your family. That brother of yours is quite talented."

"Leave him alone."

"I have no need to compel anyone, child. They will come to me. For now, let me give you a gift."

The memory dissolved and they were again at the lake, though it was nighttime now. Merlin collapsed, his balance was off due to the bindings, and he rolled onto his side, curling his knees into his chest. His pale skin was now as pasty as the dark-haired man's. He yowled in pain.

"What did you do?"

"Unfortunately," the man said in his crisp accent, "I can't kill him. But I can weaken him so your grandmother's banishment spell will work. If he were at full strength, you'd never get rid of him. The greedy little worm has amassed quite a bit of power over the years. I've just taken a large portion of it. You're welcome."

Anabel had no desire to thank the man. "Who are you? What do you want?"

The man gave her an unsettling grin. "It's not time for you to learn that. Don't worry, child. We will meet again. Sooner than you'd like, I'm sure."

He began to walk away but then looked over his shoulder. "Best wishes on your nuptials, my lady. I'll give you some time to settle in with your new husband before you see me again."

He disappeared, and he was no longer in her mind, though Merlin remained. She could feel his presence, but he was as weakened as the man had said. She closed her eyes, and when she opened them again, she was on her grandmother's bed, snuggled up next to James.

Her grandmother stared down at them fondly. "It's time. Let's banish that wizard."

Chapter 23

Rubbing her tired eyes, Anabel struggled to sit up. James awoke a moment later and bolted upright, placing a soothing hand on her back.

"Are you all right, darling?"

She was coming out of a fog. She knew Merlin's spirit, or essence, or whatever it was, had been weakened, but how? There was a vague threat in the back of her mind, but she couldn't recall any other details.

She was so lost in her thoughts that she missed the exchange between James and Gran until James was next to the bed, holding out a hand to her.

Wordlessly, she stood. She was wearing a loose night rail, her hair unbound. "Should I change?" she asked Gran.

"Nae, dear. This won't take long. We had tae wait 'til midnight so the veil would be thin enough. Once you're free of that bastard, you can return and go back tae sleep."

Still in a fog, Anabel followed them out of the tent. Most of the other fair patrons had left. The only tents still there were those belonging to her family.

Ferris approached. "The fair ended yesterday. We'll need to get moving tomorrow so we can make it to our next destination. Also, the locals will be pushing us to leave soon. I used my gift to get us an extra day, but anymore, and people will start talking."

She nodded at her cousin and kept walking toward her family. A salt circle had been drawn in the grass, and all her family members had gathered around. Fiona and Suraya were on the far side. Fergus stood next to Fiona with his wife, Ada. Her aunt Effie was next to Fergus. They held hands, ringing the salt circle.

"In you go," Gran said to Anabel before grabbing James's hand. She dragged him over to where Suraya waited next to Isaac, pointedly not holding hands. Suraya had her back to Anabel's brother.

Gran placed James between Suraya and Isaac and instructed him to complete the circle.

"I don't have magic," James protested. "How will I be able to help?"

"You'll help," Gran said, as she walked away.

Anabel gave him an encouraging smile.

"I love you," James said, his eyes pinned on her.

"I love you too," she replied.

"Love is important," Gran said as she took her place in the circle, joining hands with Ferris and Effie. "We must focus on our love if we are tae make this spell work. Anabel's hosting a vile entity within her mind, and our purpose is tae banish him. But if we focus on our hatred and disgust for this man, we will fail." Her voice resonated throughout the clearing, more formally than she usually spoke.

"Focus instead on our dear Anabel. She came tae us five years ago, knowing naught of our family but trusting us. Dearest Anabel, who, despite her privileged upbringing, hasn't been afraid tae do a chore that needed doing. She has helped care for animals, helped raise our weens, and cooked for us all. Anabel has touched each of our lives in an important way, and tis our job now tae help her. My children, focus on the love you hold for our Anabel, and send that love her way."

Gran looked up to the moon and sang a song in Old Arabic. The words were familiar, though Anabel did not know their meaning. She hummed as the rest of the family took up the words, singing along. James, bless him, even tried to keep up, though his tongue tripped over the unfamiliar syllables.

She felt the outpouring of love from her family as if it were a tangible thing. A comforting swirl of mist gathered around her in the circle. Suddenly, as if he'd been formed by the mist, Merlin was next to her. He was the beautiful young man with the golden hair, severely weakened. He no longer wore the bindings. He stared at her, dark shadows underneath his hollow eyes.

"He will come for you," Merlin said, his voice raspy. The singing continued, though she couldn't see her family through the haze. The sound was so loud she had to strain her ears to make out the wizard's words. "He will come for you all."

"Who will? Who is he?" Did this have something to do with the vague threat in the back of her mind?

Merlin's face fell. "He's blocked your memory."

"Tell me who he is!" she demanded. She had to shout. The mist was swirling faster, and the sound joined the singing and created a cacophony.

"It's too late," Merlin said, wavering on his feet. She heard a loud *thud* as his incorporeal knees hit the ground. He tilted his head back and screamed, the sound blood-curdling.

His scream joined with the other noises in a pitch that hurt Anabel's ears. She wanted to tell everyone to stop. She wanted to press him more about this vague threat, but he was right. It was too late. He turned grey and began pulling apart, like ashes scattering from a fire. The pieces were picked up by the swirling mist around them. The mist increased its velocity, and Anabel had to cover her ears as the spell continued.

Then, suddenly, it was over. The mist spun up into the sky, and she remained in the middle of the circle, bathed in moonlight and surrounded by the people she loved. The night was quiet.

"Did it work?" Fiona asked.

Anabel looked to Gran, but the old woman returned her gaze pointedly. "You tell us, child. Did it work?"

Anabel explored her mind. She could find no trace of the wizard.

"Yes," she said to Gran, tears of gratitude in her eyes. She found James and ran to him, wrapping her arms around his neck as he encircled her waist. "He's gone," she said into his neck, tears falling freely now.

James soothed her as she cried out all the tension of the past several days. She was free.

James was unsure of his feelings. The magic that had banished the wizard left goose-pimples on his skin. When the mist had blocked Anabel from his sight, he'd panicked, but Suraya had assured him Anabel was safe. He had remembered what her grandmother said about focusing on their love for Anabel, so he'd pictured her face and focused on how much he loved her. He had tried singing along with the rest of the family, but couldn't keep up, so he'd just hummed along to the tune. When the mist had cleared and Anabel stood there, whole and healthy, his heart had leapt for joy.

They bypassed the tent they had slept in before and went to another, smaller one. "I made up your bed for you," Fergus said as they entered. "Made sure tae make some room for your lad as well."

"Thank you, Uncle," Anabel replied, giving the man a quick hug.

"I still don't like the idea of him sleeping next to her," the duke said as he approached. "Why doesn't he bunk with me?"

"Cause they're gonna be married soon," Fergus said. James was grateful for his support.

"Be happy for me, Isaac. Please," Anabel said, clasping him in a tight hug. He held still for a moment before returning her embrace.

"I had no idea this is what it's like to be with the family." He spoke so low that James almost hadn't heard the man.

"Let's talk after we get back to London," Anabel said. "We have much to catch up on."

"Where are you sleeping?" James asked.

"I have a room at the inn in town."

"Then, we'll see you in the morning, Brother," Anabel said. She looked to her uncle.

"Aye, lass. I'll make sure he disnae return tae the inn alone."

"Now hang on," Montgomery said, turning to his uncle. "I can take care of myself."

"Sure you can, son," Fergus said, placing his arm over the other man's shoulders. Montgomery was tall, but Fergus was taller. The duke had no chance of resisting his relatives.

Anabel laughed, and James was so delighted he turned and embraced his love once more.

"I'm so thankful you are safe," he said.

"As am I," she said with a smile. She pulled him toward a pallet set on the ground. James removed his boots, and Anabel removed her slippers before they lay down.

James marveled at the comfort. The pile of blankets should have been lumpy, but instead, it felt like the most luxurious mattress he'd ever slept on.

"Thank the lord for Fergus's gift," Anabel said.

"Agreed," James replied, turning on his side to look at her. "It seems like it would be rather inconsequential, but it is an important talent."

"It is," she agreed. With a flick of her wrist, the opening of the tent closed. They were alone for the first time in over a day.

"His talent also includes sound proofing," Anabel said as she swung a leg over James and straddled him. He settled further on their bed and stared up at her lovely form.

"Are you saying what I think you're saying?"

"That depends. Do you think I'm saying we could make love, and no one would hear us?"

James cleared his throat. "Yes, that's what I had in mind."

"Then yes," she said as she lowered her head and took his mouth in a sweet kiss. "That's exactly what I'm saying."

James grabbed her hips and thrust his pelvis upward, letting her feel his arousal. He cupped the back of her neck to pull her in for a kiss. Anabel writhed against him, and he couldn't help the groan that escaped his lips. He was thankful no one outside could hear them, because he didn't trust himself to be quiet.

Pulling away from her mouth, he trailed his lips along Anabel's neck until he met the collar of her night rail.

"Take this off," he commanded. She complied, and James sighed at the view of her full breasts. He trailed his hands up along her side, playing with her nipples.

Anabel ground her core against him as he pinched and pulled the sensitive buds. He took one in his mouth while tormenting the other with his fingers. Anabel slid down, so she straddled his thigh, and rubbed her delectable pussy over his leg. He recognized the sound of her impending orgasm, and he switched his mouth to the other nipple. As he sucked the bud into his mouth, he rolled the other with his fingers. As her cries came closer and closer together, he bit down lightly on one and firmly pinched the other. A few more grinds of her pelvis, and Anabel was there.

Her sweet cries filled his ears, and James grinned in satisfaction. He loved this woman so much, and he would get to make love to her for the rest of his life.

The orgasm hadn't sated his love. If anything, she became more frantic as she lifted to her knees and started fumbling with the fall of his trousers.

"James, please," she panted. "I need you."

He helped her free his cock. It stood hard and thick, anticipating the slide of her wet cunt. Anabel mounted him quickly, and they both moaned.

She rode him slowly at first, then picked up speed. It wasn't enough. James sat up, doing his best to keep his cock inside of her. He rolled them over, putting Anabel on her back. The movement dislodged him, but he lifted her leg and slid back in. He set a fast rhythm, not wanting to linger too long.

"Play with your breasts," he commanded as he moved his free hand to her clitoris. Using his thumb, he rapidly massaged the little bud. He knew he'd found just the right spot and rhythm when her cunt gripped him tighter.

"James," she moaned, long and low. He hoped the soundproofing held as he sped up his thrusts while continuing to pleasure her externally.

Anabel's breath quickened, and her grip tightened to a point that made it difficult to withdraw. She gasped and then cried out her release.

He grunted when he felt the rippling of her walls along his shaft. He couldn't hold back. Throwing his head back, he fairly roared with his orgasm. When the immediate release passed, he collapsed over Anabel, kissing her deeply. "I love you," he whispered, shuddering as aftershocks pulsed through his body.

"I love you too," she replied, wrapping her arms around his neck. "Let's sleep."

James didn't even bother to put away his cock or cover them with a blanket as he fell into a deep sleep with his lady.

Waking up nude in James' arms was becoming one of Anabel's favorite things. James was still mostly clothed. He'd removed his coat and waistcoat last night but slept in his shirt and trousers. It was odd—but strangely arousing—for her to be completely nude while he was covered.

Her stretching awoke James. He pulled her into his arms, kissing her deeply. She didn't even mind that they needed to clean their teeth.

"Good morning," he said, his voice deliciously thick with sleep.

"Good morning to you," she replied. She tried to sit up, but he pulled her back down, gripping one side of her rump firmly. She laughed at his playfulness. "James, I need to put my night rail back on. My clothing is in another tent. I need to get dressed."

He pulled her tighter to his body, and she felt his firm erection against her thigh.

"I'll allow you to do so today, but once we're married, I'll expect you to be unclothed at all times while we are together in the bedchamber."

"Yes, sir," she replied, and he groaned in response.

"I'm making you my wife as soon as possible, so no one can contest my right to be close to you at all times."

She gave him another kiss before donning her night rail.

After they emerged, she made quick work of cleaning up. One of her relatives had cleaned and pressed the traveling dress she'd worn the day before, and it smelled delightful.

"Well, girl, I suppose you'll be off soon?" Gran said as she approached.

Anabel turned and wrapped the shorter woman in a tight hug. "I hope it won't be too long before we see each other again, Gran."

"Oh, you'll be seeing plenty of us when you return tae London."

"What?"

"Aye. It's Fergus's turn tae be a Representative Peer for Scotland, so we'll be in town while he attends Parliament."

James looked at Fergus, who'd come to Gran's side. "You're a Scottish peer?"

"Aye!" Fergus said with pride. "I'm the Earl of Clydesdale."

"But how were you elected to be a Representative Peer?" Anabel asked. "I didn't know you even knew any other Scottish nobility."

"I dinnae know how I was elected, but I'll do my duty tae me country, even if it means living in London for a time."

"What?" Fiona asked her father as she approached. "You're going tae London?"

Fergus puffed up his chest. "I am, and you're coming with me, girl."

"Why dae I need tae go?" the young woman asked as she put her hands on her hips. The stance was so reminiscent of Gran that Anabel had to keep herself from laughing.

"Gran says you dae," Fergus said with a nod toward his mother, "and I agree. It's time for a change for you."

Fiona was speechless, which was a feat in and of itself. She stared coldly at her father for several uncomfortable moments before storming off.

James turned to Anabel. "Your grandfather was an earl? I thought you said your mother's family was not noble."

"I said they weren't high society," Anabel replied, the tips of her ears reddening.

Gran laughed heartily. "'Her Gran-da was not an earl. He was a farmer. The earldom passed through me."

James stared at Gran, mouth agape. "This is a story I'm going to need to hear."

"Aye, you will, but later. I'll make it part of your wedding gift."

The mention of her pending nuptials triggered something in Anabel's memory, and she recalled what Merlin had said before he was banished. She turned back to Gran, grabbing the other woman's arm. "Before he left, the wizard mentioned someone else would be coming for us."

Gran's face screwed up. "Did he say who?"

"No, just that a 'he' would come for all of us. I feel I should know more about this, like it's buried in my mind, but I can't recall anything other than what he said right as he disappeared."

"'He must have been trying tae scare you. One last attempt afore he was sent off this plane of existence."

Anabel wasn't sure that was the case but decided to hold her tongue. Ferris stood behind Gran and held her eye for a moment before nodding slowly.

Isaac arrived, dressed in fresh clothing and looking every inch a duke, no matter how he tried to disguise himself.

"May I offer you and James a ride in the carriage?" he asked.

His shoulders were slumped, and he was looking at the ground. He had always looked out for Anabel when she was a child. Even when he was away at school, she'd felt his presence in the house. She flung herself at him and wrapped him in a firm hug.

"I love you, Isaac," she said as she stepped back.

"Love you too, Bel," he replied with a smile.

They said their goodbyes to the family. Anabel was overcome by a wave of comfort. She had so many people supporting her.

She wrapped Suraya in a tight embrace. When her friend pulled away, she looked serious.

"I'll be going to London with Gran and Fergus, but, whenever they decide to leave, can I stay with you?"

"Truly?" Anabel was elated at the thought of having her friend in town.

"I'd like to settle down and open the apothecary shop like we discussed."

"That would be wonderful. Let's talk about it some more after we're in town.

Suraya gave Anabel another firm hug.

They progressed through their goodbyes slowly, leaving the family more than an hour after they'd said they would. Ferris walked with Anabel, James, and Isaac to the inn where the ducal carriage was.

"If you can think of anything else about this 'him' Merlin mentioned," Ferris said, "please let me know."

"I will," Anabel said. "Will you be coming to London as well?"

His face screwed up. "I suppose I must. I didn't expect to have to do anything as the heir to an earldom."

Anabel lifted her eyebrows "You attended school in Shrewsbury for several years. That didn't suggest you might have expectations to live up to?"

Ferris frowned. "No, it didn't."

Nearly two hours after they'd intended to leave, they arrived at the inn. Ferris said his goodbyes, Isaac requested his carriage, and they went inside to wait.

"I suppose we should talk about wedding arrangements," Isaac said, as he leaned back against the chair in the private dining parlor.

"We want to go to Gretna Green," Anabel said.

Isaac's brow furrowed. "Absolutely not. You are the daughter of a duke, Anabel. You should marry in St. George's like all daughters from great families do."

"But we have been traveling together for days!" Anabel protested. "I'm sure there's already a scandal, which will be made much worse if we return to town unmarried."

"There is no scandal. Anyone who was aware of your traveling together has forgotten that information."

"You used your powers on innocent people," Anabel whispered, the sound more akin to a hiss.

"I did not harm anyone. All I did was convince them they hadn't seen you two together."

"What about my coachman?" James asked, crossing his arms.

"That is easily remedied," Isaac replied. "Despite my sister's misgivings, my ability to compel others to forget is innocuous."

James turned red. "What if she's with child?"

Isaac scoffed. "I'm going to overlook the fact that I should call you out for ruining my sister." He pointed at Anabel. "Fortunately, while pregnancy is possible, it's unlikely, due to the tea Anabel drinks every day. Isn't that right, sister? Our grandmother shared that helpful information with me."

Anabel shrunk back. She had never thought about the tea's ability to prevent pregnancy, as it had never been relevant.

"My coach is in Gretna Green," James said. "We need to at least retrieve it."

"And to get married," Anabel added. "I'm not going back to London unwed."

"Then you will certainly cause a scandal," Isaac replied. "Before he left to retrieve you, Sir James was openly courting Lady Cecilia."

Anabel turned to James, slack-jawed. "You said you were no longer courting Lady Cecilia!"

James cleared his throat. "I did not lie. I was not courting her when I told you that."

"But you failed to inform her of that?" Anabel placed her palms on the table. She looked between her brother and James. "I can't believe the two of you, playing with people's lives. Isaac, you need to stop trying to control everything. And James," she turned toward the man she'd thought loved her as much as she loved him. "How dare you build our relationship on a lie! You would have me return to town married to the man who spurned one of my closest friends?" She moved to the door. "I'm returning to Gran. I will travel to London with the family."

Fuming, she rushed out into the common room, running right into Ferris.

"Gran mentioned you might need some assistance and asked me to remain a while," he said by way of a greeting.

"Perfect," Anabel replied. Taking her cousin's arm, she turned to look at her brother and the man she'd thought she'd be marrying. "Don't follow me. I will contact you when I'm ready to see you." They both looked crestfallen as she left the inn.

Chapter 24

After Anabel had left them in York, James had parted ways with the duke, rented a horse, and ridden to Gretna Green to retrieve Taylor. Montgomery had initially pushed to alter Taylor's memory, but James had refused. He'd assured the duke that Taylor could be trusted, although Montgomery did not seem convinced. James would need to ensure his coachman and the duke never crossed paths.

Taylor had been disappointed that Anabel had not accompanied James. His enthusiasm to see James married brought to mind how eager the man had been to help when James paid calls to the ladies from the Pearson's ball. That event seemed much farther in the past than it was. So much had happened since he met Anabel.

He'd spent most of the ride back to London contemplating how to win Anabel back, but as he had gotten closer, his thoughts had drifted to how he was going to save his business. Montgomery had made no mention of their agreed-upon fee, and James had not wanted to ask. Anabel had been upset that her brother had hired James to retrieve her. He hadn't told her the entire story, and he wondered if he should have. Would she be more sympathetic to him if she knew of his dire straits?

By the time he arrived home, he was no closer to a solution than when he'd left York.

The next day, he waited impatiently for the hour deemed appropriate for calling. He arrived at Montgomery House a bit early, but still acceptable for close friends and family. James considered himself family.

He was permitted entry but left waiting in the foyer. Finally, the butler led him not to a drawing room as he'd expected, but to the study, where the duke sat behind a stately desk. Montgomery thanked his servant, and the man departed, closing the door behind him.

"Have a seat, Sir James," Montgomery said, gesturing to a wing chair in front of his desk.

"I'd rather stand," James replied. "Why am I here and not meeting with Lady Anabel?"

"My sister does not wish to see you."

"I see," James replied. A hole opened up in his chest. "I appreciate your candor, Duke,"

"I want to help you."

James's head snapped back up. He'd been too caught up in his own grief to notice when he entered, but the duke's cravat was crooked—as if he'd been tugging at it—and his hair was mussed. He had bags under his eyes, and he was currently resting his elbows on the desk and pinching the bridge of his nose.

"I'm sorry," Montgomery said.

James was moved to take a seat. "I'm not sure what you're apologizing to me for."

"I should not have asked you to go after Anabel. I should have been the one to do so."

"Why do you say that?"

"You were courting Lady Cecilia, but I saw how drawn my sister was to you. From the moment the gossip sheets reported on you two, I saw her feelings plain as day. So, when she went missing, I thought perhaps I could arrange things to ensure she stayed in London."

"As opposed to returning to the extended family?"

"Precisely. I wanted you and her to form a connection. To be truthful, I would have been happy with almost any eligible suitor if it had kept her in the city."

James scowled. "You would sell her to the highest bidder to trap her in a city she doesn't like?"

Montgomery scrubbed his hand down his face. "No. I would not have forced her to marry a man she was opposed to. But I would have supported any match she showed a preference for."

"That's not the impression I got when I met you."

"Your father gave me pause. He is not subtle about his ambitions."

"And now?"

"I only wish for my sister to be happy."

James sat back in his chair and considered the other man. "If I reconcile with Lady Anabel, I cannot guarantee we would remain in London. If she would be happier away from the city, then we would move to the country."

"I would expect nothing less," the duke replied, nodding his head. "As long as I would be permitted to visit."

"I would not bar you entry, but I cannot speak for my future wife."

"You still wish to marry her?"

"More than anything else."

"More than saving your business?"

"Yes," James replied without hesitation.

Montgomery considered him. The silence stretched out long enough that it became uncomfortable. Just as James was about to say something to break the tension, the duke spoke.

"You don't need to worry about your business. I've had my steward visit your office. He spoke with your partner and provided funds for the necessary supplies. We've also had a discussion with one of your rival firms, who I understand has been intimidating you."

"Walton and Bolt?"

"Yes. You don't need to worry about them any longer."

"Your Grace..."

"You may as well call me Isaac, since you are to be my brother-in-law."

James cleared his throat. "Isaac, then. I appreciate what you have done for my business, but I'm not sure I can accept. The fact that you hired me is a point of contention for your sister, and even if she did not object, it wouldn't feel right to accept payment given my relationship with her.

"Let's not call it payment for retrieving Anabel, then. I agree that paying you for that service is unsavory, given your intentions toward my sister. Let's say the Duke of Montgomery is investing in the firm of Marley and Reynolds. I hear there could be great returns in railroads."

James nodded. "I would like to discuss this with my lawyer and have some contracts drawn up."

"Whatever you need." Isaac rose from his chair, leaning both hands on the desk. "Now that we've resolved your business problems, let's discuss how you'll win my sister back."

James spent the rest of the afternoon in discussion with Isaac. When he left Montgomery House, his hopes were high for a reconciliation with Anabel.

Being back in London felt stranger than ever to Anabel. One month ago, she would have been delighted to have her extended family near, but now she couldn't shake the feeling that something wasn't right. She knew in her heart what that something was, but she couldn't bring herself to mention it aloud.

After a week of hiding at Montgomery House, Anabel could take it no longer and escaped for some shopping with Suraya. Her friend was delighted by the numerous stores lining Bond Street, and Anabel enjoyed a few hours of respite. Seeing Suraya's face light up at every new shop helped distract her from her melancholy. Despite Anabel's concerns that Suraya would not fit in, she seemed to be doing very well in London.

They visited a dressmaker's shop and ordered several new gowns for Suraya, at Gran's insistence. Suraya had been reluctant to spend so much, but Gran had insisted that Suraya needed to dress the part of a fine lady, since she would be one soon. Apparently, Gran intended to introduce her ward into society, a fact that did not sit well with Suraya. There was nothing to be done, however. Once Gran made up her mind, there was no changing it.

The day of shopping had been diverting, but Anabel's unease returned the moment they came upon the bookshop where she'd had her episode with Mary. Ever since returning, Mary had held herself at a distance, behaving exactly as would be expected for a proper lady's maid. There was no familiarity, or even a suggestion she'd ever been friendly with her mistress. Anabel had begged Isaac to reverse what he'd done to Mary, but he'd admitted that, once he altered a person's memories, there was no way to retrieve them. She'd been furious with her brother all over again for tampering with the mind of someone under his protection. Isaac had appeared truly apologetic, at least, but that did not fix the damage he'd done.

She wandered along the aisles, not truly looking at any titles. She kept her hands down, not touching any books, even though she felt more in control of her power. Now she could sense the invisible strings connecting her to everything around her and could ensure she only pulled on a string when it was her intention to do so.

She looked down at her hands as she pondered the revelation. More focused on her inner world than outer, she nearly collided with another lady when she turned the corner. "Oh, I'm so sorry," she said, pulling herself from her trance. She looked up and found herself face-to-face with Lady Cecilia.

"Cece," she said. The other woman's face screwed up, and Anabel cleared her throat. "Pardon me. Lady Cecilia. How do you do?" She bobbed a polite curtsy before meeting the other woman's eyes.

"I am well, thank you," Cecilia replied before dipping into a slightly lower curtsy.

"That's good."

"Indeed."

They stood there awkwardly for a moment longer before Suraya rounded the corner.

Before Anabel could introduce her two friends, someone else joined their party.

"I believe I have all the volumes you were looking for..." a man said as he approached. Anabel instantly recognized the voice.

"Sir James," she said, silently cursing her breathy tone.

James merely stared at her. Thankfully, Suraya broke the silence.

"Sir James. Lovely to see you again so soon."

"Miss Kashef," James replied, bowing. He turned to Anabel and gave her a lower bow. "Lady Anabel."

He sounded as breathless as she felt.

"That is quite a large pile of books," Suraya said. "*Conversations in Chemistry for Young Ladies,*" she continued, reading the title of the top book in the stack.

Anabel looked at James, but it was Cece who spoke.

"Sir James is helping me research a topic I've recently gained an interest in."

Anabel furrowed her brow. It was a curious subject to research in depth. Her friend seemed as interested in science as any other modern-day London resident, meaning she attended popular lectures. Her preferred reading material, however, had always been fiction.

Her curiosity was growing, but she had no idea how to broach the subject of why James and Cecilia were shopping together. She met Suraya's eye. Fortunately, her friend seemed to understand.

"Sir James," Suraya said. "I don't believe I've been introduced to your companion."

James cleared his throat. "Of course. Miss Kashef, may I introduce Lady Cecilia Manning. Lady Cecilia, this is Miss Suraya Kashef, a ward of Lady Anabel's extended family."

Pleasantries were exchanged, but Anabel's head was spinning. Why were James and Cecilia in the bookshop together?

"Would you care to join us for an ice?" Sir James asked, pulling Anabel from her trance.

"Oh, it's been years since I've had one," Suraya replied, clasping her hands together. "That sounds delightful!"

Anabel tried to grab Suraya's arm to telepathically share her displeasure at sharing a frozen treat with the man who'd broken her heart. Suraya pointedly ignored her.

"Wonderful," James replied. "Let me settle the bill, and we'll make our way to Gunter's." He carried the stack to the front counter, leaving the ladies alone.

"I am pleased to see you again," Lady Cecilia said. "It's been some time."

"Yes," Anabel said, forcing herself to meet her friend's eye. It wasn't the lady's fault, after all, that James had been unfaithful.

"Are you and Sir James well acquainted, Lady Cecilia?" Suraya asked.

"Our fathers are business partners," Cecilia responded.

"And he offered to accompany you to the bookseller today?"

"He did. I recently saw a lecture on chemistry that intrigued me greatly, and I desired to learn more on the subject."

"I would love to discuss the topic with you," Suraya said. "I have a great interest in the medicinal properties of plants, and I understand that is what some chemists study."

Anabel was barely able to follow the conversation. *Was James still courting Cece? Why was she so interested in chemistry? Did James accompany her because she was meant to be his wife?*

"All settled," James said, returning to their group. "The parcels will be delivered to your home later today, Lady Cecilia."

"Splendid," Cecilia replied, although her voice remained sedate. "Shall we proceed to Gunter's?"

She took James's arm and steered him toward the door. Anabel didn't realize she was standing in place and glaring at them until Cecilia turned back.

"Are you coming, Lady Anabel?"

"Bel," Suraya whispered. "Relax your jaw. You're going to crack a tooth."

Anabel tried to loosen up as she and Raya followed James and Cecilia. As they walked, she refused to acknowledge that seeing another woman on James's arm was the cause of her rage.

Being so close to Anabel and yet unable to touch her was torturous. He and Isaac had planned for James to begin his reconciliation the following day, when he was to attend a dinner party where the duke and his sister would also be. Isaac had promised to arrange for James to be seated next to

Anabel. He had been preparing himself to be in her presence again and to woo her properly at that time. This unexpected meeting was throwing him for a loop.

The visit to Gunter's had done nothing to ease the tension. Now, Anabel walked a few paces ahead of him, and he had no idea how to leave this encounter with his love on a good note.

"Chin up, Sir James," Cecilia said, offering him a bemused smile.

He returned the gesture with a wan smile of his own. He'd visited her home that morning to apologize and come clean about his intentions toward Anabel. To his surprise, Lady Cecilia had born no ill will toward him. Her own emotions had changed since their last meeting. She no more wanted to marry him than James wanted to wed her. She had suggested he could make up for his deceit by helping her with a project to win the object of her affections. James was intrigued, but she would say no more.

After they'd collected the volumes that interested her, he had an idea of who the mystery man might be but chose to remain silent. He'd enjoyed his afternoon, before their encounter with Anabel. James could see Cecilia becoming a close friend, and the lady seemed to share his fondness. At least, he hoped that was what her teasing meant.

"You have been a great help to me today," Cecilia said. "I am going to return the favor now." She sped up until she reached Miss Kashef. Taking the lady's free arm, Cecilia spoke animatedly about all she'd learned of the chemical properties of plants.

The conversation became intimate, and a moment later, Anabel was walking behind her friends. Her steps were slow, and she was looking at the pavement. James adjusted his stride, so he was walking at her side.

They continued in that manner for several minutes, and James was convinced that Anabel had not noticed his presence when she spoke.

"Are you and Lady Cecilia..." she began. "That is, are you..." She grunted softly.

James's heart leapt into his throat. "I met with her this morning to explain how my feelings had changed. She forgave me, but did ask that I help her with this project."

Anabel stopped walking, grabbing his arm. "Then you are not..."

James smiled down into her beaming face. "No, I am not courting her."

"So, does that mean..."

He bit back a laugh at her inability to finish her sentences. Hope swelled in his chest as he met her eyes. "My heart is yours, Anabel. Yours alone. If you will have it."

Her gaze turned watery, and James was captivated. "I do. I mean, I will. Always."

The bustling London street faded away as James looked at her shining face. There was only him and Anabel. He couldn't stop himself from lifting her hand to his mouth and placing a soft kiss on the back of it. He lowered their joined hands and continued to stare at his love. "Will you marry me?"

He had thought her smile could not get any wider, but Anabel proved him wrong. "I will."

James threw propriety to the wind, meeting her lips with his own. The kiss was brief, but a woman nearby cried out. He separated from Anabel just in time to see the lady collapse on the sidewalk, her companion kneeling by her side.

"Well done," Cecilia said. He turned to see her and Suraya grinning widely. "Shall we continue on before you scandalize all the matrons of London?"

James chuckled but acquiesced. "Your brother will be happy to hear of this."

"He will?" Anabel asked.

"He was sure it would take several weeks for me to win back your favor."

She smirked at him. "Perhaps I should make you both suffer a bit longer before I forgive you."

James stopped again and looked at her. "Take all the time you need, darling."

Anabel was relieved to be officially married. In the end, Isaac had gotten his way, and Anabel had had an elaborate society wedding. Surprisingly, Rowena had planned the entire affair, although Anabel suspected it was to avoid censure from society rather than out of love for her daughter.

Montgomery House was bustling with activity, and not just because of the wedding breakfast. Fergus had brought his entire family. Gran was there, as well as Ada, Fiona, Ferris, Suraya, and Fergus's youngest daughter, Finella. Anabel's extended family had breathed new life into the house, and she loved having them close. She and James had even decided to stay there now that they were married, albeit in another wing. Eventually they would find their own home, but for now, Anabel wanted to be close to her family.

She leaned into James, feeling content. He kissed the top of her head then straightened as a man dressed entirely in black approached. "My dear," James said. "May I present one of my closest friends, Lord Asher. Asher, allow me to introduce my wife, Lady Anabel Marley."

Anabel nodded, and he responded with a respectable bow. "A pleasure to meet you, my lady." He straightened and stood slightly taller than James. "I apologize that I cannot stay. I am still in mourning, but I wanted to convey my best wishes for you both."

"I am so sorry for your loss, my lord," Anabel replied.

"Thank you," Asher replied. He was quite handsome. He had dark hair, his blue-grey eyes were framed by thick lashes, and he had an aristocratic nose and cheekbones. He and James made a striking pair.

Before he could leave, Fiona came to her side. Her cousin wore a fashionable gown in a shade of blue that set off her skin beautifully. Her hair was swept up in a becoming style, but strands kept coming loose. Her face was framed by more than a few, and her cheeks were flushed as if she'd been running.

"Bel," she said as she grabbed Anabel's arm. "We need you."

"Is everything all right?"

"Yes, of course," Fiona replied with a smirk. She turned to James. "You can spare your bride for a few moments, aye?"

"Of course," James replied. "May I introduce my friend, Lord Asher? Asher, this is Lady Fiona Moon, one of Lady Anabel's cousins."

Anabel had to bite her cheek to keep from laughing as she observed the exchange. Asher stared at Fiona with wide eyes and parted lips. This was not the first time a man had been smitten by Fiona's beauty.

Fiona returned his stare with a coy look and subtly pushed her chest out. "I told you, James, none of that 'lady' business," she said, although her gaze never strayed from Asher.

Asher coughed and adjusted his collar. "A pleasure, Lady Fiona.."

"I'm sure it is," she replied with a wink. "If you gentlemen will excuse us." She turned, taking Anabel with her.

"Fiona," Anabel scolded. "Lord Asher is in mourning. It's not proper to flirt with him."

"Ach, society and your blasted rules. I'm sure the view he got of my bubbies helped ease his suffering."

Anabel's cheeks flamed. "What was it that you needed?"

"Nothing," Fiona replied with a sly smile. "I just wanted tae be introduced tae Lord Asher."

"You are incorrigible!" Anabel scolded.

"And you love me for it. Now, come tae the retiring room with me so your husband thinks we actually had something tae discuss."

Anabel scoffed but followed her cousin.

It was impossible for James to dim his smile.

"You look happy, Marley. I'm pleased for you."

"Thank you," James said, turning to Asher. "Perhaps one day you will find someone to make you happy as well."

"Lud, I hope not," Asher said, cringing. "That's the last thing I need. Although," he said, craning his neck to look out over the crowd, "your wife's cousin is quite enchanting."

James guffawed. "I don't think you could handle her."

Asher cocked an eyebrow at his friend. "No? What makes you say that?"

Sobering, James considered. "Fiona is... she's unlike any woman I've ever known. She's outspoken and will not hesitate to tawse you if you need it."

"I'm not hearing anything to deter me."

"She is more than capable of caring for herself, so I'll not stop your pursuit," James replied, putting a hand on his friend's shoulder. "But you may find yourself wishing you'd heeded my warning."

Asher opened his mouth, but James's father approached.

"Gentleman," Edward said as he settled on James's other side. "Lord Asher. I was sorry to hear of your brother's passing."

"Thank you," Asher said, his jaw clenched. "Although I'm sure you were happy to know your son's wastrel of a friend ended up being good for something after all." He turned to James. "Marley let's catch up sometime soon. Good day." With one more sneer at Edward, he left.

James sighed.

"Never was a title given to a more undeserving fellow," Edward said. "Now that you are affiliated with a duke, James, it's time you ended your friendship with Lord Asher. He's only a viscount, and one of the surliest ones I've met."

"I'm not abandoning one of my closest friends," James said.

"Just consider it. I'm sure your new brother-in-law can introduce you to more influential peers."

James looked at Edward more closely. "Why would I want to meet more influential peers?"

"So they can help with your petition for a title."

"I'm asking the King for a title, am I?" James asked, his eye wide.

"Aye," Edward replied. "As you chose to marry a woman who could not pass on a title to your son, we'll have to find another way."

The urge to argue rose up in James's throat, but he pushed it down. Edward would never stop. James needed to tell his father that he had no intention of ever seeking a more distinguished title, but, that would wait. "Thank you for coming, Father." James patted the old man on his shoulder and went searching for his wife.

"What a day!" Anabel exclaimed as she collapsed onto the settee in the suite of rooms she and James were sharing at Montgomery House.

James sat next to her and took her hand. "Tired, my love?"

She shook her head. "No, not tired. Happy."

He pulled her onto his lap. "As am I."

They sat in companionable silence. James's soft heartbeat soothed Anabel and tempted her to close her eyes. As she lay on the precipice between wakefulness and sleep, he spoke in a soft whisper.

"When, in disgrace with fortune and men's eyes

, I all alone beweep my outcast state

, And trouble deaf heaven with my bootless cries

, And look upon myself and curse my fate

, Wishing me like to one more rich in hope

, Featured like him, like him with friends possessed

, Desiring this man's art and that man's scope

, With what I most enjoy contented least;

Yet in these thoughts myself almost despising

, Haply I think on thee, and then my state

, (Like to the lark at break of day arising

from sullen earth) sings hymns at heaven's gate;

For thy sweet love remembered such wealth brings

That then I scorn to change my state with kings."

Anabel met his gaze. "Shakespeare?"

James swallowed thickly. "Sonnet 29. I spent a day going through a volume of them to find the right one for today." He cleared his throat. "You saved me, Anabel. I didn't know how alone I was until I met you. Your love means more to me than all the wealth in the kingdom. I love you."

Tears spilled from her eyes as she wrapped her arms around his neck. "I love you too. You saved me as well. In more ways than one."

James wiped her tears with his thumb. "We will always save each other."

"Always," Anabel replied. Nuzzling into his neck, she sighed deeply. She had finally found her place.

The Moon Family will return in Fiona and Asher's book, The Enchantress & The Rake, available July 24, 2026.

Keeping Christmas

What if Ebenezer Scrooge from A Christmas Carol had a second chance at love?

Eben Scrooge is a changed man. One year ago, after an unusual intervention, he made a promise to keep the spirit of Christmas all year long. He's done much to keep that promise, but never in his wildest dreams did he think he'd get a chance to make amends with his lost love, Belle.

Belle Santos has spent the last five years running away, trying to heal her broken heart. Her efforts are quickly undone, however, when circumstances place her back home, and back in Eben's presence. Despite her misgivings, she can't deny the passionate connection they share.

Eben is determined to convince Belle that his change is real, and to reignite the sparks between them. But can Belle let go of the past so they can move on to their future?

Acknowledgements

When I started self-publishing, I wanted to focus on the mental health of my characters. Mental Health is an issue near and dear to my heart, and I wanted to write stories about people finding love while living with long-term mental health conditions.

That was nearly four years ago. In that time, I moved across the country, lost loved ones, and was diagnosed with ADHD. It was a lot, and my writing suffered. I couldn't keep writing the series I'd had grand plans for in 2021. I needed something different.

I've always loved Regency stories. Like many of us, I grew up reading Jane Austen and watching all the excellent movie and television adaptations of her books. When I finished those stories, I turned to historical romance. I have a deep gratitude for the genre, particularly for Regency romance, which has helped me through some dark times. At the same time, I've fallen in love with contemporary witchy romance stories that are popular right now.

So, when I decided I wanted to write something new, I thought I'd try my hand at a Regency story, but with a witchy twist. Along the way, I realized that I'd still ended up writing a story about a character with a mental health challenge. Anabel certainly struggles with anxiety, and Merlin is nothing if not a personification of intrusive thoughts. I hope I've treated these subjects with the care they deserve.

Writing a book is never easy, and writing historical fiction adds another layer of complexity. I could not have completed this book without the support of several people.

Thank you to Liz Lincoln and Carla Luna, who read this book in its infancy. Your feedback and guidance were invaluable in making this story stronger, and for helping me continue working on this project.

To my beta readers, Tracy Gulovsen and Liz Czukas: thank you both for taking a look at the second draft of this book and helping me smooth out the rough edges.

To my editors, Maria and Monica: thanks for being so patient with me and my constant misuse of commas! Thank you for polishing up the story to make it shine. Any errors remaining are due to my own negligence.

Thanks to Chicago North Romance Writers whose education and support have really helped me grow as a writer. Having a resource like this group is so wonderful.

To the Live, Laugh, Lake Retreat group, Carla, Carrie, Liz C., Liz L., Melonie, and Natalie: thanks for inviting me to join and helping me work through this story. Having dedicated time to writing during the retreats has been so helpful for me. If you're a writer and you don't have a retreat, find one. Writing can be such a solitary journey. It helps to have friends.

To the Romancelandia community at large: Thank you for existing and for loving this genre. Romance is such an amazing community that I'm honored to be a part of it. Thank you to my favorite romance podcast, Fated Mates. Jen and Sarah have taught me so much about writing. I hope I have done our community justice with this book.

Thank you to my husband Mark and my daughter Daphne for supporting me during this process and tolerating me disappearing into the office for hours at a time. Thanks for always believing in me and my writing and for being my hype team. I couldn't do any of this without you. And thank you to my dog CeeCee who's been by my side so much that I ended up naming a side character after her! Your companionship—and reminders to step away and touch grass every now and then—make the hard times bearable.

Finally, thank you to You, readers, for taking a chance on my story. Every author will tell you that we can't do this without you. If you loved this book, please leave a review to help other readers find it.

About the Author

Brandy Shaw is a romance author who got her start writing fanfiction. After playing around in worlds created by other writers for years, she took the leap in 2020 to write stories about original characters. Mental health is a big focus for Brandy, as she herself lives with depression, anxiety, and ADHD. Through her writing she hopes to show how people living with mental health issues can still find their happily-ever-after.

Brandy lives in the Chicagoland area with her husband, daughter, one spoiled dog and two very spoiled cats. When she isn't writing, she enjoys baking, crafting, or procrastinating by playing games on her phone. As she is an avid reader, you will usually find her listening to an audiobook while participating in these activities.

You can follow connect with Brandy through her website (brandyshaw .com), on Instagram @branauthor, or on Facebook @authorbrandyshaw.